RID

Nick Watts

Chiselbury

Published by
Chiselbury, a division of Woodstock Leasor Limited
14 Devonia Road, London N1 8JH, United Kingdom
www.chiselbury.com

Cover design by: Jeremy Leasor
www.jeremyleasor.com

ISBN 978-1-908291-89-9

For Carrie

—

thank you for believing in me

CHAPTER ONE

Tom's eyelids drooped. The after work party had been a good one.

"You dozing?"

The sound of Anna's voice, a lilt from the highlands of Scotland, cut through his torpor. It was a good job she was driving, it'd be an expensive taxi ride back otherwise.

"Mixing the grain and the grape," she added. He could hear the smile in her voice.

"Yes doctor!" Tom remembered the wisecrack that if you marry a doctor, you spend the rest of your life having symptoms. In this case her diagnosis was correct.

Not for the first time he thought how lucky he'd been, after his wayward wandering to find someone like Anna.

"Hello......"

Fully awake now, Tom responded to Anna's tone of alarm. In the wing mirror he could see blue lights, amplified in the darkness, behind them. It really was good that Anna was driving, he'd fail a breath test. This stretch of the road was narrow and twisty, so Anna pulled over as an ambulance sped past. They watched in silence as the tail lights went round a bend.

Tom glanced at Anna, her medical instincts heightened by the passing ambulance; a reminder of her time at A&E in Glasgow. Tom too had sharpened up, his previous life in the military had accustomed him to snapping awake swiftly.

They continued driving, winding their way along the familiar road at the foot of the Downs.

Eventually they came upon the scene.

As the headlights of the car swept around the bend, Tom and Anna could see that there had been a nasty accident.

"This doesn't look good," said Tom. A policeman was in the road waving him down.

Tom opened his window, "Can we help at all? My wife is a doctor."

It was a winding road that ran along the foot of the Wessex Downs so required care especially when, like now, it was dark. Ton-up boys and jet jockeys would go roaring along this road, but every now and again you saw the aftermath in a hedge or a ditch. The flashing lights of a police car and the ambulance illuminated the area with an eerie blue light. The big yellow ambulance had just arrived, and the paramedics in their green overalls were crawling over an upturned car, which still had its lights on. The traffic policeman had just put up a blue 'Accident' notice, and was now beginning to think about traffic control. Tom and Anna's car was the first to arrive on the scene.

The policeman leant into the window to speak to Tom "if you don't mind waiting in the car, folks, while we sort this out." He wasn't in a mood to be polite.

Tom took in the scene: an upturned car, its wheels in the air, looking as if it had been turned over by a nearby tree which bore signs of scarring. His former army training gave him a sense of dispassionate calm; what is the problem, his mind seemed to ask. He shuddered involuntarily, as he recalled a previous occasion when he had been in an upturned Land rover. It had been blown off the road while he was serving in Iraq. The two in the front of the vehicle had been killed; Tom and a colleague dozing in the back had survived.

"OK?" Anna asked, sensing his unease.

Early in their relationship Anna had told Tom he needed help for PTSD, which he had reluctantly agreed to. Tom

2

could see that Anna was also watching with professional interest. He could see that all her instincts were to go and help.

The blue lights cast a ghoulish glow, making Anna's face look spectrally pale. Tom could see a female police officer sitting in the big police car with someone, who was probably the driver of another car parked nearby with its hazard flashers still on; Tom caught Anna's gaze.

"Probably a witness," he said. "He might have seen what happened, and called 999."

It was a fine clear evening with a dry road surface, not the sort of weather for a car to be skidding out of control – or that's what it looked like.

"I think I recognise the car," said Tom. In the light from the emergency service vehicles he could make out the shape and colour of the upturned car.

"Malcolm Miller, the local MP. He drives a red Jag like that."

Anna got out of the car and addressed the traffic policeman in her 'believe you me I'm a doctor' voice which sharpened her Scots accent.

"I'd make sure that the witness is OK, he could be in shock."

They all looked at the witness, sitting in the front seat of the police car. The WPC was still writing notes.

"Shall I go and have a look?" ventured Anna "the paramedics are attending to…"

She gestured in the direction of the up-turned car. The traffic policeman saw the sense of her offer.

"That would be helpful, thank you doctor…?"

"Macdonald" interjected Anna who turned on her heel and walked towards the police car.

"That's my girl!" said Tom, who had got out of the car to stretch his legs. Even in the gloomy light the PC saw the smile of pride on Tom's face.

"My wife is a GP at the health centre in Farrington, but she's done some A&E work."

The cool evening air helped to bring Tom back to his senses. Was that oil or petrol he could smell? As if in answer to his own question a big fire engine came grinding past them, waved through by the policeman. More blue lights, brightening the evening sky.

After a few minutes other cars arrived on the scene, Tom was conscious of a man walking up to join them. He was of slight build. The darkness lent him anonymity.

"Evening gents, I'm Jack Sawyer from the Vale News Agency, I heard there'd been an accident on this road."

Bad news travels fast thought Tom.

"I'm not in a position to say anything to the press," said the policeman, becoming defensive.

"I can see what's happened from here!" said Jack.

"That car is very distinctive," he carried on and caught Tom's eye, "haven't we met?"

A good trick to elicit information thought Tom, but he thought that they had met somewhere.

"Tom Scobie," he said introducing himself.

"If this is the local MP, this would be quite a scoop, if I can call it in sharpish," said Jack.

Tom had to smile. Both Anna the doctor and Jack the journalist were acting professionally, while he was merely a bystander.

"Well, it is Malcolm Miller's car," said Tom, "but we don't know who was driving."

"The Government is running out of time, there has to be an election soon," said Jack. "If the local MP is, er, dead…"

The policeman held up his hands, to signify that he was not going to comment. Tom and Jack both looked over to the police car where Anna had been joined by one of the paramedics, who was talking to the driver who had witnessed the accident. Anna detached herself from the group and walked back over to re-join Tom.

"Do you know who was driving the car?" asked Jack.

"Malcolm Miller," replied Anna matter-of-factly; "dead," she added.

By now the policeman had managed to arrange traffic cones and warning signs along the road, to allow through traffic.

"Better be getting on," said Jack, giving Tom a business card.

"Mind if I call you later to get some details Tom?"

"Anytime," said Tom, reciprocating with a card of his own.

"Thanks for your help Doctor Macdonald," said the policeman.

"Drive safely sir," he added to Tom.

Tom felt himself blush. All that time he had been standing close to a traffic copper, who had been able to smell his breath. As they drove away from the scene of the accident, Anna told Tom about her conversation with the paramedic.

"Miller wasn't wearing a seat belt, so he's as dead as a dodo. There was nothing for the medics to do."

Tom was pondering how the car went off the road.

"According to the policewoman the witness said he drove straight off the road," Anna continued.

"It sounds like what the Germans call autocide," said Tom, "I remember it happening in Germany when I was in the army. People go onto the autobahns, and drive at full speed into a bridge or something."

What would make him do such a thing? pondered Tom. A General Election was due later in the spring. The MP would be a shoo-in as the local parliamentary seat, Ridgeway, was considered very safe. Tom had got to know Miller, who had invited him to join a Working Group on Security threats to Europe, because of work he had done whilst part of a NATO Taskforce in the Balkans.

As a new Europe emerged after the Cold War, the Balkans were seen by policy makers as unfinished business, an area where weak states could harbour security threats. Tom had found Miller a distant figure, but admired his focus on what he thought was an important matter.

"That's going to be quite a story for the journalist," said Anna.

Tom thought about the journalist and his scoop; local MP dead in a car crash with no other vehicle involved. On the surface it didn't sound like much, but why was the driver not wearing a seatbelt? That would make the news more interesting.

"I'm sure we haven't heard the last of this," he said.

****

Jack Sawyer filed his story, having first of all confirmed the details with Thames Valley police, who would only say that a male was pronounced dead at the scene. The story just missed the late evening local news bulletins, but was picked up in the morning news stories. It was the top story on BBC Radio Oxford, and in the top half of national news bulletins. In the run up to an expected General Election, with an uncertain outcome, any political story was big news. Parliamentary colleagues paid generous tributes to Miller's long years of service, devoted to the well-being of his constituents. Up and down the country, political aspirants were brushing up their CVs, to establish a connection, however tenuous, with the south Oxfordshire constituency of Ridgeway.

****

A telephone call can change everything, thought Henry Makepeace, as he put down the phone. He and his wife were having breakfast the following morning.

"That was Don Johnson on the phone," he said to Muriel his wife. Henry was the Chairman of the Ridgeway Constituency Association. They had heard the news on the radio.

"He's just been to see Louisa," he was referring to the dead MP's wife.

Donald Johnson was the full-time constituency agent. Muriel's face registered shock, but not sadness thought Henry. Not the sort of news one expected to hear at the breakfast table.

"That's going to complicate matters," she mused, "the General Election can't be more than a couple of months away."

"I suppose I'd better go round and see how Louisa is managing," she said finishing her toast. "Was she at home when it happened?"

Henry replied that Miller's wife had indeed been at home when the police called. It was known that the couple had a very 'political' marriage. He lived his life and she lived hers. Henry could see that the next few days were going to be very busy indeed.

****

Lord Charles Markham also received a phone call that morning, also from Donald Johnson. Markham was President of the Ridgeway Constituency Association, an honorary title bestowed on worthy supporters of the Party.

"Thank you Don," he said solicitously, "I do hope you will let me know if there is anything I can do to be of help."

Charles Markham learnt to do business in the good old days before corporate governance tied everything and everybody down in red tape. Time was when an Englishman's word was his bond. Markham often reminded his business colleagues of one of Churchill's lesser known dictums; the English never draw a line without blurring it. He always shook hands on a deal, but never put things in writing. He kept a record of his associates' foibles and weaknesses and used the information to extract what he wanted from them. An indiscretion meant that Donald had lost his job as agent in a neighbouring seat. Markham had used his influence to get him moved to take over the vacancy in the 'sleepy' constituency of Ridgeway. Problem solved, and a debt chalked up.

Markham put the phone down. Well, well, he thought. He knew exactly who would be able to fill the shoes of the dead MP, now to get weaving.

CHAPTER TWO

"Why *don't* you have a go?"

Anna's question was buzzing in Tom's head as they were driving to Sunday lunch. It was a week since the death of Malcolm Miller. The news of the sudden death of the MP for the constituency of Ridgeway so close to a General Election, had set hearts fluttering amongst the large numbers of the Party faithful who aspired to be parliamentarians over the following days. A marching army of Prospective Parliamentary Candidates stood waiting for the call. Then the Party Leader in his continuing effort to detoxify the Party, announced that the new candidate would be chosen by an open primary. In a moment he had cocked a snook to the Party faithful in an effort to show that, under his leadership, things had changed.

"After all, you're every bit as qualified as most of the numties who'll be applying." She continued.

Tom smiled to himself enjoying Anna's use of the Scots phrase describing an imbecile. Her gentle highland lilt concealed a very sharp tongue.

"Let's talk it through with Matt and Lizzie," said Tom. His mind was in turmoil.

They had often spoken of how it might be possible to make a difference in the world. Anna had thrown herself into medicine, after her upbringing as the child of two flower people, who went on the hippy trail. General Practice gave her the satisfaction of serving a community. Tom had drifted into the army as a way of avoiding becoming a farmer, but had found his true vocation working against gunrunners and people traffickers, who had flourished in the chaos of the Balkans. Anna kidded him about being a Boy Scout, but the life of an

9

undercover operative had taken him to a dark place. He left the army to the more sedate life of a marketing executive. If the Party Leader wanted new blood and fresh ideas, thought Tom, then why *shouldn't* he have a go? His instinct told him that he could use his 'Boy Scout' talents for a good purpose. He had been fortunate enough to land a good job with a growing company. The work was interesting and it was fun. But.........

"You didn't marry a political activist, let alone an MP," he ventured.

"I married you, Tom, for better or worse!" she retorted with a smile.

He gave her a sideways look as she drove her Golf through the green country lanes. Sunglasses perched over her red fringe. He had found peace with her, after the turmoil of the Balkans and Iraq. She had found in him a safe haven, after her itinerant childhood and wayward years as a medical student. Was he about to upset the apple cart of their lives?

 "Rather a short flash to bang time," said Tom, referring to the speed with which events had unfolded.

"I think you'll make a great MP!" said Lizzie over her shoulder, as she and Anna managed the arrangements for lunch. Tom and Matt were both standing with a glass of wine.

"Why thank you ma'am!" replied Tom in a fake Mid-Western accent. "Some things just drop into your lap," said Matt "the question is what you do with them."

"Let's not get ahead of ourselves," replied Tom "I haven't put my name forward, and the competition will be fierce."

"It can't be a one horse race, can it?" asked Lizzie. "I see some fringe candidates have stepped forward already."

"It'd be a feather in someone's cap to steal a safe seat from a complacent incumbent party," added Matt.

As usual Lizzie had served up a feast. The two boys, Barney and Andrew, were preoccupied with their food while the grown-ups talked.

"Why on earth would you want to do this Tom?" asked Matt.

"You are master of your own life, with a lovely wife. If you became an MP your life won't be your own, and you will be criticised for everything you do and don't do."

It was Tom's turn to tease his cousin.

"Are you giving us a description of your life as a vicar Matt?"

"*Touché!*" cried Lizzie, giving Anna a knowing glance.

"It seems as if we have the whole benefice trooping through here sometimes," she added.

"Daddy calls them odds and sods," piped Barney, "what's a sod Anna?" They all laughed.

Tom brought them all back to the matter in hand.

"I still can't fathom what would make a sitting MP commit suicide, if that's what happened, just before a General Election. Ridgeway – or its predecessor has been a very safe seat for ever, so it's not as if Malcolm was facing defeat."

"Scandal?" asked Anna, putting her finger on Tom's unspoken thought.

"Perhaps he was about to be exposed for some underhand goings on," she ventured.

"A journalist who appeared at the scene of the accident has been poking around," added Tom.

"He called me and asked me some questions, but he didn't sound like he was on to anything."

"Yet!" said Anna.

"I always thought Miller was a bit too smarmy for his own good."

Tom didn't respond. Miller especially wanted his advice on the troublesome Balkans, so his suicide was puzzling, as they seemed to be getting close to devising a policy of 'containment' for the region. It could have become government policy, and Tom would have helped to shape it. Cousin Matt was the person, besides Anna, he felt closest to. They had always talked through life's big decisions together.

"What took you from a career in marketing to the life of a vicar Matt?" Tom asked.

"I found marketing rather soul destroying."

It was Matt's turn to ask the questions.

"Are you really thinking about life in the snake pit of politics Tom? I'd have thought you had enough excitement in your previous incarnation."

Tom looked across the table to Anna. A big career change could have an equally big impact on both their lives. He found her face annoyingly inscrutable.

"Let me think about it," he said.

****

Charles Markham was hosting Sunday lunch at Wyvern Hall. A buffet lunch with champagne was in full swing. Lady Mary fussed over a dear old thing who had hardly any teeth left, but who was a stalwart of her musical appreciation committee.

"Some more quiche lorraine, Madeleine?" she enquired solicitously.

Lord Markham, for his part, marked out his territory and stayed put. His dutiful PA Maud Cumming escorted people into his presence, so that they might receive his benediction or caution.

"I was particularly disappointed that we were unable to secure the property we looked at in Long Hampton," he said gently to a very pale looking solicitor.

These words could mean professional and social ruin to someone who failed to perform.

"It was bad luck….w-won't happen again," was as much as he could manage.

"Well, Godfrey, let's hope not, eh?" at which Markham's gaze shifted; Godfrey was dismissed.

Maud lent towards Markham "Gill Wynne would like a word".

Markham allowed himself a moment to collect his thoughts.

"Please ask Gill and her charming husband to join me," Markham beamed to Maud, who scuttled off to get them.

Gill's social ambition had led her to marry dreary Desmond, a solid enough solicitor who buried himself in a practice in Newbury. Markham made sure that he got plenty of business to keep him busy. He recalled his last conversation with Godfrey, and concluded that Desmond might be getting even more work shortly. All the better for spending some quality time with Gill.

"Gill, Desmond, come and have some champagne," called Markham, as he waved the couple into his presence.

"Maud, be a dear and send the waiter over, and you might just see that everybody is topped up?" he smiled at her as she went off to her duties. Maud moved away, glancing back as Gill approached, and wondered about what might have been had that woman not intruded onto the scene.

"Now then…." Markham began.

Gill interrupted "what are we going to do to manage this mess Charles?" she said in a tone that was a touch too shrill for Markham's liking.

He saw Desmond's colour rise, as his embarrassment became plain.

"It's hardly a mess Gill," he replied soothingly, "there are more moving parts in the puzzle, but it's by no means a mess."

He gave her a look intended to quiet a querulous pupil.

"The more runners in the field, the better your victory will look, eh Desmond?"

Markham was back to his genial persona.

"Donald is doing a very good job, as always, at marking my card and giving me the low down on the competition."

They all understood the racing allusion.

"What bothers me is not the competition."   Gill's tone had mellowed, but was still a touch too brittle for Markham.

"I'm concerned about your fellow…"

Markham interrupted her and drew closer to speak.

"I don't think you need worry about the selection process. It won't be difficult to ensure that you are one of the final group who stand."

They all knew that Donald Johnson was in Markham's pocket. His implication that the constituency agent would be working to further her cause gave Gill some reassurance. Markham signalled that their tête-à-tête was at an end by reaching out to shake Desmond's hand.

"So good to see you again Desmond, I feel that this will be a good year for us all."

As Gill and her husband wandered away Markham gave himself a moment to ponder how he would in fact manage the selection committee. It would comprise the full executive, but a core group would do the preliminary sifting. Once the election was over he would be able to use Gill's position in Westminster to access privileged information, for the benefit of his various ventures and investments.

He wasn't concerned about the independent candidates who had thrown their hats into the ring, they were small fry – this was the big game. Nothing must get in his way now, he told himself, nothing.

CHAPTER THREE

Tom's mobile phone rang as he and Anna were having supper the following evening. He fished it out of his pocket; it was Jack Sawyer the journalist who had appeared at the site of the fatal road accident, which cost Malcolm Miller his life.

"Good evening Tom, how's tricks?" came the familiar voice.

"Jack – what's up?"

"Can you speak?" asked Jack.

"I'm at home and my wife is here," said Tom, feeling a little melodramatic.

"Malcolm Miller was being blackmailed," began Jack "my sources tell me that Miller was up to his armpits in bad property loans. He had invested in property in Romania, Montenegro and Bulgaria," added Jack.

"When the banking collapse happened he was badly exposed. His debt was covered by an investment company."

"So far, so good," Tom said, scribbling notes onto the back of an envelope on the kitchen table.

Jack continued "just before his death, Miller was told that the investment company was calling in his debt."

"Coincidence?" asked Tom, who didn't believe in coincidences.

"As you may know, Tom, a serving MP cannot be insolvent," Jack continued.

"The threat was to bankrupt Miller, and render him ineligible to remain in Westminster."

Tom let the thought sink in; "it still doesn't explain why he should kill himself."

"Not immediately," replied Jack "let me do some more digging, I just wondered whether you'd picked anything up?"

"Lots of speculation, but nothing concrete," said Tom.

There would be an inquest into Miller's death. It would establish the facts, but it wouldn't explain the *why*, Tom reflected.

A thought occurred to him "what was the name of the investment company concerned? Any info about directors?"

"Thought you'd get there eventually," replied Jack. "The chairman of Falcon Holdings is one Charles Markham."

Somehow Tom didn't feel surprised at this news. He knew that Charles Markham was a business tycoon, who played by his own rules. Markham's 'Christmas card list' was alleged to be an influence network, but it seemed to be mostly rumours from people who had fallen out with him.

"Let me do a bit of digging my end," suggested Tom. "We can touch base in a few days," they agreed and ended the call.

Tom outlined the gist of Jack's call to Anna, who arched her eyebrows as only she could when she encountered something bizarre.

"Nothing would surprise me about Markham, or Miller, both as bad as each other," she said. "Friends of yours!?"

Tom saw the reproach. He had allowed himself to become involved in this group; he saw the advice he gave Miller as some form of public service. He was in reflective mood as they sat in the kitchen to eat.

"There hasn't been an inquest yet," Anna pointed out. "Will we have to give evidence? We were almost the first on the scene."

"I've not been contacted by the coroner's office," Tom replied. "Besides; there was the motorist who saw it happen, it's more likely that they'll be more interested in his version of events."

****

The following morning Lord Markham was working through papers at his desk, with Maud occasionally plying him with coffee. When the phone on his desk rang, he was lost in thought and it took him some time to collect himself.

"There's a journalist on the phone who wants to speak to you," said Maud, sounding rather anxious. "You know my rule about speaking to journalists." Markham was irritated at being disturbed, and even more irritated that Maud would ask him to take the call.

"He said that you would want to speak to him, Lord Markham," said Maud, trying to restore some *amour propre*. This sounded like some trouble-making journo, thought Markham; I'd better send him away with a flea in his ear.

"Very well," he sighed.

"Good morning Lord Markham, my name is Jack Sawyer with the Vale News Agency."

"How may I help you Mr Sawyer?" Markham's tone was civil but icy.

"I am making enquiries relating to the death of Malcolm Miller the MP," Jack began.

"A very tragic affair, Mr Sawyer, everybody who knew Malcolm admired the work he did for his constituents," interrupted Markham. He wanted to shut the matter down as swiftly as possible, but the journalist would probably be recording their conversation.

"A sitting Member of Parliament can't serve if he is declared bankrupt, isn't that the case?" asked Jack.

"I'm not an expert in the rules of parliament," Markham began.

"Malcolm Miller had invested in property in Europe, and the banking crisis left him badly exposed," continued Jack. "Miller's position was covered by loans provided by Falcon Holdings, of which you are Chairman, Lord Markham," Jack continued.

Markham allowed himself a few seconds to calculate where this line of questioning was going. His first instinct was to stonewall.

"You should really speak to the PR people at Falcon Holdings, who can tell you about their policy towards loans and investments, Mr. Sawyer," he began, hoping that any imputation of impropriety in the relationship with Miller could get lost in the labyrinth of the PR machine. If that failed then legal action would be threatened against the Vale News Agency, which was a small operation. That usually did the trick, as lawyers are expensive.

Jack was not to be put off.

"Your company covered Miller's bad debts, and then withdrew them close to a General Election. Miller would have had to resign his seat. Do you have an ulterior motive for this action, Lord Markham?"

Markham was cool.

"Mr Sawyer, that is a very serious allegation. I hope that you're not going to print that, as Falcon Holdings would be obliged to commence legal proceedings against your organisation."

He just stopped himself from saying that an expensive legal action would put the Vale News Agency out of business, but the threat was very clear.

"Is that a denial?" Jack persisted.

"I think this call is at an end," Markham said icily and he put the phone down.

Charles Markham prided himself on his ability to calculate the odds, and to gauge people's motivations. Sawyer was a journalist who wanted to make his name with a big story. Well, thought Markham, I am not going to be a big story – at least not the story Sawyer wants to write. He picked up the phone and waited while Maud answered.

"Could you have a look into the ownership of the Vale News Agency? I have a vague idea it's part of Western Media; quick as you can please." He put the phone down.

That was one matter in hand, he thought. The bigger question was more troubling to Markham. Where did Sawyer get his information from? Someone had been talking. His operation ran on the basis of absolute trust between him and his associates. He would have to get to work on finding the source of the leak, and dealing with it.

"It's a bit late for an old dog to learn any new tricks," he muttered to himself as he took another sip of coffee.

"Well, there's life in the old dog yet!" he said to himself.

He picked up his phone and dialled the number of one of his closest confidants.

"Simon?" he said as the call was answered "who is the best private detective hereabouts? I need a bit of work done in a hurry and it needs to be discrete."

He listened as the voice the other end of the line gave him a name and a number.

"That's very helpful," Markham said. "I'll have a word with the Chief Constable about that overdue promotion" and ended the call.

CHAPTER FOUR

Tom's phone went during a lull in a conference for business executives that Oxford Info was holding, in a motel on the outskirts of Newbury. It was Jack Sawyer again. It had been a few days since they had last spoken. He was cagey on the phone, and asked if he could call at their house that evening. Tom had agreed and given him directions to Shepherds Cottage where they lived. He quickly called Anna at work

"What can be so important?" she asked.

"He wasn't going to say over the phone," explained Tom.

"We've got some stew we can give him," Anna suggested.

"Good idea," replied Tom, sending a text to Jack.

Jack arrived promptly at 7 o'clock. It was the first time they had met since Miller's fatal accident. Tom opened the door and recognised the slight figure and an intelligent, enquiring countenance.

"Nice to meet you again Jack," said Tom.

Jack looked younger in the light, thought Tom.

"Is that you Jack?" asked Anna. "Come away in," she added, offering him a wide smile.

Jack was led into the kitchen.

"This is the warmest room in the house," Anna explained, by way of making Jack feel at ease.

Jack hung his down jacket on the back of his chair. He was carrying a large brown envelope, apparently bulging with papers. He saw Tom's gaze fall upon the envelope, and gave it a pat with his hand.

"I've got some stuff here that will help to fill in some of the pieces of jigsaw about Malcolm Miller's death."

Tom was puzzled as to why he was the one that Jack wanted to speak to about this. Before he could ask, Jack began.

"You need to know what Lord Charles Markham has been up to," he said, pulling a piece of paper from his envelope. Tom tried to puzzle it out.

"Is it a family tree?" he asked.

"More like a tangled web," Jack replied.

Tom poured them all a glass of red wine, while Anna dealt out the stew.

"Markham has got a reputation as a tycoon," said Jack, "but his wealth is built on criminality."

Tom gave Anna a look. She had frozen, eyes wide in puzzlement.

"Talk us through it, Jack," he said.

"You've certainly got our attention," he added, giving Anna a smile – it'll be all right he seemed to be saying.

Jack began, "Markham's established a web of influence, which fuels his business interests." Jack indicated the piece of paper.

"This is my understanding of how he does business; front companies and nominee shareholdings." "What's the connection with Miller?" asked Tom.

"Simple," Jack replied.

"Miller was overextended. He took out additional loans using his property holdings as collateral." "So when the banking crisis hit, he couldn't cover his borrowings," suggested Tom.

"Markham understood Miller's position, and used it to his advantage," added Jack.

"That's not criminality" said Anna. "Its sharp practice, but not criminal."

"The criminality lies behind where the money for the loans came from," said Jack. "Trafficking: booze, drugs, tobacco, weapons and people."

"You were working with Miller on his Security Challenges Policy Group, weren't you Tom?"

Tom felt his colour rising, there might be a connection with me he thought. Jack had a disconcerting habit of presenting facts as questions.

"Yes, I was" Tom replied, matter-of-factly.

"And you were previously doing undercover work in the Balkans, as part of a NATO team?"

Tom was cautious in his response.

"That's covered by the Official Secrets Act Jack, I can't answer that."

By way of confirmation Jack pulled out a photo copy of what looked to Tom like a military telex message with his name on it.

"Citizen Journalism at work!" said Jack.

"In the Eastern bloc, in the old days, everybody was in the business of finding out what Big Brother was up to. They just carried on with the change of regime," he explained.

Tom shrugged his shoulders as if to say – carry on.

"Miller discovered that Markham was up to his neck in trafficking, and the trafficking was financing militias and some of the Islamic fundamentalist groups we are now dealing with in the Middle East."

"Miller never shared any of this with us," said Tom, as he absorbed the information.

"We used the term 'mafia' for any bad guys. They were into whatever made money. It was the way of life for many, going back into the mists of time," Tom explained.

"Miller discovered a connection between some nasty mafia types and Markham's companies," continued Jack. He pointed towards his diagram to illustrate his point.

"When Markham threatened to foreclose on Miller, he countered by threatening to expose Markham."

"Honour among thieves!" Anna chipped in.

Tom felt deflated; he had joined Miller's group and had given him as much information about his activities as he felt he could. Miller had quizzed him at length, and Tom gained the impression that the work they were doing could make a difference to a troubled region. All the while Miller had been pursuing a vendetta against Markham. He felt like a fool.

"So who were you investigating Jack?" Anna's question brought Tom back to himself.

"I got a tip off about Markham," replied Jack "and as I dug around I came across Miller's financial travails."

"Quite a tangled web," said Tom, having regained his composure.

"Miller and Markham were a match for each other," said Jack, carrying on with his theme.

"Miller was greedy and over-extended himself. Markham used his credit as a means of exerting influence over Miller," he explained.

"Miller found himself up to his neck in debt, and the information he unearthed about Markham's involvement with criminality seemed like a get out of jail card."

"Instead of which….?" Tom wanted to get to the bottom of the matter.

"Markham stood his ground," said Jack "leaving Miller with nowhere to go."

"Like Sampson" suggested Anna, "he just pulled the whole thing down on top of him."

****

Sitting in his study that evening, Lord Markham was reflecting on what could possibly be the most important project of his life; project Portcullis. Sitting with him was Donald Johnson, whom he had summoned to join him in a glass of his very good cognac.

"Donald, I need to get someone back into Westminster, to give advance warning of anything that could impact on my investments and projects," said Markham.

It would also give him an entrée via the ability to hold events in the Palace of Westminster, either for the Party or for his own benefit. Malcolm Miller had fulfilled that role until he got greedy.

"You are my eyes and ears in the constituency," added Markham.

"Somehow I need to get onto the selection committee," he continued.

As President of the Constituency Association his position was honorary, but removed from the process of decision taking.

Johnson didn't need reminding that Markham had secured him the position of constituency agent, a paid position, upon the 'retirement' of his predecessor. Markham had created a client base of dependable associates via his proven methodology. People are fallible; everyone has their weak spot and through a combination of flattery and veiled threat, he was usually able to achieve compliance. People liked to feel that they belonged; hence he used his Christmas card list to instil a sense of camaraderie. Through the judicious use of patronage, he was able to advance people or by withdrawing his goodwill, to ostracise or in extremis, to ruin them.

"You need to find a way Don," said Markham in a gentle voice, but his meaning was clear.

Donald felt his blood go cold. Up until now, he had just ensured that money got paid to those who needed it. Now he was being dragged into the foreground and asked to risk his career for his patron. He would have to look out for himself.

He nodded his understanding, which Markham took as agreement. In reality, it was a way of internalising an important change in his life.

CHAPTER FIVE

"Penny for them?" Anna could see that Tom was brooding on something. Ever since the journalist left, he'd seemed to her to be out of sorts.

"Something he said about Miller and Markham, and the Balkans," Tom began, as if coming out of a deep sleep. "I seem to remember some talk of 'the Angliski', like they were a gang unto themselves. I definitely don't remember meeting either of them at the time, so it's possible that they used intermediaries."

"Perhaps you've buried the memories...." Anna began. "I thought you'd put that world behind you, after your experiences there." When they met, Tom was having something of a nervous breakdown as a reaction to his time working undercover. Anna had gently coaxed out of him some of the unpleasant memories, and helped him to put them behind him.

"Don't worry, I'm not regressing!" he said, realising Anna's concern. "That was a dark time, but there's a bell ringing somewhere," he pointed to his head.

"What did Miller know about your time there?" she asked. Tom sat at the table, tapping his finger on it, as if trying to recall a distant memory.

"There's only so much I could tell him, as a lot of what we did was covered by the Official Secrets Act. But he could put together times and places, if he wanted to."

"There's going to be an election soon, so there'll be a replacement and Miller will be forgotten," Anna said, dismissing the matter.

"Hmmm....." said Tom, letting the matter drop. But something was nagging in his mind. He'd kept notebooks, which were stored in an old ammunition box in the attic. He'd go and have a rummage later, just to satisfy his curiosity. Maybe he'd turn up something that could be useful. He remembered an old saying, that knowledge is power.

****

After Donald had departed, Gill Wynne arrived to see Markham. She had a pre-occupied look, which Markham recognised could spell trouble. She was dressed up, as if to go out for the evening, a look he liked. The two of them were sitting in the elegant drawing room at Wyvern Hall, Markham's house. "Now then, Gill, let's think about this….." Markham was using what he thought of as his most reassuring tone of voice.

"The plan, Charles, was for you to convince Miller to announce that he would stand down at the next General Election," she interrupted. "That hasn't worked, now it looks like he's gone and killed himself. We will have a by-election any time soon, and you've lost control of the matter!"

Markham sat back in his chair and allowed Gill to let off steam. In his experience it was always best to allow people to speak their mind, all the better to understand how to handle them. Besides, he liked her more when she was energised.

"My understanding, from my friends in the Party is that there is not enough time to have a by-election, as the General Election is likely to be in May." Markham kept his voice at an even tone. "We can manage things…."

"Ha!"

Gill's outburst was annoying. Markham knew that Gill had a tendency to fly off the handle, but he felt she could be managed like a highly spirited thoroughbred, which is what he hoped she'd prove to be.

"I think I can manage this, Gill," he continued. "I've made a life out of managing things," he gave her a penetrating glance, as if to reinforce the quiet tone of voice. "Look around you," he said, waving at their elegant surroundings. "This didn't happen by chance."

"I don't want to think that I've wasted the past few years, Charles," she said coolly. Markham's expression remained impassive. He found these expressions of regret tiresome. Gill felt that she had some sway over Markham. He allowed her to continue thinking like this, even though he could drop her at any time.

"Miller has removed himself from the picture, Gill, that's what matters," he said, regaining control of the conversation. "He saw no way out, so left the stage," he continued.

"So be it," Gill said, dismissively. "I want to be sure that I will inherit his position, so that we can continue our...... partnership."

Markham's smile reassured Gill, but in his mind was the need to continue to have someone in a place where they can be useful to his enterprise. He was banking on Gill to continue the process. He was concerned that she was not yet ready, but he had to use the cards that fate dealt him. So far he had managed to play them well.

"It's getting late" he said coolly. "I know," she replied, smiling.

****

Hidden away at the back of the attic was an old metal ammunition box, to which Tom had consigned things from his military life. Old maps, cap badges swapped with allied troops on exercises, training manuals and notebooks. He thought that one day he would drag the box out and regale his son with tales of derring-do.

Tom pulled the box into a space where he could open it. Rummaging by torchlight through the maps and manuals, he found the old notebook he had been looking for. It was the kind sold anywhere that you can shove into your pocket. He also found a map of the region, overprinted by the NATO unit he was attached to, with coloured ceasefire lines and separation zones to de-conflict the various factions who were vying for power.

When he got back downstairs, he found Anna on the phone. She waved towards the open bottle of wine on the table, and he poured himself a glass.

He wasn't sure what he was looking for. His jottings were in pencil, which lasted better on wet paper than biro. He had also scrawled hurried notes on the back of the map. He took a sip of wine and started flicking through the notebook. Names of people and places, telephone numbers, what looked like map references, times of meetings. Some comments and notes to himself.

Anna finished her phone call and wandered over to where he was sitting. She put down her glass of wine and plonked herself onto Tom's lap.

"Good evening," she said, giving him a peck on the cheek. His response was a grimace, like a school boy having to do extra homework.

"How could you ever read any of this?" she asked, looking at Tom's scribbled notes.

"It was important to get things down while they were still fresh in my memory. You can't have a conversation with someone in a back street bar and write it out, you have to do it once you're in the clear."

"Hmm, and people talk about doctors' notes!" she said, digging him in the ribs.

"OK, here we are!" said Tom triumphantly. "I didn't dream it – Angliski – English." He remembered a dingy café in Tuzla, as noted in the book. He was asked if he was with the Angliski – but that wasn't the purpose of the conversation. He wanted to pursue another line of enquiry, but his contact wanted to talk about the Angliski. Tom had used whatever language he could to get through to people, sometimes English, Russian, German, or the local slang. So his notes were often a form of Esperanto, which he had to decode when writing up his report.

"Whatever happened to this chap?" Anna asked, poking at the book as if it was a medical specimen.

"Not sure," Tom replied vaguely. He did know but didn't want to tell her. It wasn't pretty. Anna pointed at some of Tom's scribbled notes.

"Angliski – Millard"? she said. "Miller!?"

"Not that I recall" Tom replied after a moments pause. "He did travel out on a parliamentary committee visit, but he told me about that. I did pursue Millard – we looked through our database, nothing came up, not even an alias. And in time it got side lined and then dropped." Tom reached across to retrieve his wine glass.

"Could it be a mis-hearing?" asked Anna, "if it was a noisy bar,"

"Could be…." Tom replied without much enthusiasm, taking a sip of wine. He didn't like the idea that he might have missed an important piece of information, but it was certainly possible.

"Milord!" Anna said. "People often speak of English aristocracy as a 'milord', how about that?"

Tom managed not to choke on his wine, but he coughed as a penny dropped.

"Well, well doctor!" he said, grabbing her and planting a kiss on her cheek. "You may just have solved a piece of the puzzle. I'll ask our journalistic sleuth what he makes of that!"

CHAPTER SIX

Tom's phone buzzed by his bedside. He knew it would be trouble. He looked at the bedside alarm clock, the digits said 03:45.

"Hello?" he said, still trying to get his brain in gear.

"Is that Mr Scobie?" asked a woman's voice, who sounded at once scared and upset. Tom could tell in an instant that she was trying to hold herself together.

"Yes this is Tom Scobie," he replied, trying to sound reassuring.

"I'm Lena, Jack's girlfriend," she went on.

Tom could hear that she was on the verge of hysteria. He needed to overcome his own sense of foreboding, and not sound like he needed to know what was up with Jack.

"Hello Lena – what can you tell me?"

He was using a technique he had learnt when negotiating with scared village leaders in the Balkans: don't be too overbearing, but keep the conversation going.

"Jack's been killed," she blurted out. "Hit and run," she added.

Tom felt like he had been kicked in the stomach. He could hear Anna stirring beside him, cosy and warm.

"Tell me what happened Lena," he needed to coax her gently. She sounded like a scared child, probably early twenties he thought.

"Jack was coming home from work on his bike, and he was hit by a van."

"When did this happen, Lena?"

Tom kept his voice at a low key, so as not to panic her, despite his own rising sense of alarm.

"Seven thirty, he was taken to the Great Western," she added, mentioning the big hospital outside Swindon.

"I've been there all evening, but —"she broke down.

Anna was now awake, sitting up she switched on a bedside light.

"Jack's been killed," Tom said in a low voice whilst Lena collected herself. Anna put her hands up to her face, to shut out the image. It had only been a couple of days since he was downstairs having supper with them.

"Are you still there Mr Scobie?" Lena's voice was stronger now.

"Jack said that if anything happened to him, I was to give you something."

"I understand," said Tom, keeping his tone as level as his sense of alarm would allow.

"I thought he was play-acting," continued Lena, "never thought…" again she broke down.

"Where are you Lena?" asked Tom.

She gave them an address in Uffingham, close to the White Horse.

"Can I come over now?" Tom asked.

"Best to get rid of this thing," responded Lena sounding brittle.

"Give me half an hour," said Tom.

"I'm coming too" Anna was out of bed, pulling on her track suit bottoms, "sounds like she needs some tea and sympathy."

Maybe, thought Tom, but that wouldn't bring Jack back.

They took Molly, Tom's ex-MOD Land Rover, so called because of the registration letters MLY. They were both silent as Tom drove along the dark country lanes he knew so well. Even these familiar and friendly roads, which he had known all his life, could be as dangerous as anywhere he had been during his military service. The image of

35

Jack on his bike coming along a road such as the one they were now driving on, was a vivid picture in Tom's mind. He recalled their first meeting in the blue lights of the emergency vehicles at the scene of Miller's death. Had the same paramedics and policemen been present at his accident?

They reached Uffingham and drove slowly along the main street looking for the address Lena gave Tom. It was the only house with a light on. As they walked up the short path to the door it opened. A middle aged lady stood in the door way.

"Heard you coming," she said.

"I'm Lena's mum, you must be Mr Scobie," she said as she ushered them both inside a small downstairs sitting room. Lena was sitting on a sofa.

"Lena, I'm Anna, I'm Tom's wife and I'm a doctor."

When Anna went into doctor mode she was all business, focussing on her patient. Her gentle highland lilt brought some warmth to the bleakness of the room.

"Thanks for coming," said Lena in a small voice.

"Jack said that if anything..." Lena began, before she broke down again.

Tom glanced at Lena's mother, who had sat down beside her on the sofa to comfort her. Too young to be thrown into this maelstrom he thought, as he watched Lena. She sat upright as if readying herself to say something.

"I had to identify him," said Lena looking directly at Tom, with defiance in her eyes.

"My Jack, dead..." she broke down again.

"You'll not be going in to work tomorrow Lena," Anna brought the conversation back to practical matters.

"I'll call the shop," said Lena's mother. "I'm Susie by the way" she said introducing herself.

"There's an envelope full of stuff that Jack said you should have," Lena said in the same small voice. "On the table."

She nodded over to where a bulging envelope sat on a table. It was the same one Jack had brought to show them when he came to the cottage that evening, which seemed like a lifetime ago.

Anna spoke to Susie about what she could do to help Lena; the most important thing now was sleep she had said. With that they collected the envelope and left the house. As they walked back towards Molly, Tom thought he saw some movement. Had somebody been watching the house? As he got into drive, he had a look up and down the street.

"Somebody was watching," said Tom as they drove off. He kept an eye on the rear view mirror but didn't see any lights behind them.

"Are you sure?" asked Anna.

"No," replied Tom, "but….."

****

Later that day Tom got a phone call at his office.

"My name is Detective Inspector Simon Morris, Mr Scobie. Can I speak to you about the death of Jack Sawyer last night?"

Tom was curious as to what Inspector Morris wanted.

"How can I help you Inspector?" he asked.

They agreed that Morris would call into the office in the afternoon. Helping police with their enquiries thought Tom, what enquiries exactly?

The news of Jack's death was on one of the inside pages of the local papers. A hit and run accident that ended the life of a promising campaigning journalist. Tom noted that there was no further explanation or speculation.

In person Morris turned out to be a pleasant looking man, with salt and pepper hair and the look of someone who didn't miss much. Tom walked him into a meeting room through the open plan office, collecting a cup of coffee for them both along the way. None of Tom's colleagues gave the visitor a second look.

"We're treating this as a hit and run, which is a crime Mr Scobie," Morris began.

"Will there be an inquest?" Tom asked, he wanted time to work out Morris's angle.

"Mr Sawyer was a well-known investigative journalist, and I'm of the view that his death was not accidental," Morris continued.

"That's good to know," said Jack, reassured that the police were on the case so quickly.

"I understand that you met Sawyer at the scene of Malcolm Miller's fatal accident," Morris continued. Tom related their encounter just over a month ago. Was that all it was thought Tom; how life has changed.

"You kept in touch?" continued Morris.

"We did, yes." Tom's answer was no more than Morris would have been able to determine. He was becoming curious as to the line of questioning.

"Was there anything in particular that you discussed?" Morris asked.

Tom decided to keep his answers as factual as possible, until he could discern a line of enquiry.

"Jack was an investigative journalist. He was curious about the circumstances of Miller's death."

Tom decided to add a little bit to his answer.

"I had done some work with Miller, so Jack saw me as a possible source of information."

Morris kept a poker face as he continued, "were you able to enlighten him?"

Tom thought for a second; in fact it had been the other way around – Jack had enlightened him.

"No, I was unable to shed any light on the matter," Tom replied.

Morris was making notes in a small black book.

"Were there any other things that you might have discussed, anything that you might think could have been dangerous?" he ventured.

"No," Tom responded, "Jack was usually very direct with his questions, he seemed to be very well informed."

He couldn't help but smile at the memory of how well Jack seemed to know what was going on. "*Usually?*" Morris picked up on the word.

Tom paused; where was this going?

"Can you recall how many times you and Mr Sawyer spoke, Mr Scobie?" Morris's manner had become more intense.

"More than once" replied Tom, unhelpfully.

"All the time about Miller's death?" asked Morris.

Tom recognised the well-practised technique of eliciting information by asking open ended questions. Now Morris had found something he wanted to probe. Be careful Tom, he thought to himself.

"Jack wanted some context on Miller and the Party," said Tom, giving himself time to think.

"I can't honestly say how many times we spoke," he added, trying not to get trapped by speculating.

"Might Mr Sawyer have shared some information with you that touched on other matters?" asked Morris.

He's fishing, thought Tom, wondering what Morris was trying to establish. Tom looked out of the window as if trying to recall anything significant. In reality he wanted to avoid Morris's penetrating stare.

"I really… can't think…."

He was trying to sound as if he was straining to remember. He turned his gaze back to Morris and made a face, "no, sorry, no ideas!"

He could tell that Morris was not convinced.

Morris decided to end the interview. He gave Tom a card with his mobile phone number on, as Tom walked him out of the building. Once back at his desk Tom noticed that his hands were shaking. He had been too tense, the detective had sensed that he was holding something back. He needed to get to work on the material in Jack's envelope.

He had a feeling that took him back to his days in the Balkans. A wrong needed to be put right. Miller had been delving into Markham's activities in a strife torn area; profiting on the back of others misery. Jack had found out about this and was now dead. He needed to keep faith with the work Jack had begun.

"Why don't you have a go?" Anna's voice seemed to float into his mind.

One way to get to the bottom of the Miller and Markham matter would be to submit himself as a candidate for the open primary. This would enable him to delve further into the workings of whatever was going on in the Ridgeway Constituency Association. He had a nodding acquaintance with some of the folks involved in the local Party. But was he ready for what his cousin Matt called the snake pit of politics? What was that saying he recalled? All politics is local.

CHAPTER SEVEN

"This is going to be interesting," mused Henry Makepeace, doing up his black tie. "I think it's the right decision to go ahead with the Ridgeway Revels, despite Malcolm's death. It shows everybody that its business as usual".

"Poor Malcolm is hardly cold…" said Muriel.

"There's no sentiment in politics dear," replied Henry.

Muriel nodded agreement, as she applied her lipstick. She had been around the political arena long enough to know that there was only one thing worse than being an ex-MP, and that was being a dead one.

The Markhams hosted a big party every Spring, to mark the change of the seasons. A medieval celebration called the Revels was reinvented, to allow the Markhams to show off their splendid home, Wyvern Hall.

"Still, I suppose this will allow Charles Markham to parade that young filly of his like a yearling in the paddock. Why Mary puts up with it, I will never know," added Muriel.

Henry knew that Markham had ambitions for Gill Wynne, but she was not rated highly by anybody except Charles Markham.

"Charles is the President of the Association dear," Henry reminded his wife. "He is only an ex-officio officer of the Association. He won't have any say in the selection of the candidate. Besides, this open primary business means that the field will be much wider than we might have expected."

Muriel and Henry spent every spare hour either at the races, or with the trainer of their two year old up on the gallops. Henry's successful car dealership paid for the horse, and their winnings paid for their lifestyle. Muriel had a talent for spotting good horseflesh, as well as a way of talent spotting people; Henry often deferred to her judgement.

"I hear from the constituency office that there has been a sudden spike in ticket sales, since the announcement of the open primary," said Henry.

"Honestly!" said Muriel, "every Prospective Parliamentary Candidate within a hundred miles will be on their way here by now!"

They both chuckled. "Kerching!" said Henry, making the sound of a cash register.

"But your humble servant and his trusted band of advisors will get to choose the runners and riders," he added. "Come on! – we don't want to miss the champers before the concert," said Henry.

"There are bound to be a few fallers," mused Muriel.

******

"Well, don't we look fine!" said Tom, as they walked up the manicured pathway, that evening to the great front door of Wyvern Hall.

Anna gave him a rueful smile. She normally avoided Tom's party political gatherings, but the Ridgeway Revels was more social than political. As a local GP she would be able to catch up on many of the folk who came through the doors of the health centre.

"This is pure Jane Austen!" remarked Anna.

"Now, don't you come over all puritanical on me, Doctor McDonald!" teased Tom. He knew that despite the Tomboy style she cultivated, Anna enjoyed the opportunity to put her glad rags on. One of her fashionista cousins passed on some very chic frocks, one of which she was sporting this evening.

It wasn't yet warm enough to gather outside, but there were plenty of people loitering around the doorway, meeting and greeting. Tom gave their invitation to a fierce looking security guard by the door, and they walked in to a sea of men in black tie and women in varying styles of evening gowns.

Anna went straight to the ladies room, so Tom started wandering in the direction of the drinks table. He almost fell over Muriel Makepeace as she scuttled past him.

"Hello Mu – how are you?"

She nodded conspiratorially for him to follow her. She led him to the table where drinks were being served. She gave them both a glass of champagne, and led him away with a series of anxious glances around them; she beckoned him to come closer.

"Now Tom, what do you think of all these goings on? I hear you were the first to find poor Malcolm after his accident."

"Not quite," replied Tom, refusing to take her seriously.

"Anna and I were first to arrive after the ambulance. Anna offered to help as she's a doctor."

Tom paused and then added, "we did think it was odd that Malcolm should drive his car off the road, and wasn't wearing his seatbelt. It looks like it could be suicide."

The Inquest into Miller's death had been perfunctory; death by misadventure. No mention of suicide, or anything else. Tom had wondered where Inspector Morris's enquiries had gone, but let it go.

Muriel glanced around them again. The room was crowded and noisy, so there was no telling whether they could be overheard. Out of the corner of his eye Tom sensed that Don Johnson the agent, standing with Henry Makepeace, was watching them.

"This is a very rum business Tom," said Muriel looking him straight in the eye, "I don't like this at all."

"Very unfortunate," responded Tom, not wanting to get drawn any further into conspiracy theories.

"Why don't you throw you hat in the ring Tom?" Muriel said, still looking at him intently.

Tom was flummoxed; twice it had been suggested that he should fill the vacancy. He wasn't ready for the vehemence of Muriel's suggestion.

She led Tom over to where Henry was standing, "I'm hoping that I can persuade young Tom here to stand," she said to Henry and the agent.

The Ridgeway Revels was in full swing, the buzz of a vibrant social occasion swirled around them. Henry's beaming countenance radiated bonhomie. "Well, well, what do you make of that Don?"

The agent couldn't tell whether his chairman was being serious. He took a swig of his champagne, before responding.

"I'm sure there'll be lots of highly talented people putting their names forward," he replied neutrally, giving Muriel a basilisk stare.

"Well, I won't complicate matters by putting my name forward," said Tom.

Muriel maintained her social smile, but Tom could see a look of disappointment in her eyes.

For most of the evening Donald Johnson had been fobbing off the approaches of political aspirants, who had appeared from out of the woodwork at the prospect of winning the nomination for a safe parliamentary seat.

"I just need to check on something," he said by way of excusing himself from the group.

****

"All going very well," said Lord Markham to Gill Wynne, with whom he was sauntering through the central corridor running the length of the ground floor.

"Everybody thinks you'll be a wonderful successor to Malcolm," he said, as he led her towards a knot of people.

She had put on a bright blue evening gown, and done her hair in a manner reminiscent of Margaret Thatcher.

"Lovely evening, Lord Markham," said a woman with a flushed face, Markham didn't recognise her but was geniality personified in his response.

"So kind of you to say so. Can I introduce Gill Wynne, who is going to be our next Member of Parliament?"

****

Anna was watching the scene with the practised eye of a doctor. She was chatting to another woman as they left the ladies room.

"It's a bit like one of those documentaries on the telly," said the other lady, whose face was familiar.

"You mean the mating rituals of birds of paradise?" asked Anna with a smile.

As she saw Tom chatting to Muriel and Henry Makepeace, Anna noticed the agent Donald Johnson detach himself from their group and head towards Charles Markham. She had seen Donald give Tom an appraising glance as he drank his champagne. He was obviously unimpressed, while Muriel seemed positively beaming. Well, she thought, that's politics for you. As Donald left the group, Tom saw Anna and beckoned her over to join them.

"Now then Anna," said Muriel ebulliently, "can you persuade Tom to stand for the nomination."

Anna could feel her colour rising in embarrassment.

"He's as good as any – people," she just stopped herself from saying numties, "so why not?"

"Why not indeed!" echoed Muriel.

Anna's gaze was drawn past Muriel's shoulder to where Donald Johnson was now standing close to Lord Markham, who was a picture of bonhomie as he looked around the room. Something Johnson said made his face change. Its aspect went from jovial to grave. Gill Wynne, standing next to Markham glanced over to where Anna and Muriel were standing with Tom. In a second Anna caught a look of fury on Gill's face. Gill realised Anna was looking at her, and put on a smile and raised a glass in her direction.

"I don't think we're making too many friends with this talk of you standing," she murmured to Tom, as Muriel led them over to another group.

She told him what she had just seen. Tom nodded slowly; I understand, he seemed to be saying.

****

Anna was enjoying the concert. Finally a chance to sit down. The culmination of an evening of champagne and canapés, was usually a recital by up and coming young musicians that Lady Mary sponsored through one of her charitable committees. The melodious tones of Schubert's Trout Quintet flowed through the room, with its classical décor and fine Murano chandelier. The audience listened with rapt attentiveness.

But Anna could tell that Tom wasn't listening. She could see from his expression that he was replaying in his mind the conversation he had had with Muriel Makepeace. As the music flowed over her, Anna allowed herself a glance at the fine carriage clock perched on a side table. It was getting late, and it had been a long and busy week. Past ten o clock; very late for country folk, she thought. Out of the corner of her eye she saw that Lord Markham was looking in Tom's direction. His was not an appraising look she thought; it was a look of pure evil.

CHAPTER EIGHT

Sunday lunch in the Makepeace household the day after the Revels, was a very convivial affair. Henry and Muriel lived in a Georgian town house right on the square in the middle of Wandage, the market town that served as the centre for much of local life. They chose to buy a house where friends and neighbours could drop in. It served as a base for their social entertaining, and their political activities. It was testimony to Henry's success, as he progressed through the motor trade borrowing to buy dealerships, and gain acceptance among the racing fraternity through ownership of a thoroughbred stabled on the Downs. The talk was about the candidacy for the vacant seat. Even people who professed no interest in politics were eager to hear the gossip from the horse's mouth. Henry couldn't hide his enjoyment at being the centre of attention.

"We've had a lot of interest," said Henry, as he went round the table pouring wine for his lunch guests.

"A lot of people seem to have discovered long lost family connections to the area," he took his seat at the head of a long refectory table.

"Any locals?" asked a stout man down the table.

"Several," responded Muriel, allowing Henry to have a drink, "some councillors and former councillors."

"All worthy people," added Henry.

"Several no hopers," Muriel chimed in, "they won't stay the course."

"When do we get a look at'em?" asked the same stout gentleman, "when will they appear in the parade ring?"

Henry explained that first of all there would be a sift through the applications, then there would be a 'long list', which would need to be winnowed down to a short list of candidates who would be presented at an open primary.

"Sounds like the Grand National," piped up a well fed lady on Henry's right.

"Plenty of fences to get over!" added Muriel.

"What *is* an open primary?" asked an earnest young man, who might have been someone's godson.

"The idea is to encourage fresh blood into the body politic," explained Henry. "This way we are not constrained by the 'approved candidates' list supplied by Party headquarters. We can pick our own candidate, provided they support the Party, of course."

What he did not explain was the usual practice of having an approved list of candidates judged to be ideologically suitable, created a pool of willing souls who could be expected to turn up at the drop of a hat, anywhere in the country, to serve the Party's needs. In return they expected to have first dibs at a safe seat like Ridgeway. There were plenty of bruised egos making noises to Party HQ about the decision.

"It puts a lot of responsibility on your shoulders Henry," said a lady whom Henry didn't recognize, but who might be one of Muriel's bridge playing buddies.

"I will have help from the agent, who is a full time member of staff, and my colleagues on the executive committee."

"I'm pretty certain that Don has already done some weeding," Muriel chipped in, "I saw lots of eager people giving him slips of paper and business cards last night."

"They probably went straight into the bin when he got home," added Henry. "Besides, we have to consider who the other parties may put up. There might be some celebrity seeking to advance a cause they cherish. Our person would have to look credible, otherwise we'd look like we're taking the voters for granted."

During the pause between courses, Henry and Muriel both found themselves in the kitchen, Henry finding some more wine, and Muriel looking out the cheese.

"Who is that strange lady sitting next to Edward Bridges? I don't recognise her," said Henry bustling around the kitchen.

"She's one of my bridge ladies, a new arrival called Shelley, lovely girl," replied Muriel as she disappeared into the larder.

"We have Charles Markham as a common acquaintance," she added.

Henry absorbed this, and reflected that he should be cautious with his remarks about the candidates. People tend to gossip, he mused; some more than others.

The level of noise around the long refectory table was a sign of a successful gathering thought Muriel, as people chattered and laughed. There was much discussion of who was wearing what at the Revels yesterday, and who was with whom.

"Who was the gorgeous redhead with the lovely big eyes?" asked Shelley.

"That was Doctor Anna Macdonald," responded Muriel, "a very popular GP at the health centre in Farrington."

"She can take my temperature any day!" chimed one of Henry's chums from the car business, tucking into the stilton.

"She's married to Tom Scobie," explained Matthew Bridges to his neighbour. "He's a farmer's boy from up the vale," he added dismissively.

"Nothing special about him."

Henry knew that Edward Bridges' family and the Scobies were both farm owners; there was no love lost between them.

"He's a businessman," Muriel intervened, "involved in some sort of clever stuff in Oxford."

Shelley looked at Muriel, "then he's a very lucky man."

Henry saw that Edward Bridges looked unimpressed.

Henry could see that the pale Spring sun was setting through the window, and glanced at Muriel. "Coffee in the sitting room?" she said brightly.

There was a general scraping of chairs as people began to move away from the table. In the sitting room the log fire was burning brightly; Henry pulled the fireguard out of the way and took up station sitting on the fender, with a glass of wine in his hand.

"More drinks anyone, help yourself," he waved towards a side table loaded with a variety of drinks. Matthew Bridges was first to sample the cognac, joined by Henry's chum from the car business. They were soon deep in conversation about the merits of a new model of Mercedes.

One of Henry's racing pals, Gordon Parker, came and sat next to him on the fender. "This candidate business won't become a drama, will it Henry?" he asked.

"Hope not, Gordon," he replied, "no reason why it should."

"Strange business with Malcolm Miller," Gordon ventured, wanting to see what Henry knew.

"Muriel tells me that we men 'compartmentalise' things in our minds," Henry said as he took a sip of his wine.

"I guess that Malcolm had things hidden away that suddenly spilled out," he said, trying to keep his voice low.

"He and Louisa lived separate lives, but they seemed to rub along well enough, so I don't think it was woman problems."

"Money matters?" asked Gordon.

Henry shrugged and looked into his glass, "who among us doesn't have money problems at the moment?"

They both knew people who had been caught by the recent banking crisis.

"We're OK – just" said Henry, giving Gordon a rueful glance.

Gordon nodded his agreement "had to sell some stuff, at a loss, but we're in the clear."

"Well, we'll just have to win it all back on the gee gees!" Henry said, cheering up. "Now I'd better see to the guests."

It was a very happy bunch who left the Makepeace's house as the evening gloom descended. Henry walked into the kitchen where Muriel was setting the dishwasher.

"Another success I think!" he raised the glass he was still holding.

"Thank you m'dear," replied Muriel, finding her own glass and re-filling it.

"Well, here's to –?" asked Henry holding up his glass.

"To a new beginning!" replied Muriel.

"I have a good feeling about this" added Henry, as they clinked glasses.

He noticed that her face became rather solemn, "you all right Mu?" he looked anxious. His wife had had several scares with her health.

"Nothing at all" she said, "it's just - as if a ghost had walked over my grave."

CHAPTER NINE

"That's wonderful news Tom! So glad you've changed your mind," Muriel sounded positively ebullient on the phone. "I think you're just in time to submit your application."

He could hear Muriel talking to Henry about the application procedure.

"Henry will call you back Tom, what made you change your mind? – oh, you can tell me later!" she ended the call.

Tom knew he would have to get his skates on, if he was going to get the necessary paperwork sorted before the deadline. His phone call to Muriel was to short circuit the process, Tom knew that she was keen for him to stand, even if Henry was lukewarm.

Tom and Anna had discussed his candidacy as they walked on the White Horse Hill, the morning after the Revels. It was a place they always went to when something needed discussing. This was a serious matter, and they both needed to be on the same page Tom had decided.

"I said that you are as good as any of those *numties* who will be trying to win the nomination," said Anna, as they looked over the Vale of the White Horse.

"Are you doing this because you want to make a difference, or because you want to get to the bottom of the Miller – Markham connection?" she asked.

Tom allowed himself some thinking time, before he responded.

"The open primary got me interested," he began.

"Then I thought we've only just begun to live our lives together, do I really want to get wrapped up in full time politics?"

He continued, "when I learnt that Miller had discovered Markham's Balkan connection, I felt stupid. Miller had used my knowledge to unearth Markham's activities."

Anna gave him one of her looks, "hurt pride, Tom Scobie!" she said reprovingly.

Tom gave her a sheepish smile, "it's partly hurt pride, sure, but I know what has been going on in the Balkans and the idea that some of it was orchestrated from here – well, it just makes my blood boil." He paused. "If there is a connection between Miller's death, Jack's death and that copper who came calling and Markham's at the root of it, then there's something very rotten going on."

"We started to talk about this with Matt and Lizzie," said Anna, recalling their recent visit.

"Have you spoken to him about your change of heart?"

"I think I need to speak to you, before I speak to Matt," replied Tom, "this is *our* lives we're talking about"

Tom's cousin Matt was the other person he felt comfortable speaking to about big decisions. He called Matt later in the day, just as Lizzie was putting the boys to bed.

"I'll have to go and read bedtime stories in a minute, but shoot".

You had to take Matt when you could get him, reflected Tom, was that about to become their lives too? He summarised developments since they last met. The option of standing for the vacancy was still open, if he hurried.

"Are you committing yourself to a life of public service Tom, or are you on a crusade?" was Matt's typically challenging response.

"Both!" was Tom's adamant reply.

"What does Anna say?" another question, straight to the point.

"She said I was as good as any of the others, so why not have a go." Even as he spoke he felt underwhelmed at his justification.

Matt had undertaken a change of life when he quit his high flying job to become a vicar. They both had a strong sense of right and wrong, since their childhood. Matt had involved himself in voluntary work, and had become in Tom's words a God botherer. Ironically whilst Tom was doing undercover work in the Balkans, Matt had become involved in reconciliation ministry, which took him to areas of the world that were much more dangerous. 'Blessed are the peacemakers' was their mutual motto. After a long pause Matt responded, "go for it Tom, if it feels right."

****

Tom and Henry Makepeace had initially bonded over motor cars. Henry had come across Tom and Anna sitting on the tailgate of Tom's Land Rover, at a local point-to-point. Henry dealt in upmarket cars, and in his view an ex-MOD Land Rover was anything but. Henry had invited them to come and join his gathering which included Malcolm Miller, the local MP, who swiftly recruited Tom to join a Policy Working Group he was leading, looking at security challenges. So it was that when Tom knocked on the door the following evening, Henry greeted him with a broad smile.

"Still driving that old wagon of yours?" he said, as he opened the door wide in welcome.

"Wouldn't swap it for the world!" replied Tom, entering the generously proportioned Georgian hallway. Henry gestured Tom into the snug at the back of the hallway, and poured them both a good measure of whisky.

"We must get together and do some more target practice," Henry said, as he handed over the glass. He kept a collection of old pistols in a safe in his snug, and he had taken Tom to a nearby pistol club, an exercise Tom thought of as converting live rounds into empty cartridge cases.

"Now, let's get down to business," he said raising his glass, "to success!"

Tom was unsure how much of this bonhomie was genuine, or put on to please Muriel who supported Tom's application. He had mapped out in his own mind how he wanted to play the conversation with Henry. He would keep quiet about Jack's revelations, and rely on his instinct to judge whether Henry was implicated.

"What do we know about Malcolm's death?" Tom was quick off the mark.

Henry's face darkened, "I'm still not sure that I've got to the bottom of it, Tom and it troubles me."

If your MP kills himself, thought Tom, you ought to be troubled.

"It was well known that he and Louisa lived separate lives, so I don't think blackmail could have been a problem."

Tom decided there was no point pussyfooting any longer.

"What's this I hear about Malcolm being threatened with bankruptcy?"

Henry gave Tom a look of surprise.

"You found out about that? Well, it would have come out sooner or later," said Henry. "Some of us were trying to put together a finance package to stave off the threat, but all the doors were closed," he added.

"Was it meant to be a well-kept secret?" asked Tom, only just managing to keep the sarcasm out of his voice.

One rule for us; another for the little people, he thought. Henry's reply sounded sheepish.

"We all hoped that the storm would pass. On the eve of a General Election...."

"Ridgeway has been rock solid for years," Tom interrupted.

"There was discontent in the Association, that Malcolm was neglecting his constituency duties," explained Henry.

"We were hoping that he might choose to stand down at this election, but he showed no sign of doing so."

"Charles Markham is the person who provided the loans and who then withdrew them," added Tom. "Was he the driving force behind this?"

Henry looked uncomfortable. Tom wondered just how wide Markham's influence reached, maybe Henry was also under his sway.

"What about Donald Johnson the agent?" Tom pressed Henry. "He seems to be in cahoots with Charles Markham."

Tom related what he and Anna had seen at the Ridgeway Revels.

"Remember that it was Charles Markham who got Don the job here," Henry explained.

"Don had lost his job at a seat in mid-Hampshire or somewhere, and Charles thought he deserved a second chance."

So far, so plausible thought Tom, but not exactly a ringing endorsement.

Muriel's invitation to stay for some shepherd's pie was accepted with alacrity by Tom, it would allow them to continue talking. A quick text exchange with Anna meant that she could stay and chat after her evening at college, where she was studying for a post grad qualification in public health. Muriel invited them into the kitchen, where the table was already set for three.

"I hope you boys are getting matters sorted?" asked Muriel, over her shoulder as she pulled a shepherd's pie out of the Aga.

"I was just explaining to Tom that thanks to the Party Leader's decision, we have the chance to put the house in order," said Henry.

"You make me sound like the sheriff of Dodge City!" said Tom, amused at the idea of cleaning up the town.

"Seriously though Henry," said Tom, "what am I getting involved in?"

"Charles Markham is too powerful," said Muriel as she dished out the supper. "He needs bringing down a peg or two," she added, with a glance at Henry.

"We all thought that his patronage would do the Party some good," said Henry, by way of explanation. Do yourselves some good, thought Tom.

"Malcolm fell in with him, and then – fell out with him," Muriel chipped in, as she sat down at the table.

Tom took in the scene in his mind's eye; three of them in a fine Georgian kitchen, discussing corruption and suicide, as if it was the most normal thing in the world.

Muriel leant towards Tom, in a conspiratorial manner.

"Charles is backing Gill Wynne as the favoured candidate. In the normal run of things, the local association would draw up the short list for interview. That would put Gill in as the hot favourite. But the Party leaders thought otherwise."

Henry shifted uncomfortably in his seat.

"I have to be seen to be playing by the rules," he said. "Several of Markham's pals have signed Gill's nomination papers, so I can hardly block her," he added.

Tom frowned as he tried to recollect Gill's face. They had been at some events together, and he recalled a rather affected woman, who asked rather obvious questions, playing to the gallery.

"Er, I think I've got her," he said hesitantly. "Not going to set the world on fire......"

"Charles thinks she's the cat's pyjamas," said Muriel waspishly.

"You are untainted by any of this Tom, and if you really want to help the Party restore its integrity, we can help you to do it," said Muriel, with a tone in her voice that was at once a rallying cry, and partly a plea.

"How do you think I should play my hand?" he asked.

"We want to arrange a little *soirée* for you, to meet some of the members of the Executive Committee," said Muriel. "Some of them you will have met during your work with Malcolm, but this will be a chance to get to know them properly."

Tom saw the sense of this, and it was a generous offer.

"We will have an open house and ask people to drop in, so as to comply with best practice," added Henry. Tom knew that the Makepeaces were keen followers of the turf, so concluded that he wouldn't look a gift horse in the mouth.

During supper, the atmosphere lightened as Henry and Muriel plied Tom with as much gossip and scuttlebutt about the executive committee, as he felt he could usefully absorb before meeting them. They were now conspirators, set on a joint venture.

"In my army days I used to say, the team that connives together survives together," said Tom, alluding to their new partnership.

"Was that when you were dealing with the enemy?" asked Henry.

"No," replied Tom, "the Company Commander, who was an idiot!"

A date had been agreed for the 'At Home', and another text to Anna had secured her presence. A great boon thought Tom, people tended to open their souls to Anna.

CHAPTER TEN

"Tom, come to bed – its past one!"

Anna came padding across the kitchen floor. Tom was seated at the pine table, where he had spread out Jack's papers.

"Hello," said Tom, distracted.

"Is this Jack's stuff?" she asked, picking up a piece of paper.

She sat herself down in Tom's lap to study it. Tom put an arm around her waist to hold her. Jack's notes were written in a very methodical way, lots of lines connecting boxes. It seemed to Anna that Jack had just stepped out of the room.

"An unquiet spirit," said Anna almost to herself, "no wonder I couldn't sleep. There's a restless spirit in the house."

Anna seemed to sense things that Tom did not; sometimes an atmosphere when they entered a building, or when they were at a social occasion. He put it down to the confused mixture of spirituality and superstition that she absorbed from her hippie parents, and her highland grandmother.

"I'll have to get Matt to read you one of his Sermons," he teased.

"Are we going to be all right with this Tom? I know that I suggested you apply for the seat, but after what happened to Jack, and Malcolm….."

Tom gave her a reassuring squeeze.

"Look at this," he said in an encouraging tone, tapping the paper with a pencil.

"Markham thinks he has been very clever, but Jack was even cleverer. He has been able to map out His Lordship's influence network."

"Why didn't he go to the police?" asked Anna.

"A lot of this is legal tax avoidance and off-shore accounts," Tom began.

"Where the criminality lies is in the purpose to which this," he indicated the spider's web diagram Jack had originally shown them, "gets used."

"Hmmm?" Anna was sounding more reassured.

"He uses money to buy people, or to control them," said Tom.

"But there has to be a mechanism for the transmission of funds. However you wrap it up, unless you pay cash, there will be a trail. Jack followed the money."

"The root of all evil," Anna mused.

"Matt would correct you; the *love* of money is the root of all evil. But essentially you're right."

Anna gave him a playful slap on the arm, "it's way too late in the day to be giving me scripture lessons, Tom Scobie."

Tom was relieved that Anna's mood seemed to improve. He would need her support for the 'At Home' that Henry and Muriel were arranging for him.

"Can you join the dots?" asked Anna. "Can you connect the legal and the illegal stuff?"

"I'm going to have a jolly good try," replied Tom. "I just need to lift up one corner of the tent, and see inside." He was speaking to reassure himself as much as Anna.

"My application to the Constituency Association will enable me to lift up the tent edge a little bit," he added.

"OK," said Anna seemingly mollified. "I'd like to think that this will bring Jack some peace," she said almost to herself. "Don't be much longer please, we've both got work tomorrow."

Tom watched her walk off to go back upstairs. He turned his attention back to the audit trail Jack had done for Falcon Holdings, the company involved in the affairs of Malcolm Miller. With the help of Jack's annotated notes, he could see how funds had been paid out to Miller's property investment fund, and then withdrawn.

He looked at his watch; it really was getting late. He began to sweep up the papers and place them back into Jack's envelope. As he did so, he came across another spider's web diagram, which was underneath other papers. In the corner Jack had scribbled in red marker pen UPDATED, with a more recent date. Tom gave it a cursory glance, wondering what the update was.

A red circle drew his attention to an entry: WEST VALE MOTORS – the company belonging to Henry Makepeace. Falcon Holdings held 57% of the share capital, accumulated through a series of nominee front companies. Tom wondered whether Henry knew the extent to which he was in hock to Charles Markham.

****

"And who else was there Shelley?" asked Lord Markham.
"Well, most of the people who were at the lunch party they gave, plus some of the people who were at the revels," replied Shelley.

Rather obtuse thought Markham. He had asked Shelley to let him know how the Makepeace's 'At Home' had gone, the previous evening. In a conspiratorial way he had said that he was 'not invited', and Shelley had offered to fill him in on all of the gossip. Except that she hadn't done a good job at picking any up.

Markham had scooped Shelley up at a race meeting nearby. Newly divorced, he had introduced her to the Makepeaces as another bridge player. She was also on the hunt for romance and excitement. Markham had said that he would see what he could do for her.

"That lovely red head was there with her husband," Shelley continued in her giggly manner.

Markham had to think.

"You know, Anna somebody, doctor lady," she continued. This was becoming wearing thought Markham, still he did ask for a report.

"Married to Tom Scooby-do," she giggled again.

"Ah ha!" Markham responded, as if they were sharing some deep indiscretion.

"Well thank you Shelley, we'll make a special agent of you yet!" he added conspiratorially. They ended the call.

He pulled a black notebook out of the drawer in his escritoire. He made a pencil note:

TOM SCOBIE – anything known?

He picked up the phone and punched out the numbers for another of his 'special agents' in the Association.

"Hello Gordon, hope you're keeping well?" he enquired, geniality itself.

"Oh, er, hello Charles, how nice to hear from you."

Markham could detect a hint of a tremor in the voice; just how he liked things, establish who's boss early in the proceedings.

"Were you at Henry and Muriel's little *soirée* yesterday?" straight to the point.

"Yes, we were both there," came the reply, almost as if his wife would be an alibi.

"Was there any specific occasion?" Markham asked, a short question – no room to hide.

"I got the impression that it was just a chance to catch up with everybody, but my other half spoke to Muriel, who was rhapsodic about Tom Scobie," came the reply.

Bingo thought Markham.

"What did you make of Captain Scobie?" asked Markham, becoming more pleasant, to extract more revelations.

"Seemed quite serious," came the reply "he was bothered about Malcolm's death, as he had worked with him on something."

"Go on," suggested Markham.

"It seems he is involved in some high falutin' company, based in Oxford, which supplies information to companies that want to pay for it. A bit daft if you ask me, can't they read the papers?"

Markham made a note to find out more about Oxford Info, he had heard of it as a supplier of business intelligence. This was interesting news.

"His wife's a bit of a looker," said Gordon, warming to his task of informant.

"Just tell me how Henry and Muriel introduced Tom to others in the room," said Markham, trying to contain his impatience.

"Something about needing a new broom to clean out the stables."

Markham winced at the mixed metaphor, but it seemed clear to him that the Makepeaces were promoting Tom Scobie as a possible contender for the Ridgeway seat.

"Well, I won't keep you further Gordon, good to speak," said Markham as he ended the call.

He was aware of Tom Scobie, having seen him at one of Malcolm Miller's barbecues. He was also at the Revels. Muriel had mentioned something to Donald Johnson about getting him to stand as a candidate. He had him down as a rather dull ex-army type, son of a local farmer. He could be a dark horse if the Makepeaces had persuaded him to stand, thought Markham. Was that their game?

CHAPTER ELEVEN

Lord Markham was not happy.

"Gill is on the long list, which has to be good news," said Donald Johnson.

He was standing before Lord Markham in his study in Wyvern Hall, like an errant school boy. The deadline for applications had closed. Interest for the opportunity to stand for parliament among a wide cross-section of the public, who would not normally consider themselves eligible, had been huge. The imminence of an election meant that many desperate candidates on the approved list had submitted applications. Whittling these down to a manageable long list had been quite a chore, reflected Donald. Budding Wilberforces had applied as had numerous Walter Mitty types. The discriminator, however, had been to prove a strong local connection.

"Who were the people that were opposed?" asked Markham.

Johnson fished a small black notebook from his jacket pocket, and itemised the names. As Johnson read the names out, Markham noted that they were not on the Christmas card list.

"The Chairman was sitting on his hands," added Johnson.

"He was waiting to see which way the wind was blowing."

"This is too bad," said Markham, "he didn't speak earlier in the discussion?"

Johnson consulted his notes.

"He waited until others had voted."

"Is there *no way* that I can be on the committee, even as an ex-officio member?" asked Markham.

"I'll need to check the rules" replied Johnson. "It's not normal practice, especially with the public interest in this case."

"I'll need to see the list Don," Markham said, in a tone of voice which would brook no nonsense. Donald obediently handed over a photocopied list, which Markham scrutinised.

"This is the list of people we will invite for interview next Saturday," explained Donald.

"Short notice," Markham said, as he continued to scan the list.

"Exactly," said Donald, in a conspiratorial tone.

"The Party Leader said he wants this buttoned up in short order, who are we to disagree?"

Donald had checked with the Party hierarchy as to the availability of the Area Campaign Director, who would oversee the process.

"Gilbert Burch is available, so I've taken the liberty of setting things up," continued Donald. "We can use the council offices for the interviews."

Markham had finished looking at the list, "there are a couple we might be able to persuade to stand down," he poked at the paper with his pencil.

"These people are no hopers," he drew a line through some names on the list.

He noted that Tom Scobie was on the list.

"I need to be sure about the Chairman, should it come to a tied vote – which is not unknown in selections," he added.

Donald nodded in agreement but said nothing. It was his job to see that his master's bidding was done and to report any information, however insignificant. Markham, he knew, had a certain way of operating, but the stakes were getting higher.

"I need you to investigate what circumstances, however unusual, might be cited as a reason for me to be on the selection committee Don."

Markham's tone left Donald in no doubt about the seriousness with which Markham was approaching the forthcoming selection. He would be expected to deliver the right result, or heaven help him.

****

"Well Chairman that concludes our list of interviewees," Donald Johnson's voice sounded relieved but weary.

Far from being an exercise in citizens' participation in the democratic process, the selection process seemed to be a torpor inducing experience.

"Perhaps we can allow ourselves a short leg stretch, and then we'd better have a look over the list." Donald was all business, as the Executive Committee of Ridgeway Constituency Association adjourned with a collective sigh, and much scraping of chairs around the room. It had been a long day cloistered in a drab 1970s utilitarian low rise building that comprised the District Council offices. The Constituency Association had booked the room for the whole of Saturday.

"Well done Chairman! You managed the interview process immaculately."

Gilbert Burch was the Area Campaign Director, sent by the Party to oversee the constituency selection process. Henry Makepeace hadn't taken to Burch, who he saw as the exemplar of a paper pusher with a weasely face.

"Thank you Mr Burch, we've still got some work to do," said Henry.

Tom had found the interview process pleasant enough. After Henry and Muriel's *soirée*, which they arranged to introduce him to members of the committee, he made sure to establish eye contact with those members of the interview panel whom he recognised. Henry had tutored Tom on local planning matters, likely to be of concern to the inquisitors. Muriel had talked him through the relationship between the County Council and the local District Council, as two councillors were on the panel. Anna had provided a run down on health matters; Tom's brothers Tony and Sam had let him into the mysteries of agricultural and countryside matters. Thus equipped, he felt well briefed on any local matters likely to be thrown at him. He had made an effort to remain up to date on current news stories, likely to arise during questioning.

Henry Makepeace was studiously impartial, as Tom answered questions about his upbringing locally, and his motivation to stand for parliament.

"I've seen what happens when a country descends into chaos," he said. "We're lucky enough to have a deeply rooted tradition of representative democracy in this country" he went on.

"At least since the 1920s!" he added, with a nod at the women in the room.

"The best guarantee for the health of our democracy is by people trusting those that they send to Westminster on their behalf. But trust has to be earned, and I hope that I can win the trust of the people I grew up living amongst."

Tom had thought about this particular question, or something like it. He didn't want to sound too pompous, but he needed to convey to the interviewing panel a feeling that he was conscious of the responsibility he would be shouldering, should he be selected. There was also an unspoken reference to the fact that Malcolm Miller had seemed remote to many people, as he had been in Westminster for as long as many of them could remember.

"Any more questions anyone?"

Henry had looked around the room, seeking to draw the interview to an end. Tom's interview was in the middle of the day, and there were plenty of other candidates to get through. Already people were beginning to get fidgety. The clock on the wall of the committee room, which the interview panel could see, but which the candidates could not, had seemed to crawl its way through the morning. Tom saw a young girl who was sitting at one end of the table. She was probably a representative of the Party's Young Movement, as her complexion was marked with acne.

"Mr Scobie," she began timidly, sensing the disapproval of the others who were keen to get onto the next candidate. "What makes you angry?"

Tom turned to the girl, who looked at him sheepishly.

"Goodness, that's a great question!" said Tom, giving the girl credit and a winning smile. He was just about to launch into a speech about injustice, but felt that it would sound too contrived. Then he began to speak.

"Evil," he replied, addressing the girl directly. "I'm reminded of Edmund Burke's remark - all that is necessary for evil to flourish is that good men do nothing."

Tom turned to face the whole panel.

"I have seen evil at work in the Balkans. Not just the work of evil men who led their country, but those good men who were servants of the state, who went along with things. I thought that we had learnt this lesson in the 1930s and 40s, but apparently not. The International Community stood by, and wrung its hands, while people were forced out of their houses and murdered."

He saw that he had the attention of everybody in the room; no doodling or staring out of the window. He went on.

"Powerful people seize upon a big idea, and in their mind the end justifies the means. To them ordinary people are of no more worth than cattle. What is worse is the way they seek to divide people between 'us' and 'them'. I remember talking to a lovely old chap in Bihac, in northern Bosnia, who told me that it was his neighbours who killed his family, because he was a Bosnian Muslim and they were Croats; as simple as that."

As he spoke Tom could see the aged face of the gentle old man in his mind's eye. He brought himself back to the present.

"That's the sort of thing that makes me angry," he said, turning back towards the girl who had asked the question. He could see that her whole aspect had changed. No longer did she look shy and timid, stuck in the corner; but was sitting bolt upright, her eyes shining. Others in the room were also sitting up, his point had gone home.

As he left the committee room, Tom thought he saw Henry wink at him, but he might have imagined it. He needed to let Henry know about what he'd found in Jack's notes. There was no way of sweetening the pill; Henry was up to his neck in debt, and Markham held his fate in his hands. This was not the time, however, as he left the room.

Anna was waiting outside like an anxious parent. As they walked out along the functional looking corridor, another candidate was being ushered in by one of the stewards. Tom thought he looked terrified, not a good basis to begin from, he thought. Once they were driving in Anna's car, she started quizzing him on how he felt his interview had gone. Tom replayed the questions and answers, to Anna's satisfaction.

"Well done Tom Scobie!" she said proudly, as if he had secured the nomination by dint of a few well answered questions.

"If I get through this round, the next one will be in front of a random cross-section of our fellow citizens," he reflected.

"You'll have as good a chance as the others," Anna was enthusiastic. "When will you hear?"

"Very soon," replied Tom, still a little bit surprised to be even speaking of having a shot at standing for parliament.

His eyes wandered over the fields and hedgerows, beginning to show the signs of spring.

"But first I've got to have a conversation with Henry."

CHAPTER TWELVE

"We've both dealt with dodgy people before, Tom."

Matt's voice was reassuringly emollient over the phone. While Tom was in the Balkans, Matt went in and out of the Middle East, brokering back channel peace talks. This got him close to those who didn't always like the way the talks were going. A man of the cloth was regarded as a trusted intermediary.

"Henry's not a *dodgy* character Matt, rather he's – naïve."

Tom had outlined his dilemma to Matt, as he sat in the cosy comfort of Shepherds Cottage. It was later the same evening, and Tom felt drained after the selection interview, rather like he had done when he'd taken exams at school. He now needed to summon the mental stamina to think through what he did next.

As he was speaking, Anna came over with a glass of whisky for both of them, and sat down on the old sofa beside him.

"Anna says hi, by the way," said Tom, as he took the offered glass from her.

"You just be sure to look after that lovely lady, Tom!"

The comment was jocular, but Tom felt a sharp stab of remorse as he remembered Ivana, his interpreter, who had been gunned down in the Balkans.

"Oh! Sorry Tom." Matt stumbled over an apology; he knew what he'd said, but too late.

"Water under the bridge," said Tom, pulling Anna closer to him.

"Remind me of the husband and wife combination," Matt said, getting back to the purpose of the call.

Tom outlined his dealings with Muriel and Henry, and of his rather stilted conversation with them, when he had agreed to stand for selection.

"So it's Muriel who has been championing you, and Henry has been following along?" Matt summarized.

"Sounds to me that she is the one with the emotional intelligence, and he is content to exude bonhomie to all," he added.

"I haven't revealed to them what I've learnt from the papers I retrieved from Jack," said Tom.

"I have a sense that if you spoke to Muriel, it would allow her to broach the matter with Henry," Matt said.

"After all, he's the Chairman of the Association, so you're risking a conflict of interests if you spoke to him. It'd be like you were holding this knowledge over him, to secure your candidacy."

That's exactly what Markham does, thought Tom, seeing the sense of Matt's observation.

"Besides," continued Matt, "you've got to allow him to work out for himself how to behave now that he knows that you know...."

Anna, who could hear the exchange, nodded her agreement.

"The risk is that it could all blow up in your face, Tom, and you'd be excluded from the next stage of the selection, but at least you've given Henry and Muriel some space to think."

Again, Anna nodded her agreement. Tom felt that Matt's advice was something he should sleep on, and as it was getting late, they finished the call.

"Hmmmm...." said Anna. "What a tangled web we weave," she continued.

"I can't believe that Mu didn't know something was *gan on*," she mused. "*She's aye too canny fae a' that.*"

"That's the whisky talking!" Tom teased; Anna became very heilan' when she relaxed with a dram.

She jabbed him in the ribs, as they both laughed.

"Matt's got a point, though," she said, bringing them back to earth.

"I think you'd do a very good job as an MP, but you've got to decide whether this is about getting to Westminster, or unravelling Markham's activities, so that he faces justice. I'd like to think that we're going to keep faith with what Jack started."

Like the good doctor that she was, Anna had diagnosed the situation succinctly.

"I'm going to sleep on it," he said.

****

"There were a few obvious non-starters," began Donald.

Markham enjoyed walking across his land, and a Sunday morning stroll was a tonic for him, after too many hours cooped up in meetings. Spring was definitely in the air, the birds were cheeping and flitting about, busy nest building. Donald did his best to keep up, as they marched across the springy turf.

Markham had not been present at the selection interviews, his position was *ex-officio*, so this was a chance for Donald to give him his take on how the candidates shaped up.

"How did our girl do?" Markham came straight to the point.

Rather underwhelming was Donald's instinctive response, but he kept this particular thought to himself.

"She gave a good account of herself," he replied.

Donald wondered if he should ask Markham whether Gill was the right horse to back. But his thought was extinguished by Markham's response.

"Good stuff! We must see to it that her nomination is beyond doubt."

He marched on, like a man on a mission. Donald realised that there was only one outcome Markham wanted, and it was his job to deliver it.

Again, he felt a cold wave wash over him; Markham was obsessed with this woman. What had begun as a flirtation had turned into a dangerous liaison. As if no one else was aware of what was going on between them, Markham assumed that this was the natural order of things. But Donald sensed that Gill was dangerous if scorned. Should this plan fail, she'd turn on him.

Miller's death or as the coroner's verdict had it, suicide, was fortuitous, even if it had been engineered. Donald felt no qualms about it. Jack Sawyer had proven to be an unpleasant diversion, as Markham had not bargained for a turncoat amongst his close associates. The information that the journalist had got hold of could well have derailed the whole organisation; Donald knew that he was implicated and would wind up in jail, if this became public knowledge. His connection with the 'road accident' was safe, as long as the driver kept schtum.

"We're in the final straight, and we're on the inside track!" he said, trying to sound bullish.

Getting Gill Wynne past the winning post was going to require a lot of persuasion. In a moment of realisation, he understood who would be accountable if Markham's plans failed. He had a good life, and he wanted to keep it, not wind up in jail. Maybe it was time to double check on his own arrangements to disappear.

****

"How would you diagnose Henry?"

Tom and Anna were also out for a Sunday stroll. Shepherds Cottage was at the foot of the Downs, so they started climbing as soon as they got past the gate.

"I'm not a psychotherapist, Tom!"

"But when you meet a patient, what are your first impressions?" he continued.

A screech overhead alerted them both to a red kite circling in the sky. They gazed wordlessly at the creature floating freely on the wind above them.

"Henry wants people to like him," Anna began.

"Social status is something he's been working on all his life. He married up, when he got together with Mu, she's the one who is in the horsey set around here."

"Very perceptive!" said Tom.

"It's the gossip you pick up at the health centre," explained Anna. "People like to natter about their acquaintances – no great science to it."

"It's always useful to get a second opinion!" said Tom, as they reached the top of the hill.

"Mu is a smart cookie," continued Anna, ignoring Tom's jibe. "She was well educated, but in her social set, young gals got married and kept house."

Tom let the thought sink in. There was something about Henry that didn't quite add up in his mind. He parked the thought for the time being.

"And what about Miller?" he asked.

"A chancer from what I saw of him, and from what I've heard, I'm not surprised at the way things played out."

Tom saw Anna's countenance pale, as she remembered their discovery of the overturned car that evening.

"A waste," she said, almost to herself.

"And Markham?" he continued.

"Ha! That one!" Tom was surprised at the vehemence of her reaction.

"In Scotland we'd call him a right toe-rag," she replied.

"That tells me all I need to know!"

Between him, Anna and Matt, they had all seen the good and the bad in human nature. Anna had dealt with all sorts, when she was working at an A&E post in Glasgow. Tom had won the trust of his soldiers, who were a right bunch of villains. Then he had found himself, almost by accident, in the midst of the turmoil of the Balkans. Matt told Tom that he preferred the knife edge uncertainty of working in the Middle East to the politics of parish life. He knew that everybody hated everybody else, when he was brokering peace talks, but parish life could be much more stressful.

They walked on silently, enjoying the Spring morning. Anna could see that Tom was turning ideas over in his mind; he became very quiet when he was preoccupied.

"Penny for them?" Anna said, at last.

He stopped walking, and they both looked out over the Vale of the White Horse. Spring was unfolding before them, the blue of the sky was a little more promising and the clouds were more white than grey. Birds flitted from the hedgerows, and they could hear the sheep pulling at the grass as they fed.

"It looks so peaceful on a day like this. I can't believe that there was so much evil going on, and people just put up with it."

Anna wasn't sure what to say, she could see that Tom was lost in his own thoughts. They continued walking.

"You're not alone Tom," she said to break the silence.

Her voice seemed to break the spell. He looked over to her, took her hand and kissed it.

"That's good to know."

CHAPTER THIRTEEN

As Tom and Anna walked back into Shepherds Cottage, his phone went. There was little signal up on the Downs. The number shown on the screen was the one Jack had used. He answered the phone, wondering who this ghost might be.

"Mr Scobie?" a woman's voice enquired, "I'm Georgina Casey, a colleague of Jack's," she explained. Tom overcame the momentary shock of seeing a familiar number, and hearing an unfamiliar voice. He assured Georgina that he was indeed Tom Scobie. He wasn't sure how much she knew about the work he had been doing.

"I've picked up some of the work Jack was doing. Lena gave me his phone and PIN. You're in his address book," she explained.

"Concerning the death of Malcolm Miller, and Jack's own death, I can draw a dotted line of causality, but I can't prove anything," she continued.

Tom was in two minds as to how much he should reveal, in case this call was a spoof by one of Markham's cronies.

"Can we meet?" he asked, looking across to where Anna was getting lunch ready.

"Whenever you like," she sounded all business.

As they spoke about the arrangements for a rendezvous, Tom reached for his laptop and got it going. He dawdled over the conversation, while the laptop powered up. Finally he was able to put her name into a search engine.

"Ah! Got you," he said.

"I imagined that you'd want to check me out, before saying anything," she seemed to relax, knowing that Tom was being cautious.

"Jack worked for the news agency, but my little team of elves are specialists."

Looking at her web entry, he recalled some recent exposés that she had been behind. He wondered why Jack had kept his notes on Miller and Markham to himself, and not asked Lena to pass them on to her. He decided to say nothing, until Georgina had put her cards on the table.

They agreed to meet later that afternoon. Maybe talking it through would clarify his thoughts.

Anna wandered outside towards the compost heap, with a handful of carrot and potato peelings, as Tom shut down his laptop. He flopped down onto the old sofa which they kept in the kitchen, the warmest room in the house. He let his eyes droop. It had been a draining few days. Was he really up for this?

He heard Anna scream.

He was out of the kitchen and into the garden in a second, his heart pounding.

"It was a deer, right by the house!" Anna explained, laughing nervously. "I jumped clear out of my skin!"

Tom remembered to breathe.

"Me too!" he said.

They both understood how jumpy they were. The garden of Shepherds Cottage was a jumble of bushes and shrubs, what Anna called a wild garden. It gave plenty of cover for someone to get close to the house.

"Sorry if I startled you," Anna looked sheepish.

"You managed to wake me up," he said. "I might just take a walk around for a bit."

Anna nodded and headed back in. Tom began to wander around the garden, seeing it afresh. There were plenty of covered approaches to the house. Maybe it was time to install some lights, something they'd talked about, but never quite managed.

He had been teased at school as a farm boy, but his aptitude for field craft had got him command of the reconnaissance platoon in the army. As he paced around the familiar garden, he saw the marks where the deer had bounded away. He would need to be more vigilant, for a different kind of mark in future.

****

Tom made sure he was early for his appointment with Georgina. He had chosen a gastro pub just off the Ridgeway, which offered snacks to long distance walkers and to locals out for a stroll. There were plenty of cars in the car park, as people took advantage of the Spring sunshine. Tom parked Molly where he could watch the arrivals and departures.

Just a few minutes after three, he spotted Georgina getting out of a yellow Triumph Spitfire. She was recognisable from the head and shoulders photo on the website he'd seen earlier. Talk about making an entrance, he thought. He followed her into the café and sat down beside her.

"Oh, you startled me!" she said.

"I'd be very surprised if you're ever caught off guard," replied Tom, introducing himself. They shook hands rather formally, but Tom saw an intelligent pair of hazel eyes sizing him up.

He got them both a cup of coffee, and joined her at a small table in the middle of the busy room.

Tom looked at her as they both sipped their coffee. She looked every inch the country girl, complete with rosy features, not at all the counter cultural person he'd been expecting.

"I started out as an anti-nuclear greenie, sitting outside power stations," she explained when asked about her route into investigative journalism.

"Then I thought I could really make a difference by getting the inside scoop on bad people, and it went from there," she added.

"And several awards along the way?"

She allowed herself an awkward smile, signifying a measure of embarrassment. As she adjusted her seat, she nudged her handbag towards Tom. He nodded towards it.

"Are you going to turn it off?" he raised his hand, as if to reach for the bag.

She snatched it back towards her, causing several people to look in their direction.

"You're sharp, Mr Scobie!" she smiled.

"I guess we both know the game," he smiled at her.

She reached down into the bag, and turned off the recorder. Satisfied that she was *bona fide*, Tom decided to begin by explaining how he came to meet Jack. As he did so, Georgina got out a note book, which Tom smiled his approval at, and began to take notes.

"Jack began to get stuff from someone close to Markham about a year ago," Georgina replied to Tom's opening remarks.

"A bit remote, about people trafficking in Eastern Europe, then Miller's name began to appear," she continued.

"He kept it very tight, so I don't know how you and Jack got involved, apart from both being at the scene of Miller's accident, er, suicide."

As she was speaking, Tom was weighing up how much he should reveal. She could be a real asset when it came to getting to the bottom of Markham's activities. She had done a thorough exposé of a local waste management company that had been dumping hospital waste in the local landfill, and double charging the hospital and the local authority. There had been resignations and prosecutions as a result. There would be a right time, he thought, but not now.

"What do you know about Markham?" Tom asked.

"Spiv made good," she said, as if describing an unpleasant lunch.

"Surrounds himself with weak and feeble types, whose role is to do his bidding and tell him how great he is. In return, he offers them a social caché, by inviting them to swanky parties at his mansion, or the Houses of Parliament."

"He used Miller for the Westminster angle," added Tom.

"He uses everybody he can," she added, with unexpected vehemence. "Jack was getting close to something, and then…" her voice trailed off.

As with Miller's death, the Inquiry into Jack's death had concluded it was an accident. She regretted the fact that no other stories had surfaced after Jack's death, no linkage to Miller.

"I'm sure that Markham managed to get the story spiked, but I can't prove it. Like I let Jack down….."

She recovered her poise.

"He used a clunky old mobile phone, which Lena gave me".

Tom nodded, he didn't want to reveal that he had also met Lena.

"My techie colleague, Geoff, downloaded all the phone numbers and texts, and up you popped, Mr Scobie, so what's the story then?"

She had a 'gotcha' expression, which made Tom flinch involuntarily.

"I can see how you won those awards!" was all he could say.

CHAPTER FOURTEEN

Back in the kitchen of Shepherds Cottage, Tom was working out how to phrase the news he had to break. Muriel answered the phone when he called.

"We can't talk about the candidacy Tom, it wouldn't be proper," she said swiftly.

"This is about Henry's business affairs, Mu," he began.

He could sense her hesitating, so he pressed ahead.

"Markham has got the majority of the debt of Henry's dealership", he said bluntly.

He heard her gasp; she understood the import of what he was telling her.

"How....?" She began.

"Look Mu, the journalist who was investigating Miller's death had discovered the same pattern, debt used to buy compliance."

He hadn't revealed that Jack had been in touch with him, after Miller's death, when he'd been with them. Not the right time, he had decided.

"You mean that chap who was killed......" again, he heard Muriel gasp.

He could hear Henry's voice in the background, enquiring if everything was all right. There was a muffled conversation, and the sound of the phone being passed across.

"Hello Tom?" Henry's voice was tentative.

Anna had suggested that when breaking bad news, it was best to get matters clear very quickly. There would be time for kind words afterwards.

"Henry, Markham has got hold of most of the debt of West Vale Motors."

"What? How, it was spread around!" he sounded flabbergasted.

Tom spelt out what he had been able to discover from Jack's notes, this gave Henry time to let the full impact of the discovery sink in.

"Plenty of businesses run on debt finance, Tom," Henry said, by way of explanation. "Especially now, when credit is tight," he added.

"What is it that Markham wants you to do for him, Henry?"

He could hear Henry's breathing down the phone line. They both knew what would be on Markham's mind.

"Can I speak to Mu?"

He heard the sound of the phone being passed.

"Hello Tom?" Mu's voice had regained some composure.

"You and Henry have got to sort this out, Mu, I can't get involved because of my candidacy."

He was hoping that if the line was bugged, as he suspected, that he would not subsequently be disbarred from standing for election.

****

"The association will need to convene an Extraordinary General Meeting to regularise matters, Lord Markham, but I don't think there should be any objection in principle to your assuming the Chair in the circumstances."

Charles Markham and Donald Johnson were sitting in the Association office in the market square in Wandage, with the Area Campaign Director the day after the announcement of Henry's resignation, on health grounds, was made known. Gilbert Burch was flicking through papers as he spoke. Look at me while you're speaking to me you little toad, thought Markham to himself.

"That's most helpful of you Mr Burch," he replied, with as much sincerity as he could summon. "There's been so much upset lately, but we don't want the ship to be blown off course, so close to an election," he added.

"We should proceed with the open primary as the Party Leader wishes," added Markham, summoning a higher authority to bolster his need to get on with things.

"Don will be at your disposal, and I will get in touch with the officers personally to explain matters," Markham said, in a mood to wrap up the meeting swiftly.

"Of course we need to finalise the short list of candidates," suggested Donald, anxious to get the Area Campaign Director's approval for them to move on. He didn't want to be faulted by not observing due process.

"Quite right Don," said Burch.

He reached into his bag and produced a piece of paper. Markham and Donald both recognised Henry's spidery writing. Markham shot a glance at Donald; had Henry outfoxed them by producing a short list, and giving it to Burch as a *fait accompli*?

"The Chairman took some soundings after the interviews were concluded," said Burch, holding the paper up as if it was a holy relic.

Neither Markham nor Johnson could read what had been written.

"He said that it was the settled view of the majority of his colleagues," added Burch helpfully, "but he had not managed to canvass them all".

Markham saw an opening, "does that mean that the list is invalid?"

He tried to keep his voice as neutral as he could.

"It means that the list will need to be formally endorsed by the full Executive Committee," added Burch.

Markham's head was pounding. This twerp was pedantically insisting on a piece of functionless triviality, he could see his point. But he couldn't make out the names written down.

"I think I should make a copy," said Burch.

"Donald will you please assist Mr Burch?" suggested Markham in a helpful manner, concealing his anxiety. They both wandered off in the direction of the photocopier, for Markham time seemed to stand still.

As they returned, Donald ushered Burch ahead of him. Behind his back he gave Markham a smile. Only slightly mollified Charles Markham gave Gilbert Burch what he hoped was an approving smile. "May we be let in on the secret?" he asked.

A copy of the list was placed before him, and Donald had another copy. Gilbert retained the original. Markham saw Gill's name was on the list; he did his best to retain his composure, but he was exultant. He had kept his pledge to her, debt discharged he thought. The list was evenly balanced, two men, two women. All with a strong local connection, and no pundits from Party HQ. One lady was a local councillor, one man was a local teacher. As well as Gill Wynne there was another local businessman, Tom Scobie.

CHAPTER FIFTEEN

"Runners and riders Don?" Markham was seated behind his desk, in the study at Wyvern Hall. It was two days after a shocked Extraordinary General Meeting had endorsed Markham as acting Chairman. There didn't seem to be any other plausible candidate, and they had been persuaded by Donald that time was pressing. As well as Donald, Gill Wynne was sitting around the desk. There was no doubt among the group as to who was in charge. Nor was there any question that they were on the verge of what Gill saw as the reward for long years of loyal service. Donald read through the short list.

"As well as Gill, we've got Mary Hughes a local councillor, Paul Kaye a school teacher and Tom Scobie, marketing director based in Oxford."

"I'll get the private detective to work on that lot," said Markham matter-of-factly. "There are bound to be some skeletons we can unearth," he added.

"The councillor should be easy to pick off," said Donald. "There'll be her voting record on some of the controversial local planning disputes for starters."

"Which controversial disputes?" asked Gill, looking up from some papers on her lap.

"They're *all* controversial around here!" said Donald with a smile.

"What about the teacher?" asked Markham.

"Divorced," responded Donald. "Bound to be bad blood there," he added dismissively.

"Scobie?" asked Markham.

"Been away in the army too long, works for an international company, no real local form," replied Donald.

Gill could hardly believe her luck, "this couldn't be better!" she chirped.

Markham's tone shifted from business like to a more avuncular tone.

"Now Gill we need to work on your presentation. Perhaps Don can talk us through the process?"

Donald explained that the four candidates would be interviewed on the stage of the town hall by a former MP, who had become a well-known newspaper commentator. The tone was to be more conversational, and the moderator would take questions for the candidates from the audience. Afterwards there would be a simple vote. Voters would get to order their preferences. If there was no clear winner on the first count, second preferences would be included – and so on until a winner emerged.

"We'll need some supporters in the audience," said Markham.

"This is going to be a maximum effort for our friends – a must win," thumping his fist on the desk top to make his point.

"We'll need to arrange the order in which the candidates present themselves," said Markham.

"The Area Campaign Director will want to be informed of this," said Donald, injecting a note of caution. "We must ensure that he has no chance of calling a foul," he looked at them both in turn.

"Quite right Don," Markham responded, clearly irritated at the reminder that although he was now Acting Chairman, he wasn't the ultimate arbiter.

"We'll also need a list of questions," added Gill.

"The Moderator will probably draw up his own talking points," replied Don. "After all, he used to be one of our MPs, so he knows the Party well."

Markham saw the drawback of this.

"Will he ask each of the candidates the same questions?" he asked.

"Near enough," replied Donald. Markham made a note on his jotter pad.

Donald went on to explain. "One trick with the questions from the audience, is to ensure enough people sit at the front. Once the Moderator asks for questions, their hands have got to go straight up and stay up."

He explained, "like a fast bowler, the first question can put someone off their stride."

Markham saw the point of this. "You never quite recover," he said, completing Donald's explanation.

Gill was making notes and smiling to herself. "I'm looking forward to this" she said brightly.

****

Tom was poring over the pile of papers from Jack's envelope. He had been thorough, if not entirely methodical, so it was a bit of a jigsaw puzzle. There were scraps of notes, photocopies of company shareholdings and accounts, as well as memos that Jack had written. The key to it all seemed to be the spider's web diagram, which he had shown Tom and Anna when he came to visit, which seemed so long ago but was only a few short weeks. What Tom was looking for was clear evidence of a connection, rather than just hearsay. Tom took a sip from the glass of whisky and looked at his watch. It was gone one o'clock and Anna was asleep upstairs.

His phone peeped, and he saw that it was a call from Muriel Makepeace.

"Hello Mu, how are you?" he asked gently.

"I've found some of Henry's papers that I think you ought to see."

She sounded as if she had just woken from a deep sleep, tired and confused.

"They might be useful," she added, implying that he should come as soon as possible.

"Well, I'm still awake, so I can come over now, or in the morning if you like."

He didn't want to be too intrusive, but he was curious to see what else might emerge in this murky saga.

"Well, I'm awake too Tom, so why don't you come over?"

Scribbling a quick note for Anna, explaining his absence, he found a quilted jacket and headed out.

Tom did some of his best thinking while he drove Molly. There was something refreshing about the no nonsense practicality of his trusty Land Rover. It was the first thing he had bought when he left the army, and had the benefit of being very useful on winter roads around the Downs. It was a very cold frosty night, but Tom opened the window to allow the blast of air to wake him up, after a long evening dealing with Jack's papers. As he drove along silent roads past darkened houses, an owl startled by his headlights flew up from a tree branch into the moonlit night. He pulled up in front of the Makepeaces' house in the market square of Wandage, the only house with a light on. Tom shuddered as he recalled his last late night visit to meet Lena.

Muriel gave Tom a tired smile as she ushered him into the same snug, where he and Henry had sat a few weeks ago.

Henry had taken himself off to their timeshare in Portugal. The cover story was that the effects of managing his dealership through the financial crash had taken its toll. From his hideaway, he and Mu had started to shore up their financial position, reducing their debt. Most painful of all was selling their beloved thoroughbred racehorse.

"How are you getting on Mu?" asked Tom, realising that 'how are you' was probably not the right question.

"One day at a time," she repeated, as if it was her mantra to cope with the situation.

"It's amazing how quickly people who you thought were friends seem to vanish into thin air," she said.

Tom saw the look of disappointment on her face.

"Such good friends," she added, "fair weather ones..." She started to sob.

Tom reached out and took both of her hands in his.

"Now then Mu," he began in an encouraging tone. "This will pass, and you and Henry can rebuild."

He tried to emphasise the positive.

"All built on sand," she whispered.

Tom sat her down in the chair that Henry used, and sat facing her.

"Henry felt he had let too many people down," she continued. "He had built up his dealership using credit".

Tom saw at once what had happened.

"Markham?" he asked; she nodded silently.

"What about the Lodge?" he asked.

97

It was an open secret that Henry was a Freemason. Muriel just shook her head wordlessly, no help there.

"What happened to change things?" asked Tom, anxious to get to the bottom of the matter.

"Henry got a call two days after the interviews," she said looking at Tom, as if to remind him of how they had helped to secure him a place on the long list of interviewees. "After you warned us," she added. "He didn't say anything to me, he just walked out of the door. I'd never seen him look so lost.

"Henry's affairs were a mess," she added. She explained that they'd had to take out a mortgage on their house.

"Enough about me Tom," she said rallying. "You need to see these."

She held up a plastic folder with papers inside. Tom was unsure whether he should tell her about the papers he had received after Jack's death. This was not the time he decided.

"Donald and Lord Markham came to see me…" she paused and took a breath.

"They both came to say that given the need to get on with the selection process, there was to be an EGM of the Association. They wanted to know if Henry had any papers, accounts and so on, that they should have. Well, we didn't need them so I gave them his old briefcase, that he used for meetings."

Tom could picture the scene Donald Johnson and Charles Markham calling to pass on their best wishes, and by the way, while we're here…

"This was at the back of Henry's bureau," she continued. "I started to read, and realised they were not just any old papers."

She passed the folder to Tom, who put it on his lap. He was anxious to look inside but didn't want to stop Muriel talking.

"Henry always said that he kept an unofficial file, which I thought was something of a joke. You know how people like to say 'your name is going in my black book' – well, this is Henry's black book." Tom's face gave away his surprise.

"You'd better take this away and have a look," Muriel said. "It could prove useful in your efforts to win the candidacy, it tells you where the bodies are buried." An unfortunate analogy thought Tom.

Muriel saw Tom to the door and thanked him for coming. She reached out her hand and put it on Tom's arm, wanting him to bide a while.

"There's something about you, Tom," she said in the same small voice.

"Henry didn't see it, but I could. You're not a politician, but you have a strong moral compass and you can use it to do some good."

She looked into his eyes meaningfully.

"You've got to win the nomination Tom, there's nothing more we can do to help you."

He put his arm around her.

"You've already done more than enough Mu," he said. "I won't let you down."

He gave her a goodnight peck on the cheek and got into Molly. There was frost on the windscreen, so he got out to scrape it off. As he was doing so he thought he caught a glimpse of something moving.

Was it a fox?

CHAPTER SIXTEEN

As the Eurostar emerged from the Channel Tunnel into the daylight, Tom reflected that at least he knew where the train was going. As for his life, he was not so sure. The speed of the train mirrored the speed with which events seemed to be carrying him along. He was on his way to an important conference in Paris, which he had helped to set up. It was a feather in his cap that Oxford Info was co-sponsoring the event on European Industrial competitiveness, with one of the prestigious French Hautes Écoles, and a European aerospace manufacturer. But he had other things on his mind.

It had been an early start to get the Eurostar. Anna was dozing as he was dressing.

"Bring me back something French," she had said from beneath the duvet.

"Some champagne *Madame?*" he asked in a bad Inspector Closeau voice, "or maybe some *lingerie?*"

"No," came a grumpy response, "Puy lentils would be good, and some of that jam!"

That's my girl, thought Tom. He gave her a quick goodbye kiss, as he heard the sound of the taxi arriving.

"Take care," he said – and he meant it. He hadn't mentioned his suspicions about who or what he had seen after his visits to Lena and Muriel.

The final interview for the Ridgeway constituency vacancy was just over a week away. The death of Malcolm Miller had triggered a chain of events, which led directly to the death of Jack. Thanks to Henry and Muriel's help, Tom had secured a place on the short list. He needed to use the time available to get to the bottom of the whole murky saga. If he was able to secure the nomination, so much the better.

****

Lord Markham was a happy man as he chewed his croissant that morning. As he sat at the breakfast table in the large morning room of Wyvern Hall, he was reading through a preliminary report prepared for him by the private detective, on the three rivals to Gill for the nomination. To avoid showing any preference he had asked for a report on all four, just to make sure that there were no skeletons in Gill's closet that he did not already know about.

The lady councillor turned out to be something of an alcoholic. One of her sons had been in trouble for fare dodging on the buses locally, and her husband used his work computer to look at pornographic websites.

"That'll play well with the local press," he said to the empty room. Lady Mary was still in the south of France, and the housekeeper had retreated once she had set breakfast for him.

The school teacher was a divorcee who had started an affair with a colleague ten years his junior, causing his wife to leave him. He was mortgaged up to the hilt, with one child at university and another who had dropped out to become a rock musician.

"Better and better," mused Markham, as he wiped away a crumb with a damask cloth.

The detective was still at work on Tom Scobie, so Markham turned his attention to his note about Gill Wynne. Despite knowing her well, what he read displeased him. Gill Wynne had a reputation for explosive anger. She had been involved in a fracas with a work colleague, before she had started working for Markham. Her marriage was a sham, her husband seemed to spend most of his time in a nightclub in Reading, under the pretext of working late at his law practice. Markham was annoyed with himself that he hadn't discovered that before now. Forewarned is forearmed he thought to himself.

****

"And how was your day?" Tom asked Anna, as he flopped onto his bed in the hotel that evening.

"Busy – one thing you're going to have to do when you're elected, is sort out all the bureaucratic BS we doctors have to sort through once we're done with our patients."

"Ah now, let me see – which speech is that!?" he replied feeling better for hearing her voice.

"Don't start on me Tom Scobie!" she was in good form, he could hear.

"It's the BMA and the NHS you'll have to go into battle with!"

They both laughed at the idea of him haranguing some anonymous civil servant.

"How've you got on with the puzzle?" she asked, referring to his efforts to decode Henry's papers.

"I'm about to bring my mighty intellect to bear on the matter" he responded. She wished him good night and good luck.

Henry had made notes in longhand rather than using a computer. More from a need to preserve secrecy than technophobia thought Tom, as he had seen Henry using a computer in the Constituency office. He had drawn up a table with a list of names down the left hand side of the pages. Tom recognised these as the officers of the Association and ward chairmen. Across the top several columns were ruled off. Each described an attribute, positive or negative. It really was a black list, thought Tom. Each person's foibles were noted, together with some comments on what Henry had done, or could do to keep them in line. Useful, but no silver bullets.

His phone peeped. He looked at his watch and saw that it would be 10:00 pm in the UK, and it wasn't Anna. The screen on his phone showed a number he didn't recognise.

"Hello?" he said, not revealing his name or the number of his phone.

"Is that you Pathfinder?" came a familiar voice from long ago. Only one person called him that.

"Hello Sid! What are you up to these days?"

Sid was a Corporal, who had served with Tom in the Balkans. Sid gave Tom the nickname when his much vaunted map reading skills deserted him on a reconnaissance mission, and they both wound up in the middle of a hostile village.

"Can you talk – where are you?" he sounded like he was in a crowded place.

"I'm in a hotel in Paris, where are you?" Tom replied.

"I'm in a pub in Newbury," came the careful reply.

After Sid left the army, he had set himself up as a private security advisor.

"Listen, I'm doing a job for a mate of mine over Lambourn way, real Dick Francis stuff" Sid began.

"What, dodgy jockeys?" asked Tom intrigued.

"You don't need to know" was the curt response.

Fair enough thought Tom.

"My colleague has also got a job on with one of the local bigwigs hereabouts, and is a bit stretched. He asked if I

103

could help, sort of sub-contracting; I'm always game for a laugh," said Sid, reminding Tom of his sardonic humour.

"What's the extra job?" asked Tom.

"You are," was the short answer.

Tom was momentarily shaken, but he recalled seeing somebody lurking around after his late night visits to Lena and Muriel.

"You and the other faces who are in the running for the MP job in Ridgeway," Sid continued.

"Was that you I spotted?" asked Tom, still recovering from the idea that he was being followed.

"No, you wouldn't see me!" replied Sid, clearly hurt by the thought. "It's another bloke, ex flatfoot, hired by my colleague."

Tom could tell that Sid was warning him as far as his professional sense would allow.

"I've done a number on the blonde lady," Tom recognised a description of Gill Wynne.

"Interesting" said Tom, playing for time.

He needed to choose his questions carefully, so that Sid could protect his client if he chose to do so. "Any idea of who this particular client is?" he asked cautiously; encouraging Sid to give him a clue.

"Drives a nice new racing green Bentley," said Sid.

Tom got it straight away.

"Name of Charles or Charlie?" prompted Tom.

"You've got it. Watch your back, Pathfinder," and he rang off.

****

The next morning on the gallops above Lambourn it was crisp and frosty.

"No racing today I think?"

Markham's question was more of an observation than an enquiry.

"Too hard," came the terse reply.

The trainer had got his string of horses out on to the all-weather track, just for a bit of exercise.

"How about the other matter?" asked Markham.

The trainer just nodded as if to signify he was pleased with progress.

"The one in the blue cap, he's the bad'un", they were both looking at one of the stable lads riding out on a chestnut gelding.

"Best to be discrete about it," was Markham's comment as he turned to go back to his car.

As he drove back along the lanes towards Wyvern Hall, Markham's mobile phone rang. It was in a hands free cradle so he punched the button

"Yes?" he spoke into the phone.

"I've got an update for you, sir," it was the voice of the private detective.

"I'm faxing it to your private number now."

"Very good, I'll have a look when I get back."

They ended the call, both preferring to keep phone conversations short. Once he had got as much information as possible about the three rivals for the vacancy, he could prime Gill and organise the questions from the floor. They would all zero in on a key weakness, personal or professional, of the rival candidates, stumping them with the first ball. However good their recovery was, the audience would be in no doubt about their unsuitability.

He parked the Bentley on the gravel drive, outside the stable block where his private office was located. Maud Cumming was in early today, and had a fax waiting for him.

"This just came in," she said dutifully, handing him a folder with the fax inside.

"Jolly chilly this morning," was his greeting to her. She gave him her usual smile, which never quite reached her downcast eyes.

"I'll be over in the study, please get Don to join me when he arrives," with that he left.

Donald arrived shortly after, and at Maud's direction went straight into the study.

"I think we should start the information campaign," Markham said briskly as Donald entered.

"The teacher first," he pointed to a chart he had drawn up with three names on.

"Local media should lap up the details of his fling with a colleague, get some snaps of them as they go to the shops, that sort of thing."

Donald nodded as he took notes, I hope I never get on the wrong side of you he was thinking.

"See if there's anything about the son who is a musician: drug use, old girlfriends." Again Donald nodded dutifully. Markham turned his attention to the latest report.

"Ah, Scobie – now let's see."

He waved to Donald to join him in some breakfast which he did, gladly helping himself to some hot coffee and a warm croissant. Donald could tell that Markham was not pleased with what he was reading.

"Bloody goody two shoes!" he said in frustration.

 "Oh now, wait a minute."

Donald paused with a piece of croissant half way to his mouth. Markham was drawing a line in the margin of the report.

"The good doctor, now here's something."

Donald could see Markham's mind was at work.

"I think we've just discovered Captain Scobie's weak flank."

CHAPTER SEVENTEEN

Another day in the office thought Anna. Wednesday was usually her low point, and with Tom not due back from Paris until tomorrow evening, she was finding it hard to concentrate. She did not feel her usual feisty self. So much had happened, and she found that talking things through with Tom always had a therapeutic effect. She managed to give her patients the attention they deserved, but come lunchtime she was feeling worn out. As she walked out with her last patient that morning, she saw Janine, her favourite co-conspirator at the Health Centre, waving a message slip at her.

"That Penny Pocock was on the phone," said Janine excitedly. "You know, the one who writes for the Sunday glossies?"

Anna was curious. "What'd she want?"

She took the message slip from Janine as they went into the staff room to have their lunch.

"Wants to do a profile of you, as the wife of someone in the news," Janine's excitement was infectious.

"That's Tom, going to be an MP an' all!" gushed Janine, thrilled to have spoken to a Fleet Street columnist in person.

"Well, I'd best have my lunch first!" said Anna "I'm really whacked this morning."

After her lunch, Anna called the number on the slip. It was a mobile number and a female voice answered. She sounded like she was driving.

"Hello Anna! Thank you so much for calling me, during your busy day!"

The honeyed tones of a practised flatterer rang warmly in Anna's ear.

"I'm interested in doing a profile of you for this Sunday's edition, if you can fit me in?"

Anna felt herself blushing, but was flattered to be the subject of a profile story about her. The warm voice suggested an 'us girls' conversation, which Anna found reassuring. Penny suggested that they might meet after work, if that would be convenient. Since Tom was away Anna agreed, suggesting a wine bar in Farrington. "Sounds perfect!" said Penny "my treat!"

Anna recognised Penny as she walked into the wine bar, very blonde and very tanned. Penny fixed Anna with her big brown eyes, and invited her to sit down.

"What a bit of luck, I was in the area and I just thought I'd chance it and ask you to meet," gushed Penny in her smoky voice.

A bottle of champagne appeared and the waiter poured both of them a full glass.

"Well, here's to you!" said Penny raising her glass. Anna felt she was half a step behind, so took a drink to allow time to collect herself.

"Anna – may I call you Anna?" began Penny. "Your husband Tom seems to have come out of nowhere, to be one of the candidates for a *very* safe parliamentary seat, how does that make you feel?"

"Good," was Anna's hesitant reply, "it makes me feel proud of him."

"What attracted you to Tom – do you call him that?" Penny continued.

Anna felt she needed to regain control of the conversation, but was carried along by Penny's encouraging voice.

"I didn't like him at first!" she replied.

"We met at a friend's party. I was helping to pour wine, and Tom was passing the nibbles, so we kept getting in each other's way!"

She smiled as she remembered a very crowded party, where she and Tom first met. Penny topped up Anna's glass, to encourage her with her story.

"Were you Capulet and Montague?" Penny asked, taking a sip of her drink.

"Not really," responded Anna, trying to find her way through the narrative.

"We were from very different backgrounds."

"English and Scottish?" Penny was leading Anna to define the difference between them.

"Tom's background seemed to be such a cliché to me," said Anna, feeling as if she was betraying a confidence, but the champagne was numbing her inhibitions.

"He was a younger son who joined the army," she explained.

As she reminisced about the past, Anna felt herself relaxing. Questions followed about her medical work followed – she was interested in how health policy can help children from deprived households have better health. She was beginning to sound like a bureaucrat she thought.

"And what about your background Anna?" asked Penny pouring some more champagne, as another bottle appeared.

"Very bohemian," replied Anna.

"My parents, or at least my birth mother and father, were hippies who dropped out."

She related her early childhood in the idyllic setting of New Caledonia in the Pacific, where her parents were part of an anthropological research project. In reality it was their way of dropping out.

Penny's face registered surprise, inviting more revelations. "Eventually I moved to live with my maternal grandmother in Argyllshire, so that I could go to school. That's really where I grew up."

Anna took a pull at her champagne, and Penny topped her glass up.

"I went to Glasgow University to read medicine. My grandfather was a doctor, but he'd died by the time I arrived in Connell Ferry," she explained.

"And how did you enjoy University?" asked Penny, taking another sip of her drink.

"Loved it!" came the response.

****

As Penny Pocock drove through the dark country lanes, she reflected on a good evening's work. The tried and trusted practice of plying her opposite number with fizz had worked a treat. Her mobile phone rang. She glanced at where it sat in its hands free cradle, Markham was calling. She punched the button and answered.

"How did we get on with little miss twinkle toes?" came the familiar voice.

"Just what the doctor ordered," replied Penny, pleased at the allusion.

"Your informant was right, she was quite a hell raiser at University. I'll get some picture research done," Penny continued.

"Should be able to unearth something in time for the weekend edition."

CHAPTER EIGHTEEN

Markham ended the call with Penny. The study door opened and Maud Cumming entered silently. "A courier just delivered this" she said walking over to Markham's escritoire.

"Thank you Maud," replied Markham giving her a quick smile, "I think that should be all for today".

Maud left as silently as she had entered. Markham picked up the envelope, which he recognised as coming from the private investigator. As Gill and Donald watched, he opened the envelope and pulled out a thin sheaf of papers.

"Ah ha," he said neutrally, "the phone records of the late Jack Sawyer, at last."

Donald knew the significance of this, it would tell them who Jack had spoken to before and after the time he called Markham to level his allegations.

"Hmmmm...."

Markham was perusing the list with his pencil. He drew a line at the point where Jack had called him. Going up and down the list, he could see the numbers called beforehand as well as subsequently. The private detective had highlighted those numbers called frequently.

"Calls made to the PR people at Falcon," he said, referring to his holding company. He also noted some calls to the offices of the solicitors who were company registrars, they would have referred Jack back to the PR Company. Other calls were to colleagues at the Vale News Agency.

"Calls and texts to Tom Scobie," said Markham.

"They were both at the scene of Malcolm's road accident," explained Donald. "Those must be journalistic enquiries for comment,"

Markham looked up from the sheet.

"I seem to recall the detective reported that Sawyer went to Scobie's house, and after his death, Scobie went to the house of his girlfriend."

Donald noticed that Markham's expression had changed.

"I think we need to pay closer attention to the gallant captain," Markham said in a tone that brooked no argument.

****

"Tell me again what happened?" said Tom.

It had been a long day, and he was still thinking in French. The conference had been a great success. He was in the process of writing up his marketing report, to send to the sales people. He had done his job of lead generation, now it was over to the sales folks to capitalize on the day's work. Anna sounded very woozy on the phone, like she had had too much to drink. Anna explained about the call from Penny Pocock, and their subsequent evening in the wine bar.

"Did she have a note book?" he asked.

"No, we just chatted," Anna replied, a little crest fallen that Tom was being so forensic in his questions.

"So she must've had a recorder?" he persisted.

"I didn't see one," was Anna's hurt reply.

"Did she say anything about what angle she was exploring?" he asked.

"She said she was interested in doing a profile on me." Tom could hear Anna's rising impatience, he slowed down his line of questioning.

Tom understood what had happened. Someone, probably Markham, was scraping around for material to discredit the candidates who were in the final of the selection. Much of his work in the Balkans would be covered by the Official Secrets Act. He knew that Anna had a colourful past, as they had both been open with each other about their previous lives. It could have been just a coincidence that he was out of the country when the columnist called, but Anna had been caught by a very old trick.

"Tom, do you think it was a set up?" Anna's voice was clearly upset. She felt foolish.

"Let me make a few calls," said Tom, trying to let Anna down gently. Somehow she had been caught off guard, very out of character for her. He felt guilty for putting her in this position.

"We can talk about it when I get back, but *dinnae fass yersel.*"

"Good night Tom – see you tomorrow."

She sounded better at the thought of having Tom back home again. They ended the call.

Tom's mind was ice cold with anger. Coming after me is one thing, he thought; it is normal practice in business and politics to find out who you are dealing with. But going after my wife – well, that is something quite different.

Tom needed to think. The final interview for Ridgeway was just days away. Was this a ruse to throw him off balance? A story in the weekend papers would be distressing for Anna, and he wouldn't allow that, so it

114

must be shut down swiftly. Suddenly Tom felt as if he was one of the names enmeshed in the spider's web which Jack had mapped out. Markham was playing him.

"Well, M'lord," said Tom to himself, "if you want to play by big boys' rules, two can play at this game"

****

"My whole story has disappeared from my laptop Charles," Penny sounded anxious. "The file is corrupted and I can't even open it," she continued. "I've got the audio tape, but I'll need to re-do the whole story."

Markham needed to think. "Have you called the police?"

"Not yet," she replied, calming down.

"Don't call them," was his reply as he thought through the implications of this development.

"Besides," she continued, "my phone is dead – the landline I mean."

This was troubling to Markham. He could see that disabling her landline would make Penny call him on her mobile. Which meant someone might be listening.

"I received a text message," added Penny.

"Go on," Markham was curious.

"It said 'tell your patron that I'm onto him' – that's all."

Markham was wide awake now.

"Tell your editor that the story isn't ready," he suggested "and get your land line fixed, we'll speak in the morning." He ended the call.

****

Sitting inside an anonymous looking van around the corner from Penny's flat, Tom and Sid had indeed been listening to her conversation with Markham.

"Good job, Sid," said Tom, as Sid spooled back the cassette on which he had recorded the call.

"It's an old trick, just loosen a few cables and the line goes dead. I'll reconnect them in a bit, don't want to create any suspicion now do we?"

After Tom had called him late on Wednesday evening, Sid had got to work. It had taken him all of 30 minutes to discover the whereabouts of Penny's flat through public records and her social media feed.

"It's called doxxing," explained Sid. "She's got one of those new smart phones," Sid explained, "got her whole address book on it."

Sid had gone phishing, having found Penny's private e-mail address. He saw that she was looking at a foreign holiday. He sent an e-mail to her laptop with an attachment purporting to offer a luxury holiday in Oman. The attachment hid a piece of software which downloaded itself onto her computer. It was then a simple matter to identify the interview with Anna and corrupt her notes.

"What next?" asked Sid.

Tom paused, "well we've spooked them, but we need to see how they respond."

"Well, you know where to find me," said Sid, as he got up to open the side door of the van.

"If you want me to recommend you?" said Tom, as he too got out of the van.

"Well, I reckon I owe you."

Tom had vouched for Sid's good conduct when he was court martialled for conduct prejudicial to good military discipline, to wit striking a superior officer. Sid was acquitted but his brother officer, who Tom rated as a prize plonker, never forgave him.

"I know your style – you bend the rules, but don't break them," Sid said as Tom was leaving.

"Going after Anna was offside," replied Tom. "I just wanted to send a message" he added.

"Message received and understood I should think," replied Sid.

"Not so sure," said Tom, sliding the door shut.

CHAPTER NINETEEN

"Lord Markham would be glad if you could join him for a drink," Maud Cumming's voice in Tom's phone was courtesy itself.

"Each of the finalists in the selection on Saturday is being asked," she went on.

The call came out of the blue, but as Maud explained, Lord Markham was acting Chairman of the Association. He wanted the chance to get to know the candidates better. Tom was free that evening, so he jumped at the chance. He had planned to spend the last Monday evening before the selection telephone canvassing. He had drawn up his own list of people to call based on Henry's notes. The opportunity to get into Markham's camp was a welcome chance to have a good look at the man he knew was his *real* opponent on Saturday. Tom agreed to arrive at Wyvern Hall at 7:00.

Tom had time to call Anna and tell her that he would be going directly to meet Markham after work. "Keep your wits about you Tom," was her reply.

He could tell from the tone in her voice, that Anna was still embarrassed and hurt by the episode with Penny Pocock. He hated to hear her sounding so down. He had explained to her that he had persuaded Penny to pull the story, which was true. He didn't feel that the time was right to fill in the details of the means by which he transmitted his message.

"You can be sure that I will – see you later." He replied warmly.

He also gave Matt a call and caught him at home.

"Be as wise as a serpent Tom," came the reply.

"I'll take that as a benediction Matt," he responded. He felt reassured that Matt had got his heavenly antenna tuned in, he would need all the wisdom he could muster.

The evening was chilly for spring, as Tom drove Molly up the long driveway to Wyvern Hall at five minutes to seven. As he parked the Land Rover in the spot marked for visitors, he made a point of parking close to the wall, so that no one could approach from the passenger side. He didn't trust Markham, or one of his cronies, not to try something. As he approached the front door it opened to reveal Maud Cumming, fixing him with a neutral stare.

"Good evening Mr Scobie, nice and punctual."

Maud Cumming was in her late fifties and dressed in what he'd call a mumsy, unfussy style. Short brown hair and brown eyes that gave him an appraising look. You're smarter than you look, thought Tom.

She turned on her heel and led him into the large hallway. Tom recalled the last occasion he was here, the Ridgeway Revels seemed a lifetime ago.

"Lord Markham won't keep you Mr Scobie, do please sit down," said Maud indicating a rather severe looking upright chair.

"May I take your coat?" she added almost as an afterthought.

It must be the footman's night off thought Tom. There was usually an elderly old bod who opened the door at Wyvern Hall.

"Very kind," Tom replied mustering as much grace as he could, he handed her his coat.

As he sat waiting he took in the surroundings. The hallway was tastefully furnished with muted colours, so as not to overwhelm the artworks. The walls showed a

119

mixture of landscape paintings and some of Lady Mary's more modern compositions.

Tom allowed himself the time to collect his thoughts. In any business meeting, he recalled, you need to have some clear messages in mind. At the same time you need to be reading how the other person is responding. Tom wanted the chance to pick up any clues as to Markham's state of mind before the selection. Was he calm, certain that he had got things sewn up, or had his text message to Penny Pocock been passed on? As the polished doors to the main reception room opened, Tom stood up automatically.

"How nice to meet you properly at last," Markham exuded good natured benevolence. "Come in and have a drink."

Tom accepted a whisky and water. As Markham poured them both a drink from a crystal decanter, which caught the light, Tom ran his eye over him. He was probably in his early seventies but looked fit enough. A thinning head of silver-grey hair gave him the look of a B movie star, certainly enough to win over ladies of a certain age. He was wearing a well-cut charcoal grey suit and a pair of highly polished lace up shoes.

"Here we are," said Markham, holding out a fine crystal tumbler of aromatic golden liquid. He indicated that Tom should add his own water.

"First today!" said Tom, trying to inject a note of levity into their encounter. He held Markham's gaze, piercing blue eyes stared back at him.

"Let's walk into the Orangery," suggested Markham, adopting the air of a host anxious to make his guest feel at ease.

OK, thought Tom, now let's start dancing.

"These are painted by Lady Mary?" he asked, as they entered the Orangery, which was a showcase of works of art. Bright swirling colours were framed in modern looking metal; muted pastels were mounted in darker traditional frames.

"I spotted them at the Revels," added Tom, "very confident." He hoped that he had said the right thing.

"Mary enjoys creating tangible images that provoke a reaction," responded Markham, "I'm glad she succeeded with you!"

Tom could see from Markham's expression that fine arts were definitely not his strong point.

"This is a fine Orangery," said Tom, deciding to see how architecture worked as a topic of conversation.

"Yes, we put it on," replied Markham showing some enthusiasm. He explained that the cast iron frame came from France in a pantechnicon full of furniture, after Lady Mary had gone looking for *objets*.

"Now Tom, may I call you Tom?" Markham began, "tell me about you."

It sounded like the opening line in a job interview, which in a sense it was thought Tom.

"The Scobies came to this part of the world after the civil war, in the 1650s," Tom began, he needed to emphasise the local connection up-front.

"We've been mostly farmers ever since!" he added, giving Markham a sideways look as they continued to stroll among the artworks.

"That long? Goodness!" replied Markham.

"You chose a different path…" Markham prompted Tom to tell him more about his background.

"By the time I came along, the family was large enough to man the farm, so I was allowed to run around, climb trees, that sort of thing. My paternal grandfather taught me about nature and wildlife, and my   got me interested in history. Mother's family are from Nottinghamshire, my mother came to work for my father as an agricultural administrator."

"Why politics?" asked Markham. "You don't have a background in political activity."

Tom had talked through this with Anna and Matt. "Public service," he began. "The army gave me a lot, and I'd like to think that the country I was serving is worth my giving it back something in return."

He saw that Markham had registered the point. As they continued walking Markham gestured that they should go into the Library, which ran parallel to the Orangery.

Tom continued, "You get to deal with many of the sort of matters that MPs have to deal with in their constituency case work. Family matters, housing and so forth."

As they entered the long Library Tom could see the walls lined with volumes of different sizes, suggestive of great learning, or convenient acquisition. Table lamps cast a cosy glow, throwing out pools of light onto carpet and furniture. His eye was drawn to a trestle table at the end of the room with a disassembled volume laid out for rebinding.

"You're certainly a good steward of all this," said Tom.

Markham saw the direction of his gaze, "I like to think so," he replied, momentarily disarmed by the flattery.

Tom's eye caught sight of one of the book spines "may I?" he asked.

He pulled out a handsomely bound edition of Pilgrims Progress, "one of my favourites," he said, as he carefully turned the pages.

He replaced the volume and they walked through into the wood panelled Music Room. A concert grand piano stood to one side of the polished parquet floor. Tom noticed that the room was cooler, to preserve the piano. Nothing is left to chance he thought.

Walking into what seemed to be a sitting room, Markham waved them both to a comfortable seat on either side of an occasional table.

"You've done extremely well to get through a very rigorous selection process, Tom," Markham began.

"The agent has been keeping tabs on the candidates," he continued, "the Party has chosen to use an open primary process. Do you think that you can persuade people that they should select you, and vote for you?"

Tom took a sip of his whisky to allow himself time to unpack the question, and compose a plausible answer. He didn't want to give Markham any clues as to how he would address this aspect of his candidacy at the final interview. "The circumstances that have led to this selection, present the Association with an opportunity," he began.

He wanted to see how Markham reacted to a reminder of what had triggered the process in the first place. He detected no discernible signs, as he continued.

"The imminence of a General Election, which must come soon means that the Party needs someone who can get things organised sharpish and encourage the troops," he deliberately used a military metaphor to indicate that this was what he would be good at.

For the rest of their time together Markham plied Tom with innocuous questions on matters of Party policy, things he had briefed himself on, and on which Anna and others had given him their perspectives. He felt comfortable with his answers, but knew that the general public, who would be at the open primary, could ask questions that he would not be prepared for. At length Markham stood up.

"I've detained you long enough Tom," he said extending his hand. "I must let you get home to, remind me of your wife's name?"

An innocuous enough remark, but Tom felt a sting of anger as he remembered the episode with Penny Pocock.

"Anna," he replied neutrally holding Markham's gaze, "her name is Anna."

Markham walked him back to the hallway, where Maud was holding his coat.

"The best of luck on Saturday Tom," said Markham, with an empty smile.

Maud held out Tom's coat which he put over his arm. Markham gave Tom a brief wave and turned to walk back into the Music Room. Maud opened the door, avoiding eye contact and indicated that Tom could go now.

Tom stepped out into the cold. He was none the wiser as to what made the old fox tick, there had been no dropping of Markham's guard. He hoped that his own defences had been good enough.

As he walked across the gravel he had a good look at Molly in the light of the lamps in the driveway. There were no obvious signs of any interference, but Sid had suggested that once he got clear of the house, he should stop and have a good look around for bugs or trackers.

He drove about a mile along a darkened road following the beams of the headlights as they led him back towards Shepherds Cottage. He pulled in at a lonely looking bus stop and got out with his Maglite torch. He knew the nooks and crannies where a device might be secreted, he was content that nothing had been planted, and that there had been no interference with the vehicle. He texted Anna that he was on his way back. The temperature had dropped considerably, and he was still in his jacket. He reached over to put his coat on. As he did so he heard the rustling of paper in one of the pockets. A quick search found an envelope in the inside pocket.

He pulled out the envelope and put his torch on. The envelope was blank on the outside but the flap had been stuck down. He felt the envelope, it was too flimsy to be any kind of explosive device. Putting the torch on the dashboard, he fished a pencil out of his pocket. Gingerly he pushed the pencil into the back of the envelope to open it. Inside he could see a slip of paper. By the light of the torch he read:

MEET ME TONIGHT AT 12:00 – MEMBURY SERVICES - NORTH SIDE

CHAPTER TWENTY

Tom knew the back road which leads into Membury services. Motorists came off the eastbound M4 to refuel or take a break, but the access road was often used by locals to get into the service station if they needed petrol. Once he had got home, he and Anna had speculated whether Maud had put the envelope into his coat, either on her own behalf, or for someone else. He decided that he would keep the rendezvous, but that he would take a circuitous route and ensure that he was not followed.

"You'll be off boy-scouting?" was Anna's response once he had made his mind up.

"You know I'll be *canny*," he said, using the scots word to convey his understanding of her worry.

"I'll be waiting," she replied, with a tight smile.

He gave her a big hug, and went out to get into Molly. Anna stood in the doorway, swaddled in a scarf against the cold, as he drove off, then shut the door.

As he approached the back entrance to Membury, he switched his lights to the sidelight setting. As it was, the lights of the service area and motorway made it almost as bright as day. He drove steadily into the main car park. He was ten minutes early. There was a scattering of cars spread across the tarmac. He circled the Land Rover and backed into a parking bay on the edge of the car park. He would see anybody approaching. As he switched off the lights and engine, he was startled as the passenger door opened and a slight figure slipped in; in the half-light he could see it was Maud Cumming.

"I'm sorry for all the cloak and dagger stuff," she said, as Tom recovered himself.

She must have watched him as he parked and moved to a blind spot while he backed in.

"Well, congratulations on your tradecraft," he said.

"You weren't followed?" she asked tensely keeping her voice low, but unhurried.

"No, I took several wide detours and doubled back on myself twice before I came here."

He sensed that he was dealing with someone who knew her business.

"I was helping Jack, before..."

She left the sentence unfinished.

"I know that he was talking to you, he thought you could help him get to the bottom of things," she went on. Tom decided to let her speak, rather than interrupt the flow.

"Muriel also thinks you're the bee's knees," she said, her breath sending out clouds of vapour in the cold night air.

You can't judge a book by its cover thought Tom. If ever the word mousey was appropriate to describe anybody, it was Maud Cumming.

"Was Markham behind what happened to Malcolm Miller?" asked Tom, feeling that he needed to start from the beginning.

"There are never any fingerprints," was her Delphic reply.

As she was speaking a car drove into the car park and went once around the outside, as if looking for somebody. They were both silent, watching as the car headlights swung in their direction. As the beams swept past, they both averted their eyes to avoid temporary night blindness.

"Probably a drug dealer looking for somebody," remarked Maud, matter-of-factly.

"The way to get Charles Markham is through his business connections," she continued. "He always uses proxies, but if you can prove a link, the whole edifice will come down like a house of cards."

Tom realised that Maud was possibly the one person who could illuminate the whole dubious saga, and send Markham to jail. But first of all he needed to win her confidence; don't rush your fences, he told himself.

"I want to do what I can to ensure that Charles Markham is brought to justice," he began, gently but firmly. "Jack thought he was onto something, and was killed," he went on.

Tom could hear Maud breathing. She was weighing how much she felt she could tell him.

"Markham must be stopped," she said flatly. "I don't know how much I can help, but I know that he thinks the laws of the land don't apply to him."

"Maybe we can do this together Maud," Tom said in a gentle voice.

"Maybe" she replied.

"Why do you want to do this now, Maud?" Tom asked hoping that she would open up a little. In his experience there was usually a catalyst that triggers people to break with their associates.

"Malcolm and Charles were as bad as each other," she began slowly.

"I knew that Charles was a bit of a buccaneer who took chances, but as time wore on he began to believe that he was untouchable."

Tom sensed that Maud was choosing her words carefully.

"Charles developed a network of patronage and favours, so that he and his associates might prosper. To my simple mind there was no harm in it, as they were all rogues, but no innocent people got hurt."

This sounds like the banality of evil, thought Tom.

"Then things changed", Maud continued. "When little miss goodie-two-shoes appeared on the scene, she seemed to bewitch him," she continued.

"You mean Gill Wynne?" Tom asked, hoping not to divert her story.

"She couldn't organise a toothache in a toffee factory," she went on, Tom could sense she was smiling at the image. "They came up with the idea of replacing Malcolm with her, and things went from there."

It all sounded too neat for Tom's liking. He wasn't sure how much he should reveal about what Jack had told him, but he felt that the Balkans connection was the key to Miller's death.

"You said that Miller and Markham were as bad as each other," Tom prompted her.

"They both got greedy," she went on.

"Markham wanted Miller to stand aside in favour of Gill, at the General Election and Miller refused. He had found out about Markham's business dealings in Eastern Europe, and his connection with traffickers in the Balkans."

Tom held his breath, this was at the heart of what he wanted to know.

"Markham threatened Miller with bankruptcy, but Miller thought that what he had uncovered about Markham's dealings would ruin him."

Tom felt a chill come over him, he had unwittingly pointed Miller towards the murky nexus between criminals and terrorist financing.

"Gill was like a banshee," Maud continued, "she told Markham that he must settle Miller, or else."

"Or else what?" Tom sensed that Maud was getting close to the limit of what she was prepared to reveal.

"She said 'I know things about you Charles', so it turned into a three way stand-off."

Honour among thieves thought Tom.

"She said all of this with you present?" he enquired.

"The door was always open to his study, so I could hear everything," said Maud, who sounded drained by the effort of telling her story.

"Gill doesn't rate me - thinks I'm one of life's losers," she added in a bitter tone.

Tom wondered how far he should push her to reveal what she knew. She had only confirmed what he already knew, but she had hinted at a wide conspiracy.

"I need something concrete to take to the police," suggested Tom.

"Ha!" she retorted. "Save your breath. D I Morris is one of Markham's associates," she added.

That would explain Morris's intrusive questioning, about the extent of Jack's contacts with Tom. This was not going to be simple, thought Tom.

He spoke to her gently.

"Look Maud, if you can help me, I will make sure that your fingerprints are nowhere to be seen, but if you want to stop Markham, I am going to need something concrete."

He saw her nodding silently.

"If you can get me some positive proof, I will take it from there," he added, she nodded again.

"How can we stay in touch?" she asked.

"Markham has got a private detective looking at you and the other two candidates."

Tom recalled his conversation with Sid, he thought that communications and movements would be monitored. He would need all of his previous operational experience to get to the bottom of the Markham – Miller saga.

"Call me on this number – it's a mobile that I don't often use, so may not be known to any snoopers."

He handed her a slip of paper. With that she slipped out of the door and disappeared into the night.

Tom realised that there was little chance of him flushing out any concrete evidence against Markham before the selection on Saturday. If Gill was implicated in his activities, it would finish her too. Tom had not revealed his full hand to Maud, in case this was a set up engineered by Markham. He had both Jack's and Henry's notes and Muriel was in a position to help him, when it came to the way senior members of the Association were thinking. He would need to keep quiet about this encounter. Muriel mustn't know about Maud. It would also enable him to verify some of Maud's statements. Henry must have been aware of a worsening atmosphere between the two men. He could also use the pretext of a telephone canvass to gauge what other members of the Association knew.

CHAPTER TWENTY-ONE

"Well, I thought I ought to report the conversation, since you are the acting Chairman," came the rather tentative voice down the phone.

"That's very proper of you Mr. Walker" replied Markham, with as much solicitude as he could muster.

It was past nine o'clock on Tuesday evening. Gerald Walker was a recently appointed Ward Chairman, one whom Markham had not seen before.

"I'm sure that Mr Scobie was perfectly within his rights as a candidate to call you, and solicit your support," Markham continued.

He made a mental note to check that Gill was doing the same thing.

"Have you been contacted by any of the others?"

"Er, yes actually by the lady councillor, whose name I forget. She called yesterday evening." Walker sounded like someone unused to speaking to Lords on the phone. Markham pictured a figure stood bolt upright by his phone.

"Was there anything that Mr Scobie asked that you thought might be improper?" asked Markham.

"I've just got off the phone to him. We spoke about local matters mostly. He asked me my opinion about things."

"*What things?*" Markham interrupted.

"Er, about the plans for a new reservoir for a start" Walker continued.

Markham realised he was getting jumpy, and he had reacted too swiftly.

"He asked me how well I knew Henry," continued Walker blithely. "He asked me how well I knew Malcolm.

I knew them both, of course, but not so well. I've only recently been appointed to be Chairman of this Ward."

"That all sounds perfectly proper Mr Walker. Do please keep me informed should you be contacted again."

He ended the call.

He sat at his escritoire tapping his pencil on his blotter. He knew from the telephone records of Jack Sawyer that the journalist had spoken to Scobie several times, and that they had met. He had levelled an accusation at him over the phone, so he must have thought he was on to something. But why all of the back and forth with Scobie? This was one piece of the puzzle that hadn't been tied down, and he didn't like loose ends. He punched the numbers of the private detective into the phone and waited while he answered.

"Good evening," came the recognisable voice through the speaker phone.

"Make Scobie your main effort," he said.

"We have enough material on the others. I want to know where he goes who he sees and who he calls."

"Will do" came the reply; he ended the call.

****

Nearly there, thought Tom.

His morning runs were becoming less frequent thanks to his travels, but he could still do it. He came to a halt by the car park at the top of White Horse Hill, and allowed himself time to catch his breath. The last few yards were a real killer if you were out of practice. He wandered into the car park and sat down on a nearby bench erected in memory of one of their neighbours.

"Well my friend," Tom said to the hovering spirit of the departed, "what do you make of all this?"

He allowed his breathing to return to normal, watching the vapour from his lungs form clouds around him. This was a landscape he had known all his life. He felt that he needed to come up to this place and remind himself of how lucky he had been in so many ways.

"They nearly got me," he said to himself, recalling how the Land Rover he had been travelling in was blown up on a mine in Iraq. He had been asleep in the back, the two in the front were not so fortunate. He thought at the time that his luck, which had served him so well in the Balkans, was beginning to run out. Leaving the army was a wrench, but there was no turning the clock back.

His eye rested on Shepherds Cottage nestling at the foot of the hill, where Anna was probably just getting up. A smile came to his lips, I really *was* lucky meeting her, he thought.

He let his eye wander over the familiar and friendly green downland where he had grown up. From the top of the hill he had a good view of the hamlet surrounding Shepherds Cottage. He could pick out the seasonal changes in the trees around the house.

He spotted a van parked on a track which ran up to a stable yard, a field's width from Shepherds Cottage. It looked like Sid's van, but he couldn't be sure. It had pulled well off the track but the thin canopy of foliage didn't provide much cover, despite the newly greening leaves. He would go past the van as he ran back down the hill.

As he got closer, he tried to recall the registration number of Sid's van. He usually formed a mnemonic in his mind as a reminder; so PGT which suggested tea bags, as Sid's number.

He could make out the shape of the van; it was a different make, so it wasn't Sid. There was nobody visible in the front. He recalled the interior of Sid's van, as having space for two seats plus the equipment fitted inside. As he jogged past he took a look at the registration number. It was partially hidden by shrubbery, but he could make out the letters KF; so definitely not Sid.

He entered through the back door into the welcoming warmth of Shepherds Cottage. Anna was in the kitchen making breakfast, padding around in one of his old rugby shirts. He gave her a good morning kiss.

"I didn't hear you go out," said Anna.

"I was awake before the alarm, so I turned it off," he replied.

"And let me oversleep! Thanks a lot!" she gave him a wide smile.

Someone is watching us he thought. Maybe listening. He needed to think about how to tell Anna about his suspicions. He had put her through a lot recently, he worried about how this might affect her. What might this stress do to their marriage?

"I'm working at home today; got to get on with my report," she called after him as he went up the stairs.

An ice cold feeling swept over him, Anna was going to be here on her own with unknown people outside. In his mind's eye he saw the face of Ivana his translator in the Balkans. He had been pulled out of the operation he was involved with at short notice.

The bad guys found Ivana and killed her. He was pole-axed at the news of Ivana's death, and felt responsible and guilty for abandoning her. He needed some time to think. The shower would provide a good opportunity.

In the bedroom he found his phone. He sent a text to Sophie the office manager at Oxford Info, telling her he had some things to sort out at home and he might be late in. He sent another text to Sid's mobile number, asking if he was in the neighbourhood by any chance. He didn't know how long it would be before he replied.

Tom decided that he didn't want Anna worrying about something that might not be a problem, so he would have to ensure that the matter was resolved, one way or the other. When he came out of the shower, he could see the light on his phone blinking; a text message. It was from Sophie, replying that it was cool with a smiley icon. Nothing yet from Sid. He pulled on some old jeans and a pullover.

Anna gave him a quizzical look, as he came back downstairs. "Dress down day?" she said smiling.

"Just checking the bins," replied Tom.

He went out of the front door, hidden from the view of the parked van. He started looking for anything out of place. He found the telephone line and spotted that the box cover had been moved. Amateurish, he thought, or was he expected to see it? He kept moving and looking around him. He decided that he didn't want to leave Anna in the house while snoopers might be watching. He went back into the house where Anna was eating her breakfast, and went back upstairs. He found an old sports bag in the spare bedroom, and pulled it out.

Back outside he walked around the back of the house and saw that the outline of the van was just visible through the trees. His phone peeped in his pocket, a text message from Sid.

NOT ME GUV!

Tom strode out towards the parked van. If the people inside were up to no good, he needed them to know that he was onto them, and they would push off. If it was just a contractor parked up for a quick kip, then he would offer him a cup of coffee. He could see that the van was an old Transit, he delved in his sports bag and pulled out something which resembled a lady's nail file. Walking around to the side door he slung the sports bag over his shoulder to free both hands – just in case.

Using his left hand, he slid the file into the lock on the side door and turned it; he slid open the door and saw two startled faces staring at him.

"Caught napping boys!" he said.

One of the two sprang out of the door, Tom sidestepped letting him stumble out into the wood.

"On your way matey!" Tom's tone of voice left the intruder in no doubt about what might happen if he stayed.

Out of the corner of his eye he caught sight of the second man coming out of the van. He looked ready to cause trouble.

Tom held out the lock pick like a knife at arm's length. I'm ready if you are, was his message.

"Let's get going," said his companion.

The second man slid the side door shut and walked around to get in the front. Tom watched as the van drove away, making sure to get the number.

Tom walked back towards the house, a place he had always felt safe. Now he was not so sure.

"Travellers parked up in the lane up to the stables," he explained as he re-entered the kitchen. "They've moved on" he added, as Anna looked up from her breakfast.

"I hope you were kind," she said cautiously, there had been reports of travellers causing trouble locally.

"Gentleness personified," he gave her a smile, "now I need some breakfast."

CHAPTER TWENTY-TWO

How ironic to be sitting here in the House of Commons, thought Tom. He had been coming up to London since Malcolm Miller invited him to join his Security Studies Group. Along with academics, retired military figures, MPs and Peers, Tom was part of a group trying to keep the Party up to date on developments in the 'real world'. Tom always felt he was something of a fraud, as there were more distinguished figures in the group than him.

"Malcolm liked your independence of mind," said Jerry Howard, the MP who had taken over the chairmanship. He was walking Tom down to the coffee bar, in the atrium of Portcullis House, after a meeting of the group he had convened to pick up the traces of their work.

"I hope that you're going to stay involved. I also like the way you approach our work," he added. "With an election in the offing, we're very close to finalising our submission on defence and security policy."

Howard was a shadow spokesman who might expect to be a minister after the election, so Tom appreciated the comments. He didn't want to fall into what he called the 'humble mumble' trap of underplaying his attributes, nor did he want to fall prey to hubris.

"I'm glad that I've got something to bring to the party," he replied, aware of the unintended pun.

"The Party is very grateful!" replied Jerry. "I've told the Leader what you've been up to."

Was this a coded message? Tom's mind spun momentarily. Were his travails with Markham being observed? Jerry seemed to read his thoughts.

"We knew that Markham was a bit of a buccaneer, and we were aware that Malcolm had trouble with his Constituency Association, it's not that uncommon.

Malcolm always seemed to brush it off. His death really got people's attention, I can tell you."

Tom saw Jerry give him a sideways glance as they descended the stairs together. As they walked across the floor of the atrium, Tom caught sight of many well-known faces deep in conversation. The sight reminded him of a bazaar he had seen in Morocco, where he and Anna had bought a carpet. They stood in line to be served at the coffee bar, just behind a TV political correspondent who was speaking conspiratorially with one of Jerry's colleagues.

"You'll be joining us after the election, I hope," Jerry's remark wasn't a question.

"Certainly hope so," replied Tom, trying not to sound as if he was enjoying the thought, although he was.

They collected their coffee and found an empty table amidst the general hubbub of the atrium.

"You've really ruffled some feathers by getting yourself onto the short list for Ridgeway," Jerry began.

"A large number of people who thought they were on the preferred candidates list will be very miffed that they have been by-passed. If there's any help I can give you, on some of the wider policy points do get in touch."

Tom was sipping his coffee so he gave a nod of acceptance. As he looked around the atrium, his gaze fell upon the back of a familiar looking blonde woman. Gill Wynne. She was deep in conversation with someone Tom recognised as an MP from a neighbouring constituency.

"*She's* clearly had the same idea," said Tom, nodding towards where Gill was sitting.

Jerry turned around and saw who he was referring to.

"I think her card has already been well marked," said Jerry as he turned back. "Ambition is a terrible thing Tom, we all suffer from it to varying degrees!"

Tom wasn't sure from Jerry's remarks whether he would be aware of the material that Jack had accumulated about Markham's connections with criminality, so he decided to test the waters.

"You know Jerry, Malcolm wasn't straight with me when he asked me about my activities in the Balkans," he began.

"Something hush-hush, I understood?" replied Jerry inviting Tom to confide in him.

"I was seconded to a NATO sponsored group, looking into the links between militias and criminal activity. Trafficking, extortion, kidnapping – nasty stuff," Tom began. "Pretty soon we discovered a link between armed factions and the control of alcohol, tobacco and other rackets. Markham was mixed up in this world." Jerry's shocked expression told Tom that this was news to him. "Miller found this out and wanted proof. Markham worked out what Miller was up to, so there was a stand-off."

"Does the Party Chairman know anything about this?" asked Jerry, who knew it was a stupid question as soon as he uttered the words.

"Miller was trying to get proof of Markham's activity," Tom explained, sure that he had got Jerry's attention.

"A journalist was onto Markham." Jerry's face registered even more horror. The expenses scandal had been bad enough for the reputation of parliament, the thought of another story linking an MP and a major donor to the criminal underworld of the Balkans, however indirectly, would be a disaster for the Party at any time, but especially now so close to an election.

"The journalist was killed in a hit and run 'accident'," Tom continued.

Jerry's expression showed he was still absorbing this information. If this story became public in the run up to an election, it would do great damage to the Party Leader's 'detoxification' exercise.

"But he shared his information with me," continued Tom. "I'm still digging."

Tom could see that Jerry didn't quite know what to make of this revelation. Jerry's gaze shifted to where Gill was sitting.

"How much of this does *she* know?" he asked.

"Not sure," replied Tom, choosing his words carefully.

"Markham tends to compartmentalise things," he continued. "I'm not sure to what extent he would trust Gill with important information, for fear that she might let something slip."

"How close are you to getting something definitive?" asked Jerry.

"Lots of circumstantial evidence, but nothing concrete." Tom drew back from revealing too much. He had to trust that Jerry would respect the confidence.

"Keep me posted Tom," was Jerry's laconic reply. He let the subject drop and their talk turned to how Tom would approach the selection interview. Jerry let Tom do the talking, he was still processing what he had learnt.

Tom could feel the negative response from Jerry, even as they continued to chat amiably. The Party would not go out of its way to rock the boat with an inquiry into one of its officers, on the eve of an election. However much it would help to clear the air, the aim now was to get past the election, and then deal with any dirty washing.

"Once you've got past the selection interview, we should speak more about the business of campaigning," Jerry said, as he walked Tom towards the exit. As he was leaving Tom could glimpse Gill's back still seated, gesticulating with both arms. The face of the MP sitting opposite her was frozen with boredom.

"Lost him," said Tom to himself.

He walked away from the building feeling empty. He had expected more of a concerned response, but Jerry was only human. He would have a tough election battle, in a marginal seat in the Midlands. His last thought would be for dealing with trouble in another constituency.

****

The next evening, it was a rainy Thursday. A good time to be at home in the warmth of the kitchen at Shepherds Cottage. Tom's habit, when he wasn't travelling, was to do his ironing on a Thursday, leaving the rest of the weekend free.

"What is the name of the Headmaster of Wyvern College?" asked Anna.

"Charlie McFadden, a good Scot," replied Tom.

Anna was curled up in her favourite chair beside the inglenook fireplace, the wood burner was giving out a soporific warmth. She was throwing random questions at Tom, to prepare him for Saturday.

"What happened to the planning application for the wind farm?" she went on.

Tom continued with his ironing, while he tried to recall something about this thorny matter which divided opinion across the vale.

"It's been called in?" he looked at Anna tentatively.

She shuffled a stack of recent newspapers. Tom saw the copy Anna was holding and recalled that Jack had been one of its reporters. Before she could answer, Tom's phone went in his pocket. He fished it out, a number he didn't recognise.

"Hello," he said without revealing his name.

"Is that Tom?" came a voice he vaguely recognised.

"This is Tom Scobie" he continued, in a non-committal voice.

"This is Louisa Miller, can you speak?"

Tom made a face at Anna and held his finger up to his lips.

"Good evening Louisa, how are you? It's been a long time."

"Lots of things have happened Tom," she sounded as if she had equipped herself with a glass or two of wine before calling.

"Listen, Tom, I've heard on the grapevine that you are on the short list for the seat. D'you know what you're letting yourself in for?" she sounded as if she was ready to unload a tirade against the officers of the Association, which might make her feel good, but would be a waste of his time.

"But I'm not calling as an angry widow," she said, as if reading his thoughts.

"I didn't get to Malcolm's funeral Louisa, I'm sorry I was away on a business trip," he said, as he walked over to the kitchen table.

He was buying time as he found a copy of Henry's list. When it came to the Constituency Association, this was what he needed if she was going to mention names. He sat down and grabbed a sheet of paper.

"I've been doing my homework," he said, inviting her to continue.

"Poor Henry, he never knew what he was getting into," Louisa began. "He just loved the good life, being part of the racing set. Charles Markham was his boon companion, but he had Henry down for a sucker from day one," she went on. "I was never quite sure where his loyalties truly lay."

A bell rang somewhere in Tom's mind, he must speak to Mu, and dig into Henry's story a bit more.

"I think I know what happened with Malcolm, but why did he...." Tom began.

"*Kill himself?*" Louisa's voice had an edge to it.

It was still a raw emotion, but if she was going to fill in any gaps in his knowledge, Tom had to lead her gently.

"Malcolm was always a high stakes player," Louisa went on, warming to her theme.

"That was what attracted me at first, sky-diving, skiing, water-skiing, he was a risk taker," she explained. "We enjoyed life and while he was away, I - enjoyed myself. As long as I showed up and smiled." She was beginning to sound maudlin. Tom needed to keep her on the subject.

"What went wrong between Malcolm and Charles Markham, Louisa?" Tom asked.

He could hear a long intake of breath down the phone, followed by a long slurp from what sounded like a glass of wine.

"Malcolm was a good poker player, but not a good chess player. Charles could see what he was going to do, once Malcolm had got to the bottom of his activities in the Balkans."

Tom felt a chill run through him as he remembered the conversations with Malcolm about the black market in the region, and the role of the NATO taskforce he belonged to, in trying to stop it.

"Charles called his bluff. Malcolm had nowhere else to go – so….." she left the words hanging in the air.

Anna was right thought Tom, he recalled her reference to Sampson pulling the temple down.

"Anyway, listen Tom," she carried on. "Markham wants to get Gill into Westminster, as his puppet."

That was not exactly a secret, thought Tom, some people often had *protégés* whom they sought to advance. That was not the basis for a criminal conspiracy.

"He needed Malcolm out of the way, and was prepared to ruin him financially if he didn't agree," Louisa continued.

Tom was making notes but he still didn't see a smoking gun anywhere that could put Markham in jail.

"Trust no one Tom," said Louisa.

Tom could sense that Louisa had said her piece and it was unlikely that he would get anything substantive out of her on this occasion. She agreed to his suggestion that they speak further in the event that he was successful on Saturday, and they ended the call.

"I think the grieving widow has just turned into the avenging angel." said Tom, in response to Anna's enquiring look.

Louisa's comment about Henry was echoing in his mind like an annoying mosquito. His instinct was to trust Mu, but Henry was more of an enigma. A mystery he would need to delve into.

****

"Talk us through the plan for Saturday please Don."

Lord Markham was in his study with Donald and Gill, that same Thursday evening. Markham and Donald were putting Gill through her paces, ahead of the final selection meeting. Markham wanted to be sure that there were no loose edges.

"Each candidate makes a short presentation, followed by a discussion with the Moderator," began Donald.

"The moderator then opens the floor to questions from the audience," he continued.

"And, we're getting our list of 'friendly' questions sorted?" asked Gill.

They were seated in a loose triangular formation. This enabled both Markham and Donald to judge how Gill came across during her speech, and how she responded to questions.

Donald was feeling uneasy, Gill was all right he told himself, but not exactly star quality. If the audience was not impressed, then she wouldn't get enough votes to win outright. If second preferences were then counted, anyone could win. Markham had better have a rabbit to pull out of the hat, he thought.

"I've got a list of questions for each candidate," said Markham, with the trace of a smile.

"Thanks to our friendly detective, we've been able to identify some tricky *issues* with which to stump our candidates," he added, giving Gill a conspiratorial grin.

"I'll make sure they are passed to our friends in the audience," Markham continued.

"Now we should turn our minds to my little supper party tomorrow evening," Markham went on.

"I've pulled together a gathering of some of our *very* good friends to meet our moderator, in the expectation that he will be receptive to their questions on Saturday," he added.

For the first time since he'd been the Constituency Agent for the Ridgeway Association, Donald Johnson wondered whether Charles Markham was overreaching himself. He kept his eyes on the papers in his lap, as if he knew Markham would be able to read his thoughts.

"Just how do we expect to pull this off?" he said to himself.

CHAPTER TWENTY-THREE

"Happy Friday!!" It was Anna's favourite time of the week.

Anna and some of the girls from the Health Centre had gathered in the bar of the Rifleman, in Farrington. It was the end of a long week, and this was their usual way of celebrating.

"How's it going, Anna?" asked Janine.

As well as Anna and Janine the practice manager, they were joined by Mary a radiographer who had recently arrived, and Belinda one of the practice nurses. Janine was Anna's confidant, who had made her feel welcome when she arrived two years ago.

Anna knew that Janine was a fan of Tom's, but she was not so sure that the other two were quite so keen, so she kept her answer short.

"I've left himself at home today, doing his homework for tomorrow," she replied, taking a sip from her glass of wine.

"What are your plans for the weekend Bel?" Anna asked.

"Not sure dearie," was the dismissive reply.

Janine gave Anna a look, but Mary seemed not to notice the put down.

"My round girls, same again?" asked Mary.

There was a general agreement and draining of glasses, as Mary stood to walk over to the bar.

"I'll come with you Mary, just to make sure you get it right," said Belinda.

Anna and Janine watched them as they weaved through the Friday evening crowd towards the bar.

"What is it with you and Bel?" asked Janine, with a concerned tone.

Anna shrugged her shoulders, and arched her eyebrow in an expression of bafflement.

"We just don't click," was all she could say by way of explanation. "Not for want of trying," she added.

"Well, I'd watch it if I were you," Janine whispered, "little grudges can get blown out of proportion".

When the others returned, the girls chattered about plans for the weekend and looking ahead to summer holidays. The mood lifted as Belinda made her excuses and left for home.

"Got to feed the hungry," she said, by way of farewell.

The others remained until their glasses were empty. Rather than have another Anna, who had to drive made her excuses and started to leave.

"Hope it goes well tomorrow," said Janine, with an encouraging smile.

"We'll both be back at work on Monday come what may!" Anna replied.

She pulled on her old parka and checked her pockets for car keys. She spotted Mary's not too subtle glance at the grungy old parka.

"I've had this since university – very comfortable," she said.

Mary gave her a blank look, and Janine gave her a wink and waved her away. Anna walked out into the damp evening air. Her car was waiting in the Health Centre car park a few streets away. Her trusty Golf started first time, unlike Tom's temperamental old Land Rover, and she was soon on her way. Like Tom she preferred to drive in silence without the radio on. It gave her thinking time. A slight drizzle started as she drove out of town towards the downs. She put the wipers and the heater on, to clear the windscreen.

She glanced at the clock on the dashboard as she turned into the lane that led towards Shepherds Cottage, just after seven – not too late. As she approached the turn into the drive she saw headlights in the mirror. Instinctively she put the indicator on. As she turned in, so the lights drew closer and continued past as she pulled up outside the house.

Not often that there was traffic in the lane this time of evening, she thought.

****

Lord Markham's *soirée* was gathering pace, as his guests arrived.

"Giles, welcome! How was your journey?" Markham enquired of the guest of honour.

Every stop had been pulled out for the occasion. A driver had collected the guest of honour, who would be acting as moderator for the selection meeting, from the railway station. The housekeeper knew how to arrange the lighting to create a welcoming atmosphere, and show off the art and the collection of *objets*.

"Thank you Lord Markham, God's Wonderful Railway managed to get me here without incident," he replied.

His coat was taken from him and a flute of champagne offered, which he took gladly. He took an appreciative glance around the Great Hall.

"Very nice – Queen Anne?" he asked.

"Spot on, with a few additions of course!" Markham responded, pleased that his special guest was feeling at ease in Wyvern Hall.

"Come and meet some people," Markham led the way into the Orangery, where the chosen group had gathered among Lady Mary's artworks. Markham led him towards a small group and made some introductions.

"Let me just see to a few things," said Markham beaming at Shelley, allowing her to take their guest in hand. He went in search of Maud, who was speaking to Donald in the hallway.

"Nearly all here," ventured Maud, as she saw Markham approaching.

"Just check with cook about the nibbles Maud," Markham said, by way of dismissal. They were all on duty, not here to enjoy themselves. He turned his attention to Donald.

"Any feedback yet?" he asked.

He was speaking about Donald's attempt to identify the person passing information to Tom and the journalist, which had been nagging him for some time. This close to the selection meeting, he didn't want to leave anything to chance. Donald's expression was downcast.

"Nothing yet."

"What matters is that Gill gets a good run tomorrow," Markham replied.

Donald saw the sense of this. Any tension or signs of anxiety would be picked up by people this evening and tomorrow. Best to concentrate on the matter in hand. Despite his concern, Donald was determined to enjoy this evening, and let tomorrow look after itself.

"Well, I shall return to our guests?" said Markham.

"Ask Maud to let me know once we're all here and I'll say a few words," with that he strode off towards the Orangery.

As if on cue, the last couple were ushered through the doorway and their coats and scarves taken. Maud returned to where Donald was standing.

"That's everybody," she remarked.

"Best tell his nibs," said Donald, who walked over to where the newcomers were being given glasses of champagne.

Maud did as she was bidden. As she walked into the Orangery she allowed herself a smile, just for a moment. Then she arranged her face, as one whose duty was to serve and say nothing.

CHAPTER TWENTY-FOUR

"How are you feeling?" asked Anna.

After a reflective pause Tom replied, "Calm."

They were driving into Wandage for the selection meeting. Anna was driving so that Tom could let his mind wander over the things he needed to do. Green shoots in the familiar hedgerows were a promise of spring.

"It was good of Muriel to call," prompted Anna, trying to keep the conversation at a low level, but anything was better than an oppressive silence.

Anna sensed that his mind was working through the chain of events that had got him to this point. He was still trying to uncover the dealings of Charles Markham and his associates. On his lap was a plain envelope that had been on the door mat this morning.

"Is that helpful?" she asked pointing to the envelope.

"It's a reminder of how I got us into this business in the first place" he replied, trying not to sound too tense.

The envelope was from Maud. It must have been dropped off in the dead of night, as neither of them heard it being delivered. It listed those present at Lord Markham's *soirée*, for the Moderator of today's event. He had been able to compare the attendees against Henry's list. They all fell into the category of 'Bandits', Henry's description for Markham's cronies.

"What is puzzling is what the inscription means – 'look out for a big surprise', very Delphic!" he mused, allowing himself a wry smile.

Tom had chosen not to burden himself with notes or papers, he knew that he was as prepared as he could hope to be. He would also have an eye out for anything he could pick up to further the quest for evidence against Markham.

"I'll drop you off and park, and I'll be in the hall," Anna said, just to remind Tom of their arrangement.

"Got your ticket?" he asked.

Anna nodded. The purpose of an open primary was to enable a wider selection of the public to take part in the selection process. Entry to this morning's proceedings was by ticket from the Constituency office.

The Saturday shopping crowd in the market square was swelled by those going to the selection meeting.

"This is you," said Anna, as Tom got himself ready to open the door.

"Oh and Tom…." She said as he was about to get out. "I'm proud of you!"

She gave him a quick kiss and a flash of those hypnotic eyes, and her winning smile. And then she drove off.

Tom made his way into the Town Hall, largely unrecognised among the throng. One of the Association stewards spotted him and waved him over to an anonymous door.

"Candidates in here," he said curtly.

Tom walked into a drab functional room with beige furnishings, where the other candidates had already arrived. The Moderator was also there, saying a few words to each of the candidates. Tom recognised the Area Campaign Director, sent from Party HQ to ensure fair play, Donald the Constituency Agent and Lord Markham, acting both as Chairman of the Constituency Association and as the President. The candidates sought to while away the time, trying to hide their nerves.

155

Tom caught sight of Gill Wynne, he wondered what she must be thinking. Gill looked overexcited like a skittish horse at the start of a race, nerves he thought to himself, good it'll make you come across badly. Tom had learned long ago to bury his nerves by remaining present in the moment, not worrying about what might happen, but ready for whatever came his way. Something which had saved his life on more than one occasion.

"Could I have all of the candidates please?" asked the Area Campaign Director.

The four candidates stood in a loose circle, allowing each of them some personal space.

Lord Markham then said a few words of encouragement.

"We've all come a long way to get to this point, so I hope that we can all be comfortable with the outcome," he said with his most genial smile.

Tom thought this was an odd formula, but he reckoned that Markham like everybody else was afflicted with pre-performance nerves.

"Ladies and Gentlemen, congratulations on getting this far," continued the Area Campaign Director, in a practised and disinterested voice.

He went through the process that was about to unfold. He welcomed the Moderator …"who needs no introduction", and explained that the candidates would remain sequestered in this room until the proceedings were concluded, and a winner announced.

"We should settle the order in which the candidates appear," he continued, glancing towards the moderator, who was shuffling some papers.

Tom noticed that Markham and Donald tensed at this announcement, perhaps they hadn't been able to finesse this part of the proceedings.

Markham started to speak, but he was too late. The moderator's gaze fell upon Gill Wynne.

"Gill, shall we have you on first." It wasn't a question.

Gill could only nod dumbly, a frozen smile on her face. Tom thought he heard Markham make a sound, which he covered by clearing his throat. Definitely not part of the plan thought Tom. The order of appearance put him on third.

"Now if everybody else could please take their seats in the hall?" said the Area Campaign Director, in the same disinterested voice.

"Matthew if you'd like to come out with me, we'll get the show on the road," he added.

"Good luck everybody," the Moderator said, as he joined the others to leave the room.

The candidates sat themselves down awkwardly on the functional chairs around the wall. They all exchanged 'good luck' smiles. Tom thought Gill looked green, but it could just have been the combination of harsh strip lighting and too much makeup. His phone buzzed in his pocket, Anna was sending him a text to say that she was in the hall. He fished the phone out of his pocket and took a look at the text message:

LOUISA M IS IN THE FRONT ROW!!

Tom glanced again at the message, trying not to show any emotion. Maybe this was the big surprise that Maud was referring to. The widow had chosen the time to make her re-appearance well. Grief put aside, this was the time for revenge.

****

Anna had learnt from Tom that if you sit at the back of a large meeting, you can decode the dynamics of the groups attending, who sits next to whom and who talks to whom, or not as the case maybe. She had tried it herself on several occasions, and it had proved very instructive.

After she had dropped Tom she took her place at the back of the hall, she could see the group of people Henry Makepeace referred to as bandits taking their places clustered just behind the front row, which was reserved for officers and guests. Her brief was to text Tom with any useful observations, as there seemed to be no bar on communications with the candidates during the meeting.

She was about to text Tom that she recognised some of the bandits who were in the room, when she became aware of a slight hubbub by the entrance. A steward was leading a lady in an exotic black silk dress accessorized with a chunky gold necklace, and a sparkling diamond brooch, up to the front row.

"It's Louisa!" said a lady sitting on Anna's left.

Louisa Miller had chosen to make an entrance, and what an entrance thought Anna. Clutching her ticket, the steward showed her down the centre aisle. Anna watched as Louisa acknowledged friendly waves from members of the audience. Anna also saw a collective look of horror on the faces of several of the bandits.

"Well, I never did!" said Anna's neighbour, "she looks fabulous."

As Anna watched, Louisa was led to a seat in the front row. She chose to sit in a seat on the aisle directly in front of the podium which the candidates would use for their short speech, and which would allow a good line of sight of the easy chairs where the discussion would take place.

Anna saw that Louisa had placed herself where the candidates couldn't help but see her.

Anna caught Louisa's gaze across the length of the room, as she took her seat. Louisa paused theatrically to glance down the length of the hall, smiling at several more people in the audience. Anna thought she saw the trace of a conspiratorial smile on Louisa's face, before she turned and sat down.

****

"How could this happen?" Markham was trying to keep his voice low, but the acidic tone was evident.

He and Donald were seated in the front row of the hall, just a few spaces to the left of Louisa Miller.

"Why didn't we know about this?" he continued.

Donald's face had gone pale. Of all the contingencies they had planned for, this was not on their list. They had both hoped to get a sense of the room, before Gill came on. Now she was coming on first, cold, into the room. Things looked like they were slipping badly out of control.

There was little Donald could do but shrug his shoulders. The Moderator was on the stage and making some opening remarks to warm up the audience, who were enjoying his reflections on life in Westminster.

"We've got our people well briefed," was the best that Donald could manage, as he sought to recover some composure.

Any further discussion was brought to a close as the moderator invited the first candidate to come out and join them.

Gill strode out purposefully onto the stage, as they had rehearsed. Her eyes were fixed on the Moderator; make eye contact early they had advised. She was dressed in a powder blue Chanel suit accessorized with a string of pearls and low blue shoes. The unspoken reference was towards a previous Leader of the Party. Anna thought that she looked rather frumpy.

The Moderator welcomed Gill to the meeting and invited her to make her opening statement. Gill turned towards the podium, they had rehearsed this yesterday afternoon in an empty hall. She counted out the paces in her mind. She gave a wide smile to the hall, to invite those present to share in the story she was about to tell them. A story of her journey to this point, and her hopes for their shared future as their MP. Every word well-rehearsed.

Then her eyes fell on Louisa Miller sitting in the front row, right in line with the podium.

She froze.

CHAPTER TWENTY-FIVE

"See how your enemies flee before you Tom!"

Matt's voice on the phone sounded both pleased and astonished. It was early afternoon on Sunday before Tom was able to tell him the news. He was perched on his desk in the sitting room.

"When did you get the feeling that it was going your way?"

Typical Matt thought Tom, no congratulations – or well done, straight down to business. Besides, there was the small matter of a General Election campaign ahead. He wasn't the MP quite yet.

"The favoured candidate fluffed her chance."

Tom decided to skip a blow-by-blow account, and cut to the chase.

"I won on second preference votes, but a win is a win," he added.

"How are you going to work with the people who have behaved so badly?"

Matt was being careful with his language, Tom could sense he was conscious others might be listening, but Sid had reassured him that his landline was safe.

"It'll be awkward, but I will have to win over the majority, and trust that the bandits are a minority."

He had spoken to Matt about Henry's list of bandits. Matt's advice was to tread carefully and trust no one, until he was certain of their motives.

"I'll be keeping my powder dry and my flints sharp!" Tom added, trying to inject a note of levity. The conversation had become very serious.

"I'll make sure that we can get over to support you during the campaign," said Matt. Tom took this as some sort of approbation.

"Thanks Matt, that means a lot."

"Well done Tom, seriously. You deserve credit for pursuing this. With Anna in support, you'll be a formidable candidate."

They ended the call. Matt was sparing with his praise, but Tom knew that he would be a wise counsel in the days ahead.

Tom had received a string of congratulatory phone calls, after the result was announced the previous afternoon. Most touching of all was a call from Lena, Jack's partner. She hoped that Tom would be able to finish the job that they had both started. Tom assured her that it was uppermost in his mind – and reminded her to vote for him when it came to the election. She agreed to think about it. That's democracy for you, thought Tom.

"One of your future constituents would like your assistance emptying the dishwasher, if it's all the same to you!"

Anna had come into the room whilst Tom had been on the phone. A ray of spring sunshine from the window caught her red hair, casting it into a hue of burnished copper. He reached out and drew her to him.

"I couldn't have done this without you, Doctor Macdonald," he said running his fingers through her hair.

"Sure you could," she replied, moving closer to him.

"I said that you were as good as any of the other numties that'd apply. You were better than all of them."

Her big eyes and her wide smile reminded Tom of the magic that drew him to her at their first encounter.

"Besides, it was worth it just to see the look on Markham's face when the announcement was made. He looked like he'd swallowed a bunch of nettles!"

They both laughed at the image. Markham had to shake Tom's hand on the stage in the hall. His eyes were completely blank, his smile a skull like rictus.

"I look forward to working with you Tom," he had said through gritted teeth.

"Likewise," Tom had replied, holding his gaze.

This is going to be interesting, he thought to himself.

****

The housekeeper at Wyvern Hall had set out lunch for Lord Markham and his guests. Despite the Spring sunshine, the atmosphere was oppressive. Markham was seated at the head of the long, polished refectory table. Gill Wynne and a crestfallen Desmond were to his right, with Donald Johnson on his left.

"Let's consider our options," he began.

"Fat lot of good that will do," Gill's tone was acidic.

Sitting opposite her, Donald could see the effect of the last 24 hours in her face and bearing. She was clearly overwrought, every move and word seemed to be an overreaction. She seemed to be on the edge of losing control.

"Where do we stand Don?" Markham continued, in a tone that he hoped was emollient.

"Scobie has now been adopted as the Prospective Parliamentary candidate," he began.

"I don't think there are any procedural obstacles that we can throw in his way now."

He noticed that Gill had dropped her eyes, as if refusing to acknowledge his observation.

"But he hasn't been elected yet," she ventured, almost to herself.

"Okay," said Markham, feeling a need to regain control of the situation.

"We have some options to consider. Gill, you could always stand as an Independent candidate, like Martin Bell and others have done, quite successfully."

"But the Party apparatus couldn't support you, and you'd be campaigning against the grain in a very safe seat," added Donald, unhelpfully.

"*Whose side are you on, Don!!??*" she almost shrieked at him across the table.

"Don is just pointing out the facts, Gill." Markham intervened, to calm matters down.

You really are beginning to lose it, thought Donald. He looked at Desmond who was morosely drinking his wine and keeping quiet.

"I will ask the private detective to dig deeper on Scobie, to see if there is anything untoward which might make him reconsider his position," suggested Markham.

"That's the best you can do!!??" sniped Gill.

"It may yet prove helpful," replied Markham, as to a slow-witted child.

"And just what am I supposed to *do* with myself Charles!??"

Again the rather shrill tone, thought Donald. He saw Markham working out an answer in his head. She is your creature, he thought, you'll have to handle this.

"There will be plenty of scope to get you around the bazaars over the pre-election period. There's many a slip twixt cup and lip," he added.

Donald could see that Markham was working on a plan. He'd best see this thing through, besides as Constituency Agent he would be working more closely with the candidate in the future.

"I'll be able to keep an eye on the gallant captain, now that he is our candidate," he ventured brightly.

"Very good Don!" Markham said, recognising the opportunity.

"It'll be better than the private detective, because he will have to tell you what his movements are."

Gill too saw the point of this.

"And those country lanes can be very tricky," she said.

CHAPTER TWENTY-SIX

"You're very kind Ted, but I think we have to be heading back," Tom put down the empty tumbler of whisky he had just drained.

Ted Mallett was one of the Party organisers, responsible for the ward on the edge of Wandage. He would be in charge of distributing literature and mobilising activists to support Tom in the election.

"Congratulations again, Tom," said Ted. "We need to focus on the election, shame about Malcolm, but we can't turn the clock back."

"Wise words Ted!" echoed Tom.

He was glad that he had brought along his brother Mike, who had offered to help out with the campaign. A couple of stiff whiskies from Ted, in the name of hospitality, meant that Mike would be well employed as Tom's driver.

"Nice to meet you too Mike, hope we'll be seeing you on the campaign trail?" Ted was shaking Mike's hand, as they were leaving.

"Someone's got to keep an eye on this kid brother of mine!" Mike replied with a wink.

They stepped out into a drizzly evening.

"How many more of these will you have to do?" asked Mike.

"Each ward has a committee, and there are eight wards in the constituency," replied Tom matter-of-factly.

"One down, seven to go!" exclaimed Mike "I can see that politics is a boozy business!"

Tom allowed himself a smile as they walked over to where Molly was parked. It was good that Mike had suggested helping. He was usually the one who did all the driving on the farm, so it made sense for him to drive Tom around. He knew the Vale as well as anyone, so could find short cuts between places.

"Home James!" said Tom, as they got into the front of the Land Rover.

"Cor, I can smell your breath from here!" said Mike, "you reek of bevvy!"

"Just as well you're driving, Bruv!"

Mike started Molly and pulled out into the road. Ted Mallett lived in a modern estate built on the edge of Wandage that gave onto the surrounding downland. They were soon out of the developed area and into the darkness of the Downs, as the rain picked up. While Tom had gone off to University and then into the army, Mike had worked on the family farm. He loved tinkering with tractors and horse boxes, so he became the de facto farm mechanic.

"Your reward, young sir, will be a fine meal of Doctor Macdonald's reviving farmhouse stew," said Tom airily, as they drove along the foot of the Downs.

"Less of the young, thank you, *youngest* brother," replied Mike.

"We knew it was real with you and Anna, when she gave her stew recipe to mum!" said Mike, anticipating a hot meal back at Shepherds Cottage.

"That's my girl!" replied Tom.

They drove in a companionable silence. Tom allowed his eyes to droop as the windscreen wipers beat a soporific rhythm. A day of meetings at the office, and the evening's activities were catching up on him.

"Aye aye!" said Mike with a tone of alarm in his voice.

Tom was awake.

He was aware of bright headlights in the wing mirror. A big Jeep-like vehicle had got close behind them. As well as headlights it had a row of spotlights on its roof. All were on full beam.

"Lampers?" asked Tom. Some of the locals drove up onto the open downland to shoot rabbits.

"He's sitting right on my tail," said Mike, who was watching the road ahead for a chance to pull off and let them pass.

The road opened out into downland, and Mike had slowed down to allow the Jeep to pass him by. Instead of doing so, it started weaving behind them. Tom was watching in the wing mirror on his side.

"Bunch of cowboys!" said Mike scornfully.

Realisation shook Tom out of his lethargy.

"They're trying to force us off the road!" he said to Mike.

"What d'you mean? This is a Land Rover, not a Fiesta," replied Mike, unaware of the danger.

The Jeep had drawn level with them, but instead of passing it stayed alongside. Tom looked over to see who was driving. He saw a face peering back at him, it was not laughing or smiling like an idiot cowboy driver. What he saw was grim determination.

"Where are we Mike?" he asked.

Mike detected the urgency in his voice, "just by Long Barrow," he replied.

Tom looked to his left and saw the open down land stretching up to Long Barrow.

"Pull off and head up towards the Barrow!" he said.

Mike turned the wheel, throwing Molly into four-wheel drive as he did so. They both knew this part of the Downs, Mike pointed Molly up the slope.

They both saw the lights of the Jeep follow them onto the downland.

"This clown is serious!" said Mike, with a note of alarm in his voice. The lights drew closer behind them.

"Fishtail!" urged Tom.

They had both driven in hill climbs in their youth. Fishtailing was a way to get extra traction without losing momentum. It usually resulted in a spray of mud and soil onto the spectators, but was effective. Looking in the wing mirror Tom could see a spray of topsoil flying towards the jeep as Mike moved the wheel back and forth.

"Chew on that lot, cowboys!" chuckled Mike.

Tom hoped that the spray of soil would cover their windscreen, and he thought he could see the Jeep's wipers working to clear the screen.

Tom looked ahead through the rain smeared windscreen and saw a dark row of trees planted as a wind break and cover for game birds. He knew it was Barrow Spinney.

"Head towards the Spinney," he said. Mike duly turned the wheel over to his left.

"We can weave through the fire break," said Mike, as he turned the wheel to point the nose of the Land Rover towards a gap in the trees.

"How's your night vision?" asked Tom.

Mike understood, once they were into the spinney, he would jink to one side, switch off the headlights and the pursuers would hopefully lose them.

"Good enough," replied Mike.

The two vehicles drove headlong towards the dark line of the spinney. The Jeep showed no sign of wavering. Tom glanced at Mike, whose face was contorted in concentration. He turned his attention back to the spinney.

Mike knew the ground, having shot over this land, so Tom was content to let him choose his line. He drove Molly at full speed into the gap in the trees. He switched off the head lights and put the wheel over to the right as they cleared the far side. They watched the Jeep follow through the gap and keep on going. The ground dipped away sharply, so the Jeep was lost to sight.

Neither Tom nor Mike saw the tree stump until it was too late. Tom sensed the front right tyre burst as it struck. Molly lurched upwards as the momentum carried them on.

"Rolling!" was all Mike could say.

Molly rolled over to the left, as the immovable force of the tree stump met the energy of the Land Rover. Tom braced himself as best he could. The side window smashed beside him as the vehicle struck the ground. The windscreen shattered, showering them both with glass.

Suddenly all was still. Tom and Mike were suspended by their seats belts, the cold rain bringing them back to their senses. The vehicle was on its side. Tom's head had been thrown against what was left of the window, and he could feel blood. Mike was moving, trying to open his door. Tom released his seat belt and gave Mike a shove, as he climbed up onto the side of the Land Rover. Mike reached down and heaved Tom out. They jumped down to the ground, and steadied themselves. Mike found a torch in his coat pocket and shone it at Tom, to see how he looked.

"You've got a cut on the side of your head, looks like you've been in a fight," he said to reassure Tom.

Tom was feeling dizzy from the bump to his head, but didn't think anything was broken. He took Mike's torch and shone it over his brother.

He was covered in blood.

"You're bleeding Mike," he said.

Mike's face registered surprise. He looked down and saw blood coming from somewhere. It was difficult to tell in the dark.

"Take your coat off," snapped Tom, realising that Mike was bleeding from a cut under his coat. Mike obeyed.

Tom saw a wound just below the collar of his shirt. Something had cut him and he was bleeding profusely.

"You've got a bad cut. Need to put some pressure on that wound."

He was aware that they were both shivering from shock.

Tom took off his scarf and told Mike to hold it very tightly against the wound. He knew that there would be no mobile phone signal on this part of the Downs, the best thing was to walk back down to the road and stop a passing car.

"Can you walk?" he said to Mike, who nodded.

Tom put Mike's coat around his shoulders. They set off towards the road, back through the spinney and down the slope. Tom saw headlights passing along the road, but they were too far away to hear or see the two of them.

"How are you feeling?" asked Tom as they plodded on. He was anxious that Mike's blood loss could be worse than he could see. Mike grunted a response, he was saving his efforts for walking. He was stumbling more often and Tom had to support him, making sure that he was still keeping pressure on his wound. They trudged on.

Some headlights were visible on the road. Tom waved the torch at them. The car slowed down. Tom could see the hazard warning lights start, and make out a figure getting out of the car.

"Help!" was all that he could manage to call, along with a feeble wave.

Another figure got out of the car and they came towards them, shining torches ahead of them as they approached.

"My brother's got a bad cut and needs an ambulance," Tom managed to say, as the pair of strangers got close enough to hear.

"We should be able to get a signal down here," said one of the strangers, as she pulled out a mobile phone.

"Have you been drinking?" asked the other voice, a man's voice.

"I have, but he's the driver and he wasn't drinking," said Tom, realising that his breath smelt of Ted Mallett's whisky.

The other passenger was speaking on the phone, while they stood waiting.

"OK, Ambulance is on its way," said the woman. "We'd better get you into the car out of the rain."

Tom was suddenly aware of just how cold it had got. Mike's face was white in the light of the car.

"Sorry about the mess," mumbled Tom. He could feel the side of his face and realised that they must be a frightening sight.

"I'm worried about that wound, its bleeding a lot," Tom said to the male stranger. In response the man got out of the car, and went to the boot and produced a first aid kit. Then it went dark.

CHAPTER TWENTY-SEVEN

"Something's got to give, sometime," said Georgina.

The journalist was sitting in the kitchen in Shepherds Cottage. She was in the same seat Jack, her dead colleague, had sat in a few weeks ago.

"Trouble is," she added, "Markham might be luckier next time".

She gave Tom a meaningful stare. His 'accident' last week had been reported in the local media, but soon got lost in the pre-election busyness. Anna was putting the finishing touches to supper as they spoke.

"No chance of the police making two and two add up, I suppose?" she asked.

"The thing is," began Georgina, "there are lots of threads that don't yet tie up into a neat bundle."

She gave them both a tight smile, as if to lessen the bleak prospect she was spelling out.

"Jack was a very good colleague of mine, a real mate, but he kept his work close to his chest for obvious reasons."

Georgina had to start from scratch, once she had got her hands on the material which Tom had passed to her.

"Markham has been careful to observe the letter of the law, and company law can be very abstruse if you're trying to follow paper trails. They all lead to offshore accounts, or nominee shareholders."

"But Jack had found a few trails to follow," suggested Tom, trying to sound positive.

He was conscious that he had not had any contact with Maud Cumming for some time. Maybe she felt it was wise to bide her time, before re-establishing contact.

"We always seem to be just one step behind our boy," said Anna, "I'd like to see him stumble."

Tom knew that was a heartfelt remark. First there was Malcolm Miller's 'accident', Jack's 'accident', and now Tom and Mike had been run off the road by a mysterious Jeep. Tom had been kept in hospital overnight with concussion. Mike needed more attention, and was kept for a few days. It was all getting a bit too close to home.

"Back in the day," began Tom.

"Oh! Here we go" interrupted Anna jauntily, "pull up a sandbag; Tom is going to give us one of his Boy Scout stories!!"

"If I may continue, Doctor Macdonald!"

Georgina saw him give her a playful smile. You're a lucky man Tom Scobie, she thought, you've found the perfect companion. Wish I could find a hubbie like you.

"When I was in the Balkans, and we were trying to unravel the structure of gangs," Tom began, "we understood that everybody was bound together by clan loyalty. They knew that if they broke faith, their own families would suffer. So it was difficult to identify a weak link."

"But not impossible?" suggested Georgina.

"Correct," said Tom.

"Jack had uncovered a source of information, right in the heart of Markham's operation."

Tom paused to see how Georgina reacted. He wasn't sure how much she knew about Maud.

"Jack mentioned 'a source' but was unspecific," added Georgina.

So you don't know who she is, thought Tom. Let's keep it that way - for now.

"What information would we want this source to give us, which would be the clincher?" he asked.

174

"I'd need to think about that a bit," said Georgina, giving Tom a searching look.

Tom had in mind arranging another midnight assignation with Maud at Membury services. With Molly off the road for repairs, he had borrowed another Land Rover from the farm, on the understandable proviso that he didn't wreck it.

He would need to ask Maud to find out something specific. She might not be able to deliver. As far as he could fathom her motivation, it was probably because Gill had come along and upset the dynamic of her existence with Markham. She had been content whilst Markham had been a buccaneering businessman, but now something had changed. So was it anger that was driving her, or jealousy? It could be a sense of injustice, but then why hadn't she been to the police? She must have plenty of evidence.

"Wow! That smells fabulous!" Georgina had caught the aroma of Anna's cooking.

"Granny Macdonald's *farmhoose* stew," said Anna, with a flourish as she put the casserole onto the kitchen table.

"Our secret weapon!" said Tom, giving Georgina a broad grin.

****

Charles Markham considered it a mixed blessing to have Lady Mary back in the house. The Wyvern Hall Spring party had taken on added significance, now that he was acting Chairman of the local Constituency Association, as well as its President.

"Will we have enough space for everybody?" she asked.

They were both sitting in his study in Wyvern Hall, his centre of gravity as she thought of it. Between them sat Maud Cumming, with pad and pencil poised as ever.

"How many on the list?" he directed his gaze to Maud.

"Just nudging two hundred," she replied.

"Does that include *my* list?" asked Lady Mary.

"Oh yes, indeed," replied Maud.

"Should be do-able," he suggested.

It was a mixed blessing, as they usually had two events, one for *his* associates and one for Lady Mary's arts and crafts lot. But, it would be convenient to shake up his list of friends, as there was clearly a rat in the pile somewhere. He had allowed Mary to fill up her list, meaning he had to prune his. By dropping judicious hints, he had set the rumour mill going. The phone soon started ringing and 'old friends' just wanted to catch up, and hoped to see him over the coming weeks.

"And how is the *new* candidate settling down?" she asked archly.

"You'll have the chance to meet the gallant captain, and his lovely wife, shortly my dear!" he replied airily.

"Invitations went out yesterday," added Maud, trying to lighten the atmosphere.

"Thank you Maud," said Markham, she was dismissed.

She walked away from the study into her office adjoining and closed the door. Something had changed she thought. The atmosphere had become decidedly frosty since Lady Mary's return. She had no doubt learned of Gill's eclipse at the candidate selection. Possibly she had heard of Louisa Miller's dramatic entrance. The two ladies had previously been on friendly terms, meeting for lunch occasionally. Might there be a new alliance, taking advantage of Markham's setback?

Now Markham was stuck with a lame duck on his hands. The balance of power had changed. Once Scobie was MP for Ridgeway, Markham's hold over the Association would wane. His proximity to power, and his ability to enthral the gullible and the socially ambitious would pale. And would this affect Markham's ability to raise money from his 'friends'? Lady Mary might just decide that her life could change for the better.

"Well, this won't get things done, will it Maud?" she said to herself, and set about her in tray, humming contentedly.

CHAPTER TWENTY-EIGHT

It was a very select group of people who gathered in the Library of Wyvern Hall for the Markhams' Spring party. The invitations stipulated black tie for gentlemen and long dresses for the ladies, a chance to dress up. The Markhams had a small coterie of a dozen of their closest friends for canapés before joining the throng. Lady Mary was only mildly surprised to find Gill Wynne and Desmond relegated to the outer circle.

"Gill, Desmond! So glad you could join us," she gushed, as the couple collected their glasses of champagne from the sideboard.

"Very good to see you too, Lady Mary," responded Desmond flatly.

Lady Mary thought Gill was uncharacteristically quiet. She offered them both a toast.

"*C'est la vie!*" and she moved away.

"Cow!" hissed Gill.

Charles Markham came over to join them.

"Well, here we all are!" he exuded *bonhomie*.

"Hmmm, I know what's on my wish list," said Gill in an acidic tone.

As if to head her off, Markham clinked his glass with hers. "The election will most likely happen in May. The Government will want to maximise the voter turnout. Holding local and parliamentary elections together will suit their purpose. But they'll still lose!"

"So, all to play for!?" Desmond chimed in, with an uncharacteristically insightful remark.

"Exactly," responded Markham "I've got a few tricks up my sleeve!"

"So have I" said Gill, not quite to herself.

"Tom, Anna! How good to see you both!" The welcome from Lady Mary was warm enough.

They were all gathered in the Orangery of Wyvern Hall, which had been artfully converted into a wonderland of spring flowers. It seemed odd to Tom to be back in Wyvern Hall, without Muriel's effervescent enthusiasm. She had diplomatically absented herself for this occasion.

"Lovely to be back again, Lady Mary," Tom's reply was warm but not effusive.

"Anna, you look *fabulous!*" added Lady Mary, loud enough for those around to hear.

Anna smiled and blushed deeply. Tom knew that when she put her mind to it, Anna could dress up with the best of them. She had selected a creation from her wardrobe of dresses and gowns that derived from the paternal side of her family, a mixture of French and White Russian, that she had inherited.

"I suspect that you know everybody?" continued Lady Mary, indicating that they really ought to mingle. She moved off towards a group of her charitable ladies.

"Wow!" said Anna, "what a difference from last time."

"Hmmm," said Tom, "just so long as you don't inhale, it can become intoxicating."

They were greeted by well-wishers as they moved around the room. Pledges of support came thick and fast.

"Good luck in the election, Tom!" said a face that he vaguely remembered.

"Don't forget – you can't vote unless you've registered," was Tom's practised reply.

Donald Johnson hove into view, bringing a man in a dog collar in his wake. He introduced him as the vicar of the church in Wandage market place.

"I do hope that you might be able to do one of the readings at our Easter service Tom?" the vicar asked.

"It's in your diary Tom!" added Donald, with a friendly smile.

"Delighted!" replied Tom. "Am I becoming part of the establishment, before I'm even elected?" he quipped.

"Mustn't be superstitious Tom," Donald said, smiling.

They moved off. Tom noticed that Anna had gone pale. He gave her arm a squeeze.

"OK?" he asked.

"It's..." she hesitated.

"What you said about before you're elected. So much has happened. Something might still happen..... That man...."

Tom followed her gaze towards where Markham was standing, surrounded by a group of red-faced men. He put his arm around her waist, to draw her closer to him. He moved to whisper into her ear.

"I think he's running out of ideas," he said.

"That's what I'm afraid of," she whispered in reply.

He gave her another squeeze to encourage her. In the corner of his eye he caught sight of Maud Cumming wandering around the edge of the gathering. She was looking at him. For a second he thought he saw her twitch her eyebrow.

"Let's meander over towards the drinks tray, we could both use a top up," he suggested.

"If you get the drinks, *I'm* going to powder my nose!" said Anna, wrinkling her nose.

Tom was glad to see that the momentary gloom had lifted, but he knew that Anna had a sense that he did not; what the Scots called *fey*, another worldly clairvoyance.

Not something to be entirely ignored. He made a mental note to get her take on things a bit more.

Holding both their glasses he could see Maud had moved herself closer to where the drinks were being served. In the throng of the room, Tom needed to keep sight of her, as she was quite petite. He noticed that she only had one glass, so he put down both empty glasses and picked up one refill in his left hand. He recognised the classic 'brush past' that he had learnt whilst serving in military intelligence. And where did you learn that Miss Cumming, he asked himself.

"So nice to see you, Mr Scobie, and your wife too!" said Maud with a smile as they passed in front of the drinks counter.

They shook hands politely, and Tom was able to palm the piece of paper that she passed him. They walked away from each other. Tom put the paper into his pocket and remembered to collect another glass for Anna.

"Ah! young Thomas," a booming voice sounded behind him.

Tom jumped, for a moment he wondered whether his exchange with Maud had been noticed by anybody. Adrian Simpson was one of the officers of the Association, who fancied his chances to replace Henry as Chairman. Judging from his flushed countenance Tom guessed that Adrian hadn't seen anything.

"Wondered if you and your lovely lassie could join us for a *wee dram* one of these days?"

Tom winced at the terrible attempt at a Scots accent. Anna would *gralloch* you if she heard that, thought Tom, as he smiled an acceptance.

"Very kind, Adrian, thanks."

Adrian gave him an avuncular slap on the back and wandered off in search of others. Tom broke the news of Adrian's invitation to Anna upon her return, as he gave her the glass of champagne.

"Into every life a little rain must fall!" said Anna ruefully, taking a sip from her glass.

She cast her gaze around the room, full of people dressed in their finery. She felt proud of Tom who had won the approbation of the open primary, something which several people among this gathering had sought to prevent.

She caught sight of Gill Wynne standing with Desmond her husband, at the far end of the room. This time there was no smile, no raised glass. Gill held Anna's gaze.

It was a look of pure hatred.

CHAPTER TWENTY-NINE

Once again Tom was sitting in the car park on the northern side of Membury services. This time it was milder. Maud's note was brief and to the point.

SAME TIME, SAME PLACE, TOMORROW

So here we are again, he thought. He had driven a dog leg route to ensure that nobody was following, and had arrived 10 minutes early. He looked down at his watch. It must be midnight by now, he thought. The passenger door opened and Maud slipped in. They both sat in the light of the carpark.

"Got to stop meeting like this!" was Tom's opening gambit.

"I needed to see you, now that you're the candidate," began Maud, with breathless urgency.

"Markham knows that there is a leak within his clique, and has begun taking steps to close it down."

"Are you safe?" asked Tom anxiously.

"I need to be careful. He has found a different private detective and Don Johnson is reporting on your movements, he sees what is in your diary."

"I think I've encountered this new regime," said Tom sombrely.

"He's not giving up!" continued Maud. "This has become personal for him. It's like you are defying him and he doesn't like it. Besides, he's got to keep that harridan happy. She really thinks that she could still be the next MP for Ridgeway, and Markham's job is to make it happen."

"We can still keep in touch?" Tom wanted to reassure himself that his 'source' was still reliable.

"Oh yes," was the confident reply.

"We're still no nearer getting anything solid on Markham," said Tom, keen to exploit the opportunity to tell Maud what he was looking for. "Anything that links Markham to criminality. All we have at the moment is circumstantial evidence and a blank wall of shell companies in the Turks and Caicos Islands and nominee shareholders, who turn out to be law firms."

"Jack Sawyer made a good start," Maud began, "the money flow will be the key."

"Who manages the money flow?" prodded Tom.

"I do," said Maud.

That admission took Tom's breath away. For a moment he was lost for words.

"Did Jack know this?" was all he could think of by way of response.

"It was too premature in his investigation for him to know that. He had to establish the extent of Markham's network first. Events got ahead of us."

Tom understood in an instant that he was dealing with a serious pro. His own dabbling in the Balkans really had been Boy Scouting by comparison. Maud was the money bags for an international criminal conspiracy. This relationship was being conducted on *her* terms.

"I can't give you any bank statements or any payment material, as it would point straight to me," she continued.

"But I can leave you this," she put a thick A4 sized envelope into his lap. "It's a printout of the phone record. Markham's friends have been ringing him recently, to ensure that they are still on his list and in favour. That should help you to go further down the rabbit hole."

She was out of the Land Rover door in an instant.

Tom was just beginning to formulate a whole range of questions, but they would have to wait. He was still no nearer to fathoming her motivation. She clearly hoped for Markham's downfall. There was no question of her taking the reins of his empire, as she was giving him information designed to dismantle it. Nothing for it but to get this material to Georgina and her investigative team.

"Happy Easter Maud," Tom said into the darkness.

He started the Land Rover and began the drive back to Shepherds Cottage. There was little traffic at this late hour, but he was extra alert after the incident when they had been driven off the road. Mike was out of hospital, but his wife Annabel had banned him from any further driving duties until the campaign proper.

As he drove along the empty road Tom saw an owl perched on a roadside fence post. It took off as he approached. Tom smiled, Anna loved owls.

****

"Loving the bow tie Tom!" Sophie the office manager at Oxford Info was well into the party spirit.

The office party was given at the end of the tax year, in April, by the partners of the company, of whom Tom was one. Held in a nearby hotel it was an opportunity to say thank you to co-workers, co-conspirators Tom called them, who had kept the company running over the last 12 months.

"It was an anniversary present from Anna," Tom said over the noisy hubbub of the hotel room they had hired for the occasion. "It's Macdonald tartan."

"Can't wait to see you in your kilt!" giggled Sophie as she swigged her glass.

185

Tom was trying to get himself another drink. He could see Anna through the crowd, in animated conversation with one of their academic contributors. Probably some learned discussion about healthcare he thought, as he recalled that his expertise was biochemistry.

He found one of the circulating wine waiters and got a refill of red wine. He could feel his phone buzzing in his pocket. He pulled it out, it was Georgina.

"Hello – wait a minute!" he was able to say through the noise.

He left the room and stood in the corridor of the hotel. With other events going on, it wasn't that much quieter, but he could hear himself think.

"That's better," he continued, "d'you get the envelope? Any help at all?"

"The best Easter present ever!" gushed Georgina. "We can match these numbers against some of our known suspects. It'll take a bit of work, but I wasn't going to be doing anything over the Easter break!"

"Seriously?" said Tom.

"We've got people's mobile phone numbers as well as landline numbers. It's a bit of a jigsaw puzzle, but we can put the pieces together. It'll help us to map out the network," she continued.

"Will that help track the money flow?" asked Tom, trying to concentrate amidst the noise.

"Short of actual bank statements and transfer notes, this will identify Markham's principal cronies," Georgina continued. She was all business. "We've got some clever little elves who can dig into this a bit, and we'll see what we wind up with. No smoking gun yet, but we're getting there."

"How much more do we need?" he was thinking of whether he could re-approach Maud so soon after getting this information.

"Too early to tell, Tom," she replied "I'll give you a call."

"You know where to find me!" They ended the call.

He went back into the noisy room and straight into Brad and Jürgen, the two ex-Rhodes Scholars who had founded Oxford Info and invited Tom to join them.

"Just about to make the big announcement Tom, so stick around!" said Brad.

Brad called the room to order, and the hubbub declined. People were still moving around and it was a few minutes more before Brad could speak.

"It's been a great year folks, and we couldn't have done it without *y'all*!" Brad played up his Carolina accent on occasions like this.

"Now we're going to embrace the digital revolution, and launch a new web-based platform!"

This was news to most people in the room, so there was an appreciative chorus of oohs and aahs.

"Oxford Info will be available via your smart phones and the navigation will be state of the art!" added Brad enthusiastically.

"He thinks he's Steve Jobs!" murmured Jürgen to Tom, "just hope that the share offering goes well!"

"It'll keep us all busy!" replied Tom.

Brad carried on in the same vein for a few minutes more, and his remarks were greeted by enthusiastic applause. They had agreed not to mention Tom's candidacy, as it would detract from the launch of the digital platform.

"Happy holidays everybody!" Brad concluded, "back to work after Easter!"

A collective groan drowned out Brad's final flourish, followed by laughter.

Tom could see Anna at the back of the room, she raised her glass and blew him a kiss.

Jürgen followed Tom's gaze, and raised his glass back to Anna.

"Lucky man" he said, slapping Tom on the back.

CHAPTER THIRTY

Just another day at the office, thought Anna. It was the end of the day and the end of the week. She still had a slight buzz in her head after Tom's office party last night. Either from the booze or from the coffee that had helped her through her day at the health centre.

"See you in the Rifleman Anna?" Janine's cheery voice came drifting into her room from the corridor.

She put her head around the door.

"All right?" asked Janine.

Anna pulled a face.

"Hair of the dog is what you need my girl!" chirped Janine pulling on her down jacket, "see you in a couple of minutes then."

It was Anna's turn to shut up the Health Centre at the end of the week. It being the Easter break, it would remain closed until after the Bank Holiday. She closed her computer, tidied up her filing tray and stood up to begin a walk around the building, to ensure all was safe and sound before locking up.

"See you in a mo, Anna!" came the voice of Marion one of the practice nurses, as they passed in the corridor. "Tom coming?" she asked.

"He's on the bus from Oxford, I've got the car. It's his turn to drive home tonight!" They had stayed overnight in a motel after the party, Anna had driven down to Farrington this morning. Tom would join the gang at the Rifleman.

Everybody was in high spirits, at the thought of a few days break for Easter. Anna was weary at the end of the week and felt out of sorts. A test had come back with a bad diagnosis for one of her patients, she would wait until after Easter to tell her the gloomy prognosis.

"Oh! You startled me!" it was Belinda, backing out of a cupboard. "On your way over?" she asked brightly.

"Right behind you," replied Anna, sounding more cheerful than she felt. "Just got to shut up the shop."

She finished her walk around the building and returned to her room. She pulled on her old parka and the cotton Arab headscarf, which she wound around her neck. She set the alarm and pulled the door shut behind her and double locked it. As she did so she was aware of how cold it had become. A cold blast of air blew the cobwebs out of her head. She tightened the scarf around her neck and pulled up the hood of her parka.

"Straight from Russia!" she heard herself say, as she shuddered in the cold.

As she walked up Market Street, Anna was aware of someone under the eaves of the butter market, who began walking on the other side of the road. Anna could see the Rifleman about a hundred yards ahead of her. She imagined that the other person was a drunk as she could see a bottle of something in one hand. Well, she thought, after a few Friday nights in Glasgow, you can handle the odd drunk.

The shadowy figure crossed the road towards her. Anna turned to see whether there was going to be any trouble. Instead of the smell of alcohol on the breath, she smelt something like drain cleaner. She saw the bottle of foul smelling liquid being raised towards her.

Instinctively, she turned her head away and felt the liquid spatter onto the hood, and run over the left shoulder of her parka. She felt a warm tingle at the same time as she smelt the odour of something like ammonia.

She heard herself let out a shriek, as she began running. The other figure disappeared into the darkness down an alley. Anna started pulling at the parka to get it off before the liquid soaked through. She crashed through the door of the Rifleman, still shrieking. The merry gang around the bar and the other customers saw her and reacted with horrified expressions.

"Acid!!" shrieked Anna.

Marion reacted first.

"Water, Beth, quickly – that ice bucket'll do," she barked at the girl behind the bar.

Janine came towards her and helped Anna to get out of her parka. She could see where the garment had been burnt. It looked like Anna had been lucky, but she was hysterical.

Marion came towards Anna with the ice bucket, ready to douse away any corrosive liquid.

"I think she's OK!" Janine said, the last thing Anna needed was to be drenched in ice cold water if it wasn't necessary. The parka was lying on the floor with vapour coming off it. Janine pointed towards the garment, and Marion emptied the contents of the ice bucket onto it, which started it fizzing and hissing anew.

Anna stood wide eyed and frozen to the spot.

The crowd of drinkers in the pub began buzzing amongst themselves about what had just happened; who had done it; did anybody see anything; anybody acting suspiciously?

"You've had a lucky escape Anna," said Marion, who took her into her arms and had a good look at her face and smelt her to make sure there had been no splashing onto her clothes or skin.

"I've called an ambulance," said Beth, from behind the bar.

Marion led Anna to a seat which had been vacated by another customer.

"Anyone called the police?" someone said.

"Give the girl a drink, someone!" called another.

"My phone," gasped Anna. "Call Tom….in the pocket."

Marion looked at the soggy parka, still sizzling on the floor.

"Can you give me the number, and I'll call him?" she said. Anna slowly gave Marion the number of Tom's mobile and she went away to call him.

"Drink this, honey!" Janine had brought Anna a cup of hot sweet tea. Barry the publican draped a piece of sacking over the parka, to smother the fumes.

"Don't want to lose any customers, do we?" His habitual cheeriness lightened the mood.

Janine took off her down jacket and draped it around Anna's shoulders. The health centre gang all knew the way to treat shock; it was the most common reaction to any significant upset such as a car accident, or nearly being doused with corrosive fluid.

"I was almost – devastated….." Anna said to herself.

****

Tom was beside himself as the bus ground its way towards Farrington. Marion had stressed the fact that Anna was unharmed, but was clearly upset. His fears about a repetition of what happened to Ivana were coming true. This had to be Markham's doing, he reasoned. There had been vague threats from animal rights activists, but something this nasty had to be the fruit of Markham's mind. Fortunately it was not long before the bus drove down Market Street. Tom could see the blue lights of the ambulance outside the Rifleman.

"Looks like a punch up in the pub!" said one passenger to another. Tom knew otherwise.

He got off at the stop just past the Rifleman, and saw Janine standing outside the ambulance. A police car was parked opposite; statements were being taken in the pub.

"I heard the bus coming, Tom," she said, "she's in the back of the ambulance."

Tom could see through the back door which was ajar, that the paramedic was still with her. He climbed in. Anna had a thermal sheet wrapped around her shoulders. Her face was white. She saw him and burst into tears.

"*Kotyonok!*" he said as he took her in his arms. His pet name for her; little pussycat in Russian, which they normally only used in private. "What's all this then?" he said gently. He could feel her shaking as she sobbed into his shoulder.

"OK, little one, no one's going to hurt you," he said soothingly, feeling totally inadequate.

"She's not been hurt by the attack, Mr Scobie," said the paramedic gently.

"I'd be happier if we could give her the once over at the hospital. Keep her in overnight."

Tom nodded in agreement, and was relieved to see that Anna was nodding too.

"We'll drive her in, if you want to follow behind?"

There was the small matter of retrieving the car keys from Anna's parka.

"OK – give me a minute," with that he blew Anna a kiss and returned to the pub.

The drive to the Great Western Hospital was uneventful, but Tom's mind was racing. Was this attack aimed at Anna, because some people disagreed with medical centres that gave out birth control advice? Animal rights activists who didn't like pharmaceutical companies who conducted research using animals?

Another thought lurked at the back of his mind.

Was this a warning to him?

****

In the event, Anna wasn't kept in overnight, as she insisted on being discharged once she had been seen by a doctor. A friendly nurse gave Tom regular updates, as he drank coffee in the waiting room which was reminiscent of many drab government or municipal building, anywhere in the world.

A police lady came and sat with Tom, and took a statement from him.

"We'll probably ask your wife to give a statement when she's good and ready," she added.

The door opened, and a young medic in scrubs entered. Tom saw at once that her face was relaxed. She introduced himself as Doctor Priya.

"Your wife is unharmed by any substance thrown at her" she began, looking at Tom and also at the WPC. "A good night's rest will see her right," she continued.

A wave of relief swept over Tom; what if he had won the seat and lost Anna?

"Given her condition, you'll have to be a little bit careful from now on," she added.

She saw the blank look on Tom's face.

"She's in the early stages of pregnancy."

"*Mazel tov!*" said the WPC, before Tom had a chance to process what he'd just heard.

He put both his hands up to his face. He saw the other two smiling. He felt himself blushing.

"You didn't know?" asked Doctor Priya.

"Typical!" said the WPC.

"We've both been, er, preoccupied." Was all Tom could think to say. His first feeling was one of happiness – a father! His mind was racing – what could he do to keep them all safe?

Doctor Priya explained to Tom, in terms that she thought he should understand, that Anna would need to mind what she ate and how much alcohol she drank.

As she spoke, the thought that Anna might have lost the baby due to the shock of the attack, stung him. He'd make sure that no more harm came to her, to them both.

CHAPTER THIRTY-ONE

"I'm not Ivana!" Anna was furious.

Any thoughts Tom might have had about the attempted acid attack scaring Anna into staying locked up at home melted in the glare from those hypnotic eyes. Any thoughts that the prospect of motherhood would make her more careful, also evaporated. He should have known what the reaction would be to his suggestion that he should ask Sid to be her bodyguard. But he felt he should make a gesture, he had been pretty wrapped up in his own life, neglecting Anna.

"I want you, us, to be safe," even as he spoke the words fell flat on the floor between them.

"You told me what happened to Ivana, and how you couldn't protect her," Anna's tone was more moderate now. "I'm pretty street wise, Tom, so please concentrate on getting Markham locked up! We've been through a lot together, so let's not allow this numtie to come between us."

Tom couldn't hide his smile, the attempted acid attack had very nearly succeeded. Anna's streetwise instinct had saved her. She had been planning to tell him about the pregnancy when the right moment arose, but it never quite happened. Well, now he knew and the baby was safe. Nevertheless, it had shaken him. If anything Anna had responded like a lioness protecting her, as yet unborn, cub.

"I just wish I'd got a better look at that person," she added.

"Are we Okay?" she said, holding out both her hands in a gesture of togetherness.

"Of course," replied Tom gently, taking her hands and drawing him to her. "It's just…."

"I know," she said, putting a finger on his lips. "Now baby and I need feeding. I think we should see if we can get into the White Horse for some supper."

The flood of messages of concern and congratulations had buoyed them both up since they returned from the hospital. Anna mourned the loss of her parka though. "Some happy times," she said wistfully as they strolled down the hill towards the pub. The first decision was not to think about names for the little one until they were sure of its gender.

"I had a great uncle Marmaduke," teased Tom.

"And I had a great Aunt Countess Natalia Pavlovna," responded Anna in kind.

"Top trumps!" said Tom "I'll stop now."

As they entered the pub, there was a brief hush. Bad news spreads fast thought Tom.

"Evening all!" called Charlie the publican, "a drink for you both!" he added, which broke the atmosphere and the hubbub of chatter picked up. Tom noticed people staring at Anna, to see for themselves that she was unharmed by the attempted acid attack. The stares dissolved into smiles, as people wanted to be welcoming, but didn't know what to say.

"Nice having an evening off," said Tom, realising that if he did win the seat family time would have to be carved out from a busy schedule.

****

"You've no idea who was behind the attack?" Matt's voice down the phone line was concerned, when Tom rang, later that evening, to ask him to be a godfather to mini-Scobie, and other news.

197

"All sorts of speculation," Tom began, "there was some talk of a fringe animal rights group who don't like modern medical methods, or some other group."

"Just the one attack so far," continued Matt, "no others?" Tom told him of his offer to arrange for Anna's safety, and how it was firmly rebuffed.

"I feel I've let her down," he began.

"Did Anna say that?"

"No but…"

"Did you ask her?" continued Matt. Tom felt this was turning into a marriage guidance session.

"I'm duly chastened," he said, hoping to head off a lecture.

"I always ask couples about the difference between listening and hearing," continued Matt. Tom dimly recalled a session with Matt before their wedding, and nodded to himself.

"Go thou and sin no more, now how're you getting on unearthing evidence against you know who?"

Tom brought Matt up to date, as much to remind himself what had happened, as to fill Matt in on developments.

"This isn't going to be a one-horse race" added Tom, "several celebrity candidates have appeared out of the woodwork, endorsing all kinds of causes. Greens, whales, nuclear power and so on."

"That's the risk you run if you're standing in a safe seat," Matt said. "People won't want a coronation and they just might unseat the incumbent party."

Thanks for nothing thought Tom.

"If you manage to get the goods on your man, would you step away from the parliamentary contest?" Matt's question brought Tom up short. "After all, you got into this to right a wrong. Suppose things wrapped up in the next day or two…."

Tom felt that there was still some way to go in unearthing the full extent of Markham's network, so the question was largely academic. Even so, having launched himself on this path, he had warmed to the idea of serving his community. He felt they'd been let down. He spelt this out to Matt, who seemed to approve of his logic and his motives.

"I'll try to get over to help when I can Tom, in the meantime look after the family!"

"One thing you can do Matt," added Tom, "keep your network on the lookout for any of these dodgy types, you just never know what might turn up."

Matt agreed and they ended the call. That last thought just seemed to drop into his mind. The more eyes and ears he had on his side the better. He just might need them.

****

"Where have we got to with your latest scoop Georgie?" The proprietor's voice was genial enough, but she knew that this call was to remind her about the cash her investigative unit was using up.

"You know how it is, Seb, plenty of hay and we're looking for needles. So far, we've had a few near misses, but I hope we can get to the bottom of it soon." She hoped that sounded convincing.

"Hmmm – nothing actionable I hope?" the last thing the proprietor wanted was an expensive legal action against his organisation.

"No," she said, a little too quickly. "We're double checking everything, which is why we haven't gone public yet," she added. "We could take a chance, but we'd be in court and *sub-judice* in half a day, if I know anything about this character."

She had made a career out of exposing wrongdoing and had accumulated some enemies along the way. Normally her proprietors were prepared to back her judgement, so this call was alarming, was the proprietor having second thoughts?

"Are you being lent on?" she asked, no point in being coy with her paymaster.

There was a pause, which she felt was a little bit too long. "Just protecting the bottom line," was the enigmatic reply. "Keep me posted, Georgie."

"Will do," she heard herself say, sounding more chirpy than she felt. As she put the phone down she saw one of her elves giving her a quizzical look.

"Big Brother checking in," she said with a wry smile. They all enjoyed the idea of a bunch of insurgents intent on overthrowing the Establishment, despite the fact that they were funded by a media plutocrat.

"Progress chasing on the new big project?" Georgina nodded as she turned her attention to her desktop PC. They were so close now, she thought. Markham's network seemed to extend into many corners of the establishment. Had he managed to reach the owner of the news agency she was working for?

CHAPTER THIRTY-TWO

Tom was glad to hear Anna laughing. It was Easter Sunday afternoon and they were at the family farm house. The hurly burly of dogs, children, friends and family gave them both a feeling of safety and continuity. The news about her pregnancy had spread, and Tom was getting his leg pulled by his brothers.

"What was in that stuffing you made Anna?" asked Mike's wife.

"*Haggis!*" replied Anna in the voice of a Highland fishwife.

"So that's why it all disappeared!" bellowed Tom's father, 'the guv'nor' across the big farmhouse kitchen. They all laughed.

"You two are a right pair!" he barked at Anna and Tom.

Anna flashed her eyes at him "I'll take that as a compliment kind sir!" she said coquettishly.

She caught Tom's eye across the kitchen and gave him a smile; I'm all right, she seemed to be saying. Tom responded in kind – ditto he implied. After his encounter on the Downs and the attack on Anna, they were both feeling fragile. A family gathering was just what they both needed.

"What about your family Anna?" asked Mike's wife

Tom caught Anna's eye, it was a thorny subject.

"My mother is with cousins in Perthshire and my Father is – wherever he is…."

Mike's wife gave her an embarrassed smile, she had forgotten about Anna's itinerant childhood. She recalled something about growing up with granny in the west of Scotland, but the details were hazy. Rightly so, Anna would have said.

"Uncle Tom, are you going to be our MP?" asked Zach who was Mike's son.

"How old are you now Greg?" asked Tom.

"Fifteen," came the confident reply.

"You won't get to vote in this election, and by the time the next one comes you might well have gone off to university," Tom began.

"I'm now the parliamentary candidate for this seat, for my Party" Tom continued.

"Haven't we got one now?" asked Zach.

"The previous MP was killed, and the writ for the new election has been held over until the General Election which will be in May."

"So are we unrepresented?" asked Mike's wife curiously.

"Actually yes," Tom replied, "but if there was something urgent one of the neighbouring MPs could take up your case."

"No point voting," said Lucy, Zach's elder sister who came swirling into the kitchen in time to pick up the conversation.

"Changes nothing, especially here – been the same party for years," she added, with an accusatory look at Tom.

"Plenty of people would like the chance to vote out their government in other parts of the world Lucy, we're lucky to have the choice," Tom began.

As he was talking, he saw Anna reach into the pocket of her jeans and pull her phone out. Lucy began what sounded like a well-rehearsed speech about why she was going to vote Green. Tom saw Anna's complexion drain as she listened and spoke on the phone.

What now thought Tom? Maybe something at the Health Centre. He saw her look at him anxiously. He walked across the kitchen ignoring Lucy's tirade. He put his arm around Anna, and led her into the hallway which was only slightly quieter.

"It's Janine on the phone," she said holding the phone away, "Belinda's been arrested!"

Tom was shocked, was this anything to do with the attack on Anna? She proffered the phone to Tom who took it.

"Happy Easter Janine," was all he could think to say.

He could hear that Janine was upset down the phone.

"The police came to my house at 8 o clock this morning, Tom, I was just telling Anna," she began.

"*On Easter day!*" he said.

"They've charged Belinda as an accessory to the attack on Anna!" Janine went on. "And Gill Wynne was found dead in the river last night, it was on the local news Tom!"

They had managed to avoid any local or national news for a few short hours, and this happens. Tom was trying to fit the pieces together.

"They think Gill was responsible?" he said, still trying to comprehend the turn of events. He pulled Anna closer to him, trying to protect her against this intrusion from the outside world. She put her arms around him and held on tight.

"It seems there was a lot of text traffic the evening of the attack between Bel's phone and Gill's" added Janine.

"Bel's terrified, she thinks that whatever happened to Gill might happen to her. She's spilled everything about it. They came to ask me if I'd noticed anything suspicious," she continued.

"I told them that I was aware of a coolness between Bel and Anna, but it didn't seem to amount to much," Janine was on the verge of tears.

"Are you ok Janine?" he asked. "You've been questioned as a witness?"

"Er, yes – they're not bothered with me. How's Anna?"

"I'm looking after her," he said in what he hoped was a soothing voice, both for Janine as well as for Anna's hearing.

"As long as you're ok then, thanks for calling Janine," said Tom. He looked at Anna to see if she wanted to say anything, but she shook her head and buried it in his shoulder. She was sobbing. He ended the call.

****

"Just the two of us, how nice!" Lady Mary raised her glass to Charles Markham.

They were in the Library of Wyvern Hall, having seen off their lunch guests.

"No sign of Gill and Desmond?" she said in an enquiring tone.

Markham's face was expressionless. The remark was both a barb to taunt him, as well as an enquiry.

"Poor Gill has been over wrought since she failed to win the nomination for the parliamentary seat," he replied.

It was true, he had noticed that her attitude became both more belligerent and remote at the same time. As if she was blaming him for her poor performance on the day, and wanting to lash out as a reaction.

"One door closes, another one opens," said Lady Mary in that hey-ho way that annoyed Markham, as if belittling his efforts.

"Well, happy Easter," he said, wanting to change the topic.

He reflected on the events of the previous 24 hours. He had to do what he did, as Gill had finally become unhinged. Like most people he had assumed that the attack on Anna had been carried out by an animal rights supporter, or someone with a grudge against doctors. D I Morris had called him to give him news of the attack. As he was acting Chairman of the Association, he might warn others but in a low-key manner.

"We're keeping the details quiet because we don't want to trigger any copycat attacks," Morris had said.

"All we're saying publicly at the moment is that Dr Macdonald is unharmed, and appealing for witnesses."

He had called Gill, to tell her. When he spoke to her, something she said turned his blood cold.

"Is that bitch badly burnt?" she had blurted out gleefully.

Markham knew. Gill had finally flipped. She was liable to do anything, and that would be dangerous. He had ended the call swiftly. He then found his black pocket-book, in which he kept a few special phone numbers. This time he didn't phone the private detective – but someone he knew as the pest controller.

'Get rid of the man, you get rid of the problem' was the dictum of Josef Stalin; in this case it was very necessary.

He poured them both a glass of wine.

"Here's to the future," he found himself saying, surprised at his own self-belief.

I may be finished with Gill, he thought to himself, but I'm not done with you, Tom Scobie, yet.

****

Who says that men can't multitask thought Tom, as he was sitting in the small constituency office one evening. He was working through a schedule with Donald, mapping out his life up until the anticipated Election Day in May.

Everybody expected the Government to call a General Election to coincide with the local and municipal elections in May. By doing so it hoped to maximise the voter turnout, but the opinion polls were not encouraging. Meanwhile the voters of the Ridgeway constituency were without an MP.

"So we have to combine fund raising and 'getting to know you' events for the next few weeks," said Tom. "We're going to be busy."

His approach to working with Donald was to play it straight: I'm the candidate, your job is to help get me elected. The atmosphere in the functional office was redolent of the ghost of Malcolm Miller. Tom imagined that the unquiet spirit of Gill also hovered, like something from a Shakespearean tragedy. The office was full of boxes of leaflets which needed delivering by the party faithful. The wall was adorned with the obligatory portraits of the Queen and Winston Churchill. Donald's manner was equally business-like. There was no warmth between them, but Tom had decided that he didn't need to make any more enemies at this stage.

"I'll be travelling a bit for work over the next week or so," Tom said, as they both studied a planning calendar on the office wall.

"Welcome to my world!" said Donald trying to create a sense of fellow feeling. Tom allowed himself an ironic smile. Their eyes remained focussed on the calendar.

"Well, I can't complain, having run for the job, now I've got to do it," he replied. "I'm travelling up to Edinburgh tomorrow and will be there until Thursday. Friday…" he tapped the calendar, "that should be OK for the Downside ward meeting."

To show who was boss, Tom tapped his watch.

"Got to get home and pack my bags. You can always reach me on my mobile."

The death of Gill had stunned those closely involved in the Association, they knew of her ambition to be the candidate. The story had made the local news, referring to Gill's candidacy in the recent selection for the new MP for Ridgeway. Once again, the story seemed to fade as soon as it had appeared. Such events were far removed from the daily concerns of the wider public. Both Muriel and Georgina had called Tom, to see if Anna was ok, and to wonder about the demise of Gill.

"I think I know who did this, but of course, no fingerprints," Georgina had lamented. Perhaps Markham's dead hand had stopped the story spreading.

After her initial delight about Anna's news, Muriel had got straight to the point, "He clearly had no more use for her," she ventured. "Watch yourself Tom, who knows what tricks he may pull."

CHAPTER THIRTY-THREE

Donald enjoyed working on a Sunday afternoon, it enabled him to catch up on himself before the week got going. As a single man, his time was his own. Especially with the election campaign close at hand. He was looking at the week's grid of activities, where the candidate would be going and which activists were out on the ground canvassing. He thought he was alone in the building, but he heard footsteps coming up the stairs.

The door opened into his office in the attic of the building. He looked up to see the figure of Louisa Miller enter, preceded by her favourite scent, dressed in country casuals. She smiled as she saw his startled expression.

"Thought I should drop in the office keys, which Malcolm won't need anymore," she said with undisguised scorn. She dropped the keys onto the desk.

"Lovely to see you Louisa," replied Donald. He had started to rise in his seat as any gentleman does when a lady enters the room, but she put a hand firmly on each shoulder and sat him back down again.

"Now you listen to me, you little squirt," she began, waving an admonitory finger in his face.

Donald's face took on a bemused air. Please continue, he seemed to say.

"I've got the goods on you, and Charles Markham can't save you this time," she said, drawing closer to him.

"*Goods*, Louisa?" he managed to reply, without squeaking.

She settled herself down in the chair opposite his. All of a sudden he felt claustrophobic, in his garret office.

"You think that you can go around killing people left and right, and leave no fingerprints Donald?"

He remained still. Where was she going with this?

"Everybody knew about me and Malcolm, it was an open secret," she began. "He enjoyed playing a high stakes game and he lost. He knew what to do to cut his losses. Fortunately for me I was not affected financially by what he got up to."

"Louisa, dear, you're clearly upset," Donald began, in an attempt to regain control of the situation.

"Damn right I'm upset Donald, *darling*, but I am going to be merciful," she hissed.

"You know what happened to Gill, once she was of no further use to Markham," she continued in a conversational voice, as if they were discussing the racing results. "Once he realises that you are no longer useful to him, he'll do the same to you."

Donald kept silent. He could feel a chill rising up his back. Louisa's manner was controlled, her big brown eyes bored into him.

"The thing is, Donald *darling*, that you're expendable. You've failed Markham. Scobie is already onto you. Markham made a big mistake going after his wife. You've been outplayed from the off. You thought Scobie was some ex-army thicko. Malcolm knew what he did in the Balkans, and he wasn't polishing his boots."

Donald was lost, he was vaguely aware of Malcolm introducing Tom into what he called the circle of trust, but hadn't paid much attention to his background.

"Your private Dicks have done you no favours, matey, they stand out like the ex-flat foots that they are."

She was beginning to sound plausible, thought Donald. She knew too much to be bluffing.

"Just remember," she said standing up, "a chain is only as strong as its weakest link, and Donald *darling*, you are the weakest link!"

"This is like Groundhog Day," said a weary voice.

Tom had joined Georgina and a small group of researchers at her 'skunk works', hidden away in an industrial estate in Didcot. The voice came from one of the researchers, as Georgina was showing Tom into the room. He had managed a day away from the office and campaigning. Nobody knew where he was.

"Don't feel guilty Tom, they love this stuff!" Georgina gave him a smile. "This is why I got into journalism, not to report on the opening of the new supermarket, but to change things."

"But you still have to do the supermarkets?" asked Tom.

"The owners want us to make money, so we do what we have to."

"So much for high moral principle," said Tom with a smile.

"Cheeky!" she replied. "I can see why Anna likes you."

Georgina led Tom to a long table covered in papers in front of a wall, covered with Post-it notes and a variety of maps and charts.

"Welcome to mission control," she said, waving her hand towards a group of pasty-faced researchers. Tom guessed they were either students or activists of some sort. As they sat down Georgina brought Tom up to date on their efforts.

"Annoyingly, we have about 95 per cent of what we need. We just need one piece of the jigsaw that will connect Markham to this lot."

At the mention of Markham several faces turned towards Tom. So this was *him* they seemed to say, the reason we're stuck in here. Tom sensed their feelings. He picked up a piece of paper with Jack's writing on it.

"Remember this is not about me," he said to the group. "It's about justice for Jack, and those others whose lives Markham has ruined."

"You'll do well in politics," said Georgina.

Tom saw that she was blinking away tears. She gave him a smile to brush the moment away. Their attention was diverted by a small voice that seemed to be musing to itself.

"Someone's been dozy."

Tom and Georgina looked at each other. All they needed was one thread which they could pick at, and unravel the whole story. They walked over to a cubicle where a girl was sitting with a stack of papers. She saw them approach and tapped what looked like a credit card statement.

"This is Gemma our forensic accountant," Georgina said hurriedly, anxious to hear what she had discovered.

"Someone checked into the Hotel Olympios in Nicosia three weeks ago," she began. "This was a new credit card with no history."

Tom smiled. Georgina looked quizzically at Gemma.

"A new credit card will function perfectly for the transaction," she continued. "No problem with the payment, but this card has no history, so the security system has flagged it. If the cardholder is on a watch list it'll get the authorities interested."

"Any name?" asked Georgina.

"Nigel Baxter," she replied.

Tom and Georgina smiled at each other, it was one of the bandits.

"It's a start," said Georgina. "I'm surprised he used his own name," she added.

"Maybe Markham is getting careless," said Tom.

"Baxter is one of his cronies, but hardly one of the high stakes operators. Maybe Markham was playing him into his network," he added.

"Sounds like a job for Theo," said Georgina. "One of our friendly ex-policemen, who want to atone for their previous errors."

"He 'retired' after a patchy career with the Cyprus police, but knows every villain on the island," she explained.

Tom held his hands up, signifying that he didn't need to know.

"Well, Thomas Scobie you certainly have brought us some luck, I just might bring myself to vote for you!" she said with a mischievous smile.

Tom couldn't help but smile at her infectious enthusiasm.

"Let's not get ahead of ourselves," he said.

"Hmmmm, Captain Sensible!"

Was she flirting with him? He'd better watch himself. They went back to the main table and joined the others.

"Maybe," Georgina said looking down at the piles of paper "just maybe……."

CHAPTER THIRTY-FOUR

Tom did his best thinking when he wasn't thinking. Whenever he had a problem to puzzle over, he let his mind go blank and just freewheel. The random combination of images and ideas acted as a filter to winnow out the chaff, until he reached the germ of the problem. So an evening of leafletting in a housing estate was just the job.

"Right folks, each side of the street and just keep going."

The Ward Chairman, Jane, had been one of Tom's early supporters. She was a no-nonsense Yorkshire girl transplanted to the south. Tom had driven over to her house after his day at the skunk works. His mind was still on the missing piece of the puzzle, so an evening of leafletting with a bunch of jolly souls was the right antidote to brooding on it.

"How's it going Tom?"

Jane's eager face made Tom smile, despite himself.

"So far so good!"

"We've got a shed load of this stuff to shift, so any time you're passing you'll be welcome!"

They both smiled ruefully at the thought of stuffing letter boxes until early May.

He needed to get a message to Maud today, without the delay of meeting in a safe place. He could deliver a message later this evening wrapped up in election leaflets. She could do likewise.

"Mind if I hang onto some of these?" he asked in what he hoped was an offhand voice.

"Fill your boots!"

He would do just that.

****

Maud was sitting in Markham's office opposite Donald, who was lounging in Markham's chair.

"Thing is Maud, whoever is leaking this stuff must know in detail what information matters. Someone in the inner circle."

Maud allowed herself a moment to collect her thoughts. She wasn't in the picture as to what the private detectives had discovered, despite her best efforts to find out.

"That would make sense Don," she said, in a flat voice.

She knew that Donald had instigated a mole hunt, and had started several false rumours which he hoped would flush the mole out. Despite his patent ineptness, she mustn't allow her guard to drop.

"Let me ask you then Maud, are *you* the mole?"

She held his gaze and kept calm. Thank heavens for all those meditation classes she attended. She slowly shook her head, "no Don", not trusting herself to say more. Donald gave her a final glance and then looked down at a piece of paper on Markham's desk, which he began to fiddle with.

"Hmmmmm" he said non-committedly.

He gave her a dismissive wave. She got up and wandered back to her office just off the study. She sat down in her chair and began moving files around to signify activity, in case Donald was listening for any sign of nervousness. She realised that her hands were shaking. Not that she was afraid of Donald, but rather she knew what happened to people who crossed Markham.

She needed to pass a message to Tom, advising him to keep his distance. Delving in her bag she found her phone, and saw a message. It was from Tom.

MSG 4 U @HOME

He had left a message at her home. How did he find it? For a moment she was seized with panic; Tom could inadvertently alert any watchers, and she would be discovered. Her breath came in short bursts, she realised she was on the verge of having a panic attack. Calm down she told herself. She sat still and breathed slowly. Donald was still fussing in Markham's office, she dared not make any untoward noises. She was on the electoral roll and Tom could probably find her home that way.

"Got the diary?"

Donald called airily from the office. Getting a bit too big for your boots, she thought.

"Coming," she called brightly.

She wandered into the office with a big smile and handed it to Donald who took it giving her the briefest of glances. She walked back into her office and sat down again.

****

As she turned into the drive outside her house on the edge of the downs, Maud looked for any obvious signs of surveillance. She had stopped on the drive back, to look for any giveaways that bugs or trackers had been attached to her car. She had not been followed as far as she could tell.

"Steady my girl" she said to herself, remembering the advice her mother, a wartime SOE operative had often given her.

She got out of the car, taking in the scene as she did so. She trusted her instincts to spot any changes. She was looking for where Tom might leave a message, but there were no obvious signs of anything moved or out of place.

"Evening Maud!"

She almost jumped out of her skin. It was Joyce her neighbour, who sometimes took in parcels for her. She was out walking her terrier.

"Lovely evening Joyce!" she managed to reply.

Opening the door she saw the mail and publicity flyers. She stepped over them to get inside and shut the door behind her. She reached down to pick up the mail and grabbed the flyers, and dropped them into the bin she kept in the hall for unwanted propaganda. She hung her coat up and walked through to her kitchen with the mail. There was no message light on the phone.

She set about the process of getting her supper ready, pulling pots out of cupboards and food out of the fridge. All the while she was wondering whether Tom had meant to signal that he was going to leave a message, or that he would do so. She looked again at the text message.

MSG 4 U@HOME

It must already be here she realised. The flyers! She went back to the bin in the hallway and retrieved the bundle of leaflets. She went through them and found a small bundle of election campaign flyers tied together with several elastic bands – of course! She smiled at Tom's artifice; hide in plain sight. She found Tom's message on a series of Post-it notes inside one of them, written in telegraphese.

WE ARE CLOSE. ONE MISSING JIGSAW PIECE.

NEED PROOF – LINK BETWEEN M & BAXTER.

USE DLB 2 REPLY @ BENCH WHITE HORSE HILL CARPK.

MARK DLB FULL.

Maud could picture the bench in the car park at the top of the White Horse Hill. It offered a panoramic view over the Vale. She was happy with the basic tradecraft. What bothered her was the information Tom was seeking. He was asking for something specific to fill a gap in the picture he was developing.

"Time to put your thinking cap on my girl"

She said to herself, hearing her mother's voice as she did so.

CHAPTER THIRTY-FIVE

At last! The campaign proper had started; the phony war was over.

"Right oh, Maud, you're in charge!" said Markham over his shoulder as he walked out of the office.

He and Donald were on their way to the launch of the campaign. A big event where everybody would be gathered to cheer Tom Scobie, as he began his campaign in the market square in Wandage. Maud was left behind "to mind the shop," as Markham had dismissively termed it.

She was alone.

Maud had worked out that everybody, including Markham, Donald and several of the bandits would be at the campaign launch. There was no danger of her being interrupted.

She had also decided upon the various pieces of evidence that she needed to retrieve and copy, to provide evidence of a link between Markham and criminality. It was the money trail which would be conclusive. There would have to be evidence of the various stages of the journey from Markham to the recipient, and the resultant criminal activity.

A copy of a telephone record showing a conversation with a number among the last bundle she had given Tom would establish the connection and the date of the call. A copy of a bank transfer from one of Markham's shell companies to a similarly recognisable bank account would give substance to the matter. The offence in UK law would be a suitably banal, tax evasion, but the related information would shine a light on the whole enterprise.

Her phone rang.

She jumped out of her skin. Calm down Maud, she told herself.

She answered the phone with as steady a voice as she could manage.

"Forgot to turn my computer off!" was Markham's brusque greeting.

"Right you are," she replied.

She replaced the phone.

Thanks for the prompt, she thought, collecting a USB memory stick from her desk drawer.

"I'm going to turn you off all right," she said to herself, as she got up from her desk.

****

Tom's campaigning routine meant he was up with the lark, and out on the ground in what he called 'dawn raids'. It got the local activists, at least the younger fitter ones, enthused about stealing a march by delivering leaflets through letter boxes, outside schools and at the railway station. He was still being paid to do a job at Oxford Info, so he pledged Brad and Jürgen that he would be free from 9:30 onwards.

This morning they were in a shopping centre catching the workers as they arrived, as well as the early shoppers and those passing through. The bright Spring sunshine brought a festive air to the occasion. The reaction from the voters was the usual mixture of polite apathy, and occasional hostility directed towards the political class as a whole. Local councillors who had joined in, were greeting passers-by who they knew. Out of the corner of his eye Tom saw Mike his brother, now restored to driving duty, tapping his watch. It was time to move to another location where a similar activity was taking place. He gave a cheery wave to the local organiser and jogged over to where Mike was waiting with a fully refurbished Molly, now festooned with placards and posters, his mobile command post.

"Finish your butty," said Mike, handing him a half-finished bacon sandwich.

As he chewed, Tom allowed himself a moment to luxuriate in the energy of being back on campaign. It reminded him of his younger self, bombing around in a Land Rover with a motivated team behind him. He was jolted out of his reverie by his phone buzzing in his pocket. He saw that it was Georgina.

"Tom! This is fabulous!" she gushed.

"It's the complete package, names, dates, account details. We've nailed him on fraud and tax evasion, which will get him into court. But nothing that will stick on, er, murder."

"Great news!" was all he could say.

He had received a text from Maud that the dead letter box was loaded, on the evening of the campaign launch. He had gone straight to the White Horse Hill as soon as he could get away. Stuff tradecraft, he thought, Maud would be well out of the way when she sent the message. As he retrieved the package the only movement came from a passing fox, who regarded him disdainfully.

"I've been in touch with the police," said Georgina coming back to the matter in hand.

"D I Morris has been, er, removed from duty pending investigations, and now there's a new team looking into Markham and his gang," she continued.

Tom knew that Maud had blown her cover by providing material that only she could access.

"Just let me check my source is safe before you call Markham please?" he asked.

"Er – OK", Georgina was taken aback.

"Like you I want to protect my source of information," he explained.

"Of course," she responded, sounding crestfallen at having her moment of glory postponed.

He fished out his other phone, and sent Maud a text.

R U IN THE CLEAR?

He put the phone on his lap and continued eating his bacon butty. A surprisingly short time later he received a reply.

YES – TTFN.

Maud would be safely away from any danger, once the lid came off the can of worms. He called Georgina and told her she could make her call.

****

Markham was beyond irritated that Maud had chosen this of all times to go on her annual leave. The short notice was particularly annoying, but in Markham's world no one was irreplaceable. Shelley was an amusing companion, but she was all fingers and thumbs when it came to the office routine. Still, he chuckled to himself, she made up for it in other ways. He looked up as she walked into his study from the adjoining office. She was wearing a colourful dress and a fragrance that spoke of promise. She smiled apologetically.

"There's something wrong with the computer," she began. "I know you think I'm being a bit ditsy, but I can't get into the Main Menu."

"Hmmm? See if our IT people can help," he said, giving her a dismissive smile.

He looked at his watch.

"Got a meeting now, I'll see you later," he said over his shoulder, as he got up from the desk and walked out with a black leather folder under his arm.

He got as far as the hallway, when his mobile phone buzzed in his breast pocket. He reached in and saw a number he didn't recognise. It puzzled him because only his closest associates had this number.

"Hello," he said tentatively.

"Lord Markham, I'm Georgina Casey of the Vale News Agency," a voice began in his ear.

How had she got this number he wondered? Oh well, he'd dealt with this lot before.

"I've spoken to your colleague before Miss Muir," he began.

"I'm recording this call, Lord Markham. We're running a story later today implicating you in criminality including perverting the course of justice, fraud and tax evasion. I just wondered whether you would like to make a comment?"

He could hear the smug tone in her voice, he went into auto-pilot mode.

"I'll have to refer you to my lawyers, Miss Casey," and ended the call.

Damn!!

What is going on? He called Donald, at campaign HQ in the market square. He got an unobtainable tone. He dialled the Constituency office number, which was answered by one of the volunteers, drafted in for the election campaign.

"I need to speak to Donald, the agent, urgently please," he said curtly.

"Not here," came the reply, "haven't seen him yet."

Donald was an early bird, he'd be in the office at the crack of dawn. He must be out and about. He walked back into the study, where Shelley was still fumbling with the PC in her office. Markham walked into the small space and smiled.

"May I have a look?" he waved at her to move out of her chair.

Sitting down at the key board he typed in the password to get into the Main Menu. When it opened the screen showed a warning icon

Drive Corrupted

Markham blinked.

"That's as far as I've got," said Shelley trying to sound intelligent.

Markham's brain was muddled. He was still processing the phone call he had just received. Had Shelley inadvertently done something to the computer?

"Maybe best to wait until the IT chaps get here," he said, getting up from her desk.

"I'm going to the Constituency office, you can reach me there," he said over his shoulder as he left.

****

Tom had just finished his second event when he got another call from Georgina.

"Good news and bad news," she began. "One of my sources tells me that Donald Johnson has just surfaced in Northern Cyprus," she said matter-of-factly.

No agent was a big deal on the eve of an election. He needed to find a replacement fast. Tom recalled that there was no extradition treaty between the UK and Northern Cyprus.

"Rats leaving the sinking ship?" he said.

"He was about to be nabbed, I think one of Markham's cronies must've tipped him off."

He could hear the frustration in her voice.

"But there's enough to pick up Markham," she added, brightly.

"He's just arrived at the Constituency office, if that's helpful," said Tom. "One of the folks there told me he was wandering around like a bear with a sore head."

"You should get over to campaign HQ now," she said, in a no-nonsense manner. "Your Constituency President and Chairman is about to be arrested. You'll need to be there to show that you're the new broom, come to clean the stables".

Tom winced at the mixed metaphors, but he saw Georgina's point. This was her moment of glory, and it would be justice for Jack. He would need to reassure the campaign team that Markham was a bad apple, but the effort was still worthwhile. Mike got Molly moving across the Downs with what he called the speed of a thousand gazelles, the Land Rover was going as fast as it could.

As they pulled into the market square, they saw ahead of them two blue and yellow police cars, with blue lights flashing swing around the square, and swerve to a stop outside the Constituency Association office. A mixture of uniformed and plain clothes police emerged. As he got out, Tom spotted Georgina among the bystanders, he gestured for her to follow him into the office.

Markham was in the hallway on his way out, when he was confronted by a petite looking woman wearing a dark jacket.

"Charles Markham? Thames Valley Police. You're under arrest for conspiracy to commit murder, perverting the course of justice, tax evasion, fraud and false accounting."

Markham looked thunder struck, as she continued.

"You do not have to say anything. But it may harm your defence if you do not mention when questioned, something which you later rely on in court. Anything you do say may be given in evidence."

Tom felt detached as he watched the scene. Two detectives took one arm each, and led Markham into the back of the front car. Two uniformed PCs went into the office.

"They'll be looking for evidence amongst Donald's files," said Georgina, who had sidled up beside him.

He nodded towards her in admiration, "well done Georgie!"

She blushed.

"Don't thank me. Thank Jack" she managed to hold back the crack in her voice, but her eyes were welling up.

CHAPTER THIRTY-SIX

The news about the arrest of Lord Markham, brought a media frenzy to sleepy Wandage. The market square filled up with TV news crews, and locals found themselves being vox popped by reporters from national and local networks. The more enterprising reporters, who dug deeper, linked the story to the disappearance of the Constituency Agent, an employee of the national Party, and the death of one of the candidates for the seat. Annoyingly for the Party Leader, the link was drawn to his attempts to detoxify the Party's image.

"There's a news wagon parked outside Wyvern Hall," reported one of the local activists as the story unfolded.

The Area Campaign Director was despatched to man the office, whilst volunteers took phone calls and stonewalled, until they were given instructions from Party functionaries, on how to direct calls. He managed to reach Tom on his mobile.

"You're going to have to call *another* EGM, to appoint a Chairman as well as an Agent," he began. "I can think of a few likely candidates, if that would be helpful?"

I don't think so, thought Tom. He needed to buy himself some thinking time. "Let me do a ring around and see what the view here is, there may be someone who is suitable."

He didn't want some flatfooted functionary upsetting the apple cart, and he needed to head off the bandits, who might have been primed by Markham for this eventuality. He told the Campaign Director that he'd call him back shortly.

As if in answer to an unprayed prayer, as Matt would say, the next call was from Muriel, to see how he and Anna were getting on.

"Hang on a minute, Mu!" the thought struck him. "Could you act as my agent? You must know the procedural ropes as well as anybody."

Her response was an immediate yes. They quickly agreed on how to play things, to keep within the rules. When Tom called the Area Campaign Director back, he was initially reluctant to agree to Tom's suggestion, but was persuaded by the momentum of the national campaign, he had other fires to fight. Tom was proposing a neat solution to the problem, if his Association would agree to it.

****

It was a very subdued group of people who assembled in the village hall the following evening, in response to Tom's ring around to the Executive Committee. The bandits had protested about proper procedure, but Tom had outflanked them. He had secured the presence of the Area Campaign Director, to ensure fair play. With no reason to object, they had no choice but to acquiesce. There were enquiries about Anna's wellbeing, some people's concern appeared genuine.

"We've got an election to fight, and were giving the opposition parties plenty of ammunition to throw at us," was his rallying cry.

At the appointed hour, Tom introduced the Area Campaign Director, who was well known to most of them. There were a few absentees, as some of the Markham's bandits had decided to boycott the proceedings; others had been caught out by other arrangements and sent apologies.

"Apologies duly noted" intoned the Area Campaign Director.

Tom thought he caught a hint of a smile, as he moved onto the main business of the evening.

"I have received one nomination for the post of Chairman," he continued, in his deadpan voice.

This was news to some in the room, but not to all. Tom saw a look of befuddlement on the faces of the bandits present. He had ensured that other members of the committee, who were not on the bandits list, were present. Two can play at this game, he told Anna.

"Er, I thought we were going to discuss who should be nominated," came a voice from the back of the room.

One of the bandits was trying to delay the proceedings. The Area Campaign Director raised a copy of the agenda, which he had circulated.

"I sent you all a copy of this agenda. Item 1 – *Election* of Association Chairman," he said, brooking no delay.

There was subdued muttering from the back of the room.

"Without objection? Do we need a show of hands?" His eyes were positively sparkling, as he glanced around the room.

"Let's get on with it!" came another voice, from the opposite side of the room.

"Who has been nominated?" asked another of the bandits.

"Henry Makepeace," came the deadpan response.

The gasp of surprise was equalled by a ragged cheer, as Henry and Muriel made a very theatrical entrance into the room.

"Do hope we're not too late chairman," Henry's avuncular tones rang around the room.

Anna's phrase about nettle suckers came to mind, as Tom saw the deadpan expression of some of the bandits.

Realising that they were thoroughly outmanoeuvred, several of them stood up noisily, and stomped out of the room. Tom noticed that one of them remained behind, probably to report back.

"Without further objection….?"

Henry was duly elected as Chairman, and to nobody's surprise, Muriel was elected as Agent *pro-tem*. Tom allowed himself a weary smile, as he shook hands with those in the room who'd supported him. The Area Campaign Director, slapped him on the back and shook his hand vigorously, as he took his leave.

"Well done, young Scobie! I think you've done us all a favour running that rogue out of town!"

"I remembered that line of yours Tom," said Muriel as the meeting broke up. "The team that connives together survives together!"

"All we've got to do now is survive!" said Tom.

****

The media storm blew away almost as soon as it had arrived. The General Election campaign soon pushed developments in Wandage down the news agenda. Henry and Muriel set to with renewed vigour, to rally the Party faithful. The bandits, having been flushed out, went to ground and vowed they would never support a 'puppet regime'.

Tom was managing to keep a foot in the camp at Oxford Info, just in case, as well as getting out and about on the campaign trail. Mike was driving him across country on a fine spring afternoon, when his mobile rang.

"Afternoon Pathfinder – saw you on the telly!" Sid's voice was as deadpan as ever. "Are you ok to speak?" Tom replied that it was.

"Word is that before he got nicked, Markham put out a contract on you."

Now he tells me, he thought.

"Any details?" was all that Tom could think of by way of reply.

"I'll see what I can pick up, but we've been here before Pathfinder, just look after your lovely lady, OK?" he ended the call.

A local warlord had put out a contract on him when he was in the Balkans, which led to him being withdrawn from his mission. His interpreter had subsequently been killed. He went cold at the memory.

"You all right!?" Mike said looking worried.

"Markham wants to kill me," he said as if in a trance.

Mike's first instinct was to look in the mirror. Nothing.

"Well, he'll have to get past me!" his reply was in earnest.

"He's tried it on once, I won't be caught again!"

The memory of their 'accident' on the Downs was fresh in both of their minds. Mike was lucky not to have bled to death.

"You've got to call the coppers," he continued, "this isn't a game, boy!"

"Hmmm," replied Tom. He didn't like the idea of the police dogging him, it would scare people away.

"Two minutes," he said, warning Tom that they'd arrive at the village hall shortly.

He called Anna, who was wandering through the house. She'd planned to take leave to help Tom in the final days of the campaign.

"A couple of the girls have come over, to give me some moral support, and for a natter."

Tom was glad to know that she wasn't alone. He would have to warn her, but he'd have to choose the time. She'd already been through so much. The attempted acid attack chilled him, but Anna reminded him that she was made of strong stuff. Even so, it would be stupid to make light of this news.

"Won't be too late," he said warmly. They ended the call. Tom closed his eyes. His whole being seemed bowed down by the thought of Markham, seemingly still able to reach him.

"We'll be fine boy!" Mike's voice cut through the gloom.

"This is our turf, we know every nook and cranny. Neighbours'll keep an eye out too."

I hope you're right, thought Tom.

****

"Looks like your agent has surfaced in Northern Cyprus," Matt's voice was business-like on the phone.

They were having supper, the following evening. This was not news, but it was good to know that Matt was on the case too.

"One of my contacts came across him in Kyrenia yesterday evening."

It was good to have Donald's location pinned down; this would be news for Georgina.

"The ecclesiastical network is on top form," replied Tom, admiringly.

"It's a network of trust Tom, you know how these things work."

Matt's work in reconciliation paralleled Tom's in military intelligence. His world involved him acting as go between in disputes where politicians were not trusted. This took him to trouble spots around the globe. In the process he had accumulated a deep and wide network of trusted contacts.

"There's no extradition arrangement with the UK," Matt reminded Tom.

"The UK doesn't recognise the regime as legitimate, so we don't deal directly with them."

"So he's safe," mused Tom.

"He can't be extradited, but that doesn't mean he's safe."

Tom was amused at Matt's characterisation of Donald's situation.

"Honour among thieves?" he prompted Matt.

"People who believe they're above the law often find that the law can't protect them," Matt replied, sardonically.

"In the meantime, young Thomas, you've got an election to win."

Tom winced, Matt was older than him by only five years, but on this occasion it seemed like a wide gap.

"Thanks for the info," Tom said, winding up the call.

All the while Anna had been going to and fro, to fetch the makings for supper. Anna had decided that any alcohol was not good for her new regime. He watched her as she got on with cooking over the small stove. She seemed to have lost her *joie de vivre*. He moved behind her and enfolded her in his arms.

"I can't cook like this!" she said giggling.

"That's better," he said, "I just wanted to hear you laugh again."

"We're not going to let that numty beat us down, are we Tom?"

"No we're not," he said kissing the back of her head.

"One more week......" Anna began.

Tom wasn't sure what that meant. If he won the election, he would have to get up to Westminster and go through the process of getting an office set up. He would need to see that things at home were in hand. He didn't want his life taken over by the Westminster machine.

He needed to tell her about Sid's warning.

"I won't be far away," he said, nuzzling the back of her head again.

"Amazing how lives can change," she said, in the same wistful tone. "Would Jack still be alive, d'you think?"

"Well we know that Miller began this by driving into a tree. That should've cleared the way for Gill to replace him," Tom began.

"We would have got on with our lives. Jack had the story, so something would have come out sooner or later."

Tom needed to lift their spirits, as he felt the conversation was verging on self-pity. He gave Anna another squeeze around the waist.

The door rattled and opened out onto the dark evening. A figure in a black hoodie came into the kitchen.

Tom felt like a fool, leaving the door unlocked.

In the confined space of the kitchen the place felt very claustrophobic. There was a wine bottle on the counter top. Tom grabbed it.

"Whoa! Tom, it's me Rob, from over the road!!"

As Rob lowered his hood, Tom relaxed and replaced the bottle. Anna looked at him in horror.

"You've gone white!"

Tom could feel his heart pounding. The adrenaline draining away made him feel faint. He lent on the counter top.

"Sorry Rob, I'm a bit jumpy," he said trying to control his breathing.

Rob was still a bit wary. He knew Tom had been in the army, he might do unarmed combat on him.

"Louise said to ask whether you'd both like to join us for a bite of supper?"

It was Anna who replied.

"I was just about to start cooking, but I'm happy not to!"

"And I was just about to open a bottle," Tom added, trying to make light of things.

"Not on my head, I hope!" Rob replied relaxing.

As they walked across to their neighbour's house, Anna took Tom's hand. She gave it a squeeze.

"Are you OK?" she whispered anxiously.

To evade a tricky conversation, Tom replied by squeezing Anna's hand in return. This was not the time to have a conversation about a threat to their lives.

CHAPTER THIRTY-SEVEN

Tom and Anna were sitting next to each other in the kitchen at Shepherds Cottage.

"Anything you want me to go over?"

Sitting opposite them was a slight looking plain clothes policewoman. She was the same one that had arrested Markham.

"Are you our *bodyguard?*" asked Anna, to break the awkward silence.

The policewoman smiled.

"You've got a pretty good bodyguard, I'd say!" She looked at Tom.

Tom gave Anna's hand a squeeze, and he winked at her.

"My job is to give you advice, and I'll respond when you think you need me."

Tom had seen bodyguards, nicknamed bullet catchers, in his travels. He had never had one assigned to him, even in the nastiest of situations. Yet, here he was discussing a threat to their lives with someone who would 'respond' if needed.

"We can think about some scenarios."

The remark was meant to be innocuous.

"*Scenarios!?*" Anna's voice was brittle.

Tom had hoped that by contacting the police, Anna would feel reassured that they would be safe. The policewoman had given them both a small pale blue booklet, and gone through some elementary do's and don'ts. Anna didn't like the idea of being told what to do, her freebooting spirit rebelled at the thought of not being allowed to do as she pleased.

"Just so we can think about what might happen, and what we could do about it," Tom said, trying to soothe the atmosphere.

"OK," added Anna, in a flat voice.

"My name's Isobel, by the way," said the policewoman, to lighten the atmosphere. "Most people call me Izzy."

Smart move, thought Tom. The bodyguard had a name, somehow more human. As a GP Anna always referred to patients by their name, and suggested they do the same.

"I'm Anna and this is Tom," said Anna, relaxing a little.

"But people don't call me Tommy!" he added, playing along.

Tom knew that Anna's moods didn't last, so he was glad that this one was passing. Izzy suggested to Anna that she went through her daily routine, so that she could suggest some things to do to keep her safe. As Anna began to speak, Tom felt his phone buzz. It was Sid.

"I'm going to step outside," he said, waving his phone.

"Evening Sid," he began, once he was in the driveway.

Sid sounded anxious, he was at what sounded like a race meeting.

"Just heard there's a bloke, a shooter who uses a motorbike, and makes a quick getaway."

Tom tried to think of any recent sightings of motorbikes, he couldn't call any to mind.

"Jumped bail, and last seen in the Midlands." Sid added.

"If he's not local, he'll stick out like a sore thumb," Tom responded, as much to reassure himself as to acknowledge the information.

"He might team up with some locals," continued Sid. "They'll know the lie of the land, and act as spotters."

That was a different proposition. There was plenty of local low life, trading in cars and drugs. He made a note to pass this on to Izzy.

They ended the call.

Tom could hear the two voices inside the house. It sounded like a normal conversation, but the topic was anything but.

A thought struck him.

He took his time to walk around the outside of the cottage. Nothing suspicious, but he took time to become familiar with the shapes and shadows of the house he thought he knew so well. He looked underneath both their cars.

Standing up and brushing the dirt off his trousers, he instinctively looked around. Childhood memories of sitting still in the woodland, listening for bird calls came back to him. His bushcraft had earned him the nickname Pathfinder, and command of the reconnaissance platoon. He'd need all of his senses now, to keep them both alive.

****

Maud was enjoying the anonymity of walking around Windsor among the tourists enjoying the spring sunshine. Like many people she had never really explored her own country, and one of her many resolutions was to rediscover it and hopefully herself.

Once she had texted Tom that she was well away from Markham and his cronies, she had gone to stay with a cousin who lived by the Thames in Datchet. She had watched the news of Markham's arrest with a sense of detachment. Her cousin had found the explanation for the sudden appearance plausible and she had ventured nothing further.

237

She found a bench by the riverside and sat down. Taking out her phone she turned it on, and waited while it powered up. She looked for a message from Tom and was reassured not to find one. Instead she found one from Louisa.

Louisa answered on the second ring. "Maud - How are you – where are you!?" she asked with a mixture of relief and exasperation.

"Been keeping my head down."

Louisa got straight to the point; "Mary is going to divorce Charles," she began. Maud understood that Markham had placed most of his assets in his wife's name to avoid tax. Mary would make sure she hung onto them in any settlement, a big hit to his wealth.

"Smart girl" replied Maud "I think she might just become my new best friend!"

"Mary's going to speak to the journalist who is in cahoots with Tom Scobie, I think she wants to reinvent herself as a lady bountiful and become a philanthropist."

"I like the sound of that," said Maud, maybe there might be a way for her to redeem herself as well.

"I wouldn't put anything past Charles Markham, he's a clever operator," Louisa continued.

"Maybe too clever…." Maud said, almost to herself. "He believes that the laws of man and nature don't apply to him, but I reckon that Scobie has psyched him out."

Whilst she spoke, Maud was continually looking around, anxious that she had not been spotted. She felt almost superstitious about invoking her former master's name, that retribution might emerge from among the teeming crowd of tourists.

"Have you met Tom Scobie?" asked Louisa suddenly.

A wave of anxiety swept over her, "er…yes actually at the Markham's Spring drinks, and he came to see Markham as a candidate before his selection". She recovered herself.

"A lot of people have underestimated him, Malcolm got to know him a bit…" she left the thought unfinished. Before all of this, they both thought.

"I think that in good time Charlie will find a lot of his friends deserting now he is of no use to them," Maud said, savouring the thought.

"Or can't control them," echoed Louisa.

"Can you put me in touch with the journalist lady?" asked Maud. "Now that the cat is out of the bag, I can add my two penn'orth. I still don't trust the police to get to the bottom of things."

Louisa said that she would get Georgina's number for her. As she listened, Maud continued looking around her. Was that person really looking at a map, or watching her?

"Donald got away, someone must've tipped him off," Maud continued.

"I think he began to see which way the wind was blowing," said Louisa. "I caught him in the office when I dropped off some keys, and gave him a piece of my mind. He might have had the sense to put two and two together."

Maud was not so sure that the matter was as cut and dried as this, she felt there was still someone out there on Markham's side. She'd need to stay vigilant.

"If Markham gets off, he and Donald could recreate his enterprise," Maud mused. "I suspect some of Markham's cronies are keeping their options open," she continued.

"Are you safe Maud?" Louisa's voice had a note of urgency. "You're the one person who knows Markham's operation inside out. You saw what happened to Gill……"

Despite the warm spring sunshine, Maud shivered.

"It's doubly important that Markham is locked up, and his gang shut down," Louisa added.

They ended the call with Maud agreeing to call again. She got up and began to stroll along the riverside, all the while conscious of others moving through the streets.

Was she being followed?

CHAPTER THIRTY-EIGHT

Tom woke with a start. Did he imagine a loud bang?

He was in the familiar bedroom at Shepherds Cottage, and could hear Anna's breathing. It had been a long and eventful day. Periodically he had a recurring dream, about being in the back of a snatch Landrover which was hit by an IED in Iraq. Anna had told him to seek help for PTSD, but he knew that there were worse cases than his.

He could smell burning. This was real.

Smoke was coming up through the floorboards.

This was not a PTSD episode. Suddenly awake, he shook Anna.

He could hear the sound of burning coming from downstairs. He flicked on the bedside light switch, nothing happened. The fuse box was above the door, maybe the power had gone. No time to speculate.

"The house is on fire," he said gently, as he shook Anna. He didn't want to frighten her.

"We've got to get out", he said to himself.

Even in the dark he could see the room was filling with smoke. He needed to quell his rising dread at the thought of being burnt alive. He found a torch and put it on, Anna's face registered the alarm they were both feeling.

"Get some clothes on and grab your phone."

"*Oh Tom…..!!*" He could hear the alarm in her voice.

He held her in his arms. He knew they mustn't panic.

"I'll slide down and get the ladder from the shed. Meanwhile you can call 999."

He tried to make it sound as matter of fact, but he could taste the smoke. They had to get out. They quickly pulled on clothes by the light of the torch. Tom gave Anna another hug.

"Back in a sec," he said, and opened the narrow window as wide as he could.

Grasping the window frame, he shoved his feet out of the window and launched himself onto the earth below, managing a commando roll to cushion the fall. He could hear Anna on the phone to the emergency operator, trying to retain her no-nonsense doctor's voice.

As he ran to the woodshed, a thought struck him. This was no accident. Suppose the arsonists were lurking, watching their handiwork. His head spun at the thought but he had to drive himself on, and get Anna out. Running into the woodshed he found the old garden ladder. Frantically he wrenched it out, yelling with the effort. He ran back and planted it firmly, letting it clatter against the wall. He scrambled up to Anna. He took her hand to steady her as she stepped onto the ladder.

He could hear voices from the other side of the house. Was it the arsonists?

As they descended the ladder torch beams found them. It was the couple from the cottage opposite. If there was any arsonists lurking, they will have scarpered by now thought Tom.

"We've called the fire brigade!" they said.

"Anybody else inside?" asked Rob the husband.

"Just us," Anna managed to reply.

"The garden hose!" said Tom, as much to himself as to the others.

"The fire seems to be around the front door," said Rob.

"Did you see anybody hanging around?" asked Tom.

"Er – no" replied Rob, not quite understanding the question.

"Take Anna in doors," he said to Louise his wife.

The two women retreated towards the neighbour's house. Anna glanced back in horror, reluctant to leave their home. Louise took her arm and gently pulled her away. Tom led Rob to the garden tap and uncoiled the hose. It was a futile gesture but Rob was right, only part of the house seemed to be burning. He had to do something to save their cottage, the home they had made together.

"Water on!" he called to Rob.

As the water spurted out of the hose, Tom gave vent to his rage.

"We're not finished!" he yelled to the flames.

Steam gushed around the door as Tom hosed the flames. Nothing else to do, but I'm not giving up his inner voice said. With an increasing sense of desperation, he played the water around the doorway to contain the fire.

After what seemed like forever he was aware of blue lights approaching along the lane. A fire engine turned into the driveway and suddenly the place was full of people, lights and noise. His efforts with the hose were joined by a superior jet of water dousing the flames, then another.

A hand on his shoulder.

"Alright Mister Scobie, we'll take it from here."

Behind him he saw a fireman. Tom dropped the hose and realised he was shivering.

"Better get warm, sir"

Rob walked up to him.

"OK Tom, I've turned the hose off, let's get you inside."

Tom was transfixed by the fire. Their home burning with everything inside, no time to save anything. Rob took him by the arm. As in a daze he felt himself walking through noise and confusion, over the road. Tom was aware that Rob was speaking to him, making reassuring noises about the fire brigade having things under control, but his mind was elsewhere. This was certainly no accident.

As he walked into the warmth and light of the neighbours' kitchen, he saw Anna sitting looking utterly forlorn. From inside a large duvet that Louise had found for her, she stood up unsteadily and managed to run to him. They held each other, without speaking.

"What about a drink Tom?" Rob spoke awkwardly, after what seemed like an age.

"Yes please".

"We're still here," Anna's head was nestled under Tom's. He could feel her shivering. He gave her a tighter hug. He realised he was shivering as well.

"I'd like Anna to see a doctor, given her condition," he suddenly felt stupid. Anna was a doctor, but she could hardly examine herself.

"I'll get an ambulance," said Louise, as she draped the duvet around Tom's shoulders. He pulled the ends together to enfold them both.

"We have a bed upstairs," Louise was tentative.

In Tom's pocket his phone was buzzing. Unwrapping himself, he led Anna back to her seat. He found the phone. It was Georgina.

"Tom! Are you alright?" Her voice was anxious.

"We're slightly kippered, but otherwise fine," he replied, giving Anna an encouraging grin.

"Your house on fire?" her voice was mingled with journalistic curiosity.

Bad news travels fast thought Tom.

The door opened to reveal a fireman. Rob pointed towards Tom on the phone.

"Mr Scobie?" he began.

"Hang on a minute Georgie," he said, putting the phone to one side.

"Looks like we've limited the damage to the doorway and hall."

"So we've still got our house?" Anna's voice was muffled by the duvet wrapped around them.

"Yes, but you might need to do some redecorating!" the fireman gave her a friendly smile.

Was this a warning, thought Tom, or an attempt to kill them both?

CHAPTER THIRTY-NINE

"I can't hide away", mused Tom. He and Izzy were sitting in the kitchen of Shepherds Cottage. It was two days after the fire. The house smelt of smoke, despite all of the windows being open. They had decided to stay in the cottage. The insurance folks had decided that this was not a scam when they saw the local news about the fire. A neighbour had lent them a caravan to sleep in, which was parked in the driveway.

"How is Anna?" her voice reflected her sense of failure at not having foreseen something like this.

"The hospital decided to keep her in, to allow her to rest, which I'm glad of," he replied. "She was quite shaken."

"You'll be watched by the bad guys wherever you go," said Izzy, bringing them back to the question of their security.

They exchanged glances. Tom saw a shrewd pair of brown eyes appraising him. Izzy looked as if a puff of wind would blow her away, yet she was a trained firearms officer. She never spoke about whether she was 'carrying' or not, and Tom didn't ask.

"I'm worried that they'll try something against Anna," said Tom. The words came unbidden, but he didn't regret admitting it.

"I can look after myself," he said almost to himself.

"You're more tactically aware," began Izzy, "but *you* are the target." Matter of fact. "Maybe if you allowed Mike to look after Anna," she continued, "or another family member?"

"My cousin Matt is coming over for Election Day, he's been in a few scrapes in his time," added Tom, grateful for the suggestion.

Izzy's phone buzzed in her pocket. She pulled it out, looked at it and took the call. Tom wandered over to the kettle to renew the tea pot. As he was pottering around the sink, he looked over his shoulder to see how Izzy was getting on. He saw that she was listening, with an expression of concern on her face.

"One of my colleagues has spoken to your agent Muriel," she began, putting her phone away. "Someone presented themselves at the campaign headquarters, asking for details of activities on Election Day.

"Muriel decided that there was something fishy about them, and called the number we've given her."

Tom nodded his acknowledgement of the news. Muriel might be overly sensitive, but perhaps she had reason to be.

"I'd trust her instinct," said Tom.

Muriel had given a good description, but Tom realised that Markham's gang of bandits would be happy to report his movements. These were people he knew. They couldn't all be arrested. In the Balkans, Tom always knew that he could leave and come home. This was home, and he was expected to be visible and accessible.

****

There had been a lot of calls from well-wishers, which Tom was grateful for, but this close to an election, he wanted to keep the air waves clear for election planning. With one of Anna's many cousins deputed to look after her, Tom felt able to get back to the campaign.

Muriel had arranged the Constituency Association office as a campaign HQ. The garret office had tables arranged around the walls with maps and charts depicting the various wards, lists of volunteers and phone numbers for each ward committee room.

"I will be based here with the data input team," began Muriel, as she addressed the final gathering before the election.

The room was full of people who would be key players on Election Day. An air of expectancy pervaded the gathering.

"Tom will be out and about," she added, nodding to where Tom stood leaning against a wall.

What they weren't told was that Tom and Muriel had decided on this approach, as a means of making him a harder target for Markham's hit man. Anna would travel with him, until the polls finally closed at 10 p.m., when she would be spirited away to Muriel's house. Mike and Matt would stay with her.

"It's going to be fun!" Tom's voice was all eager encouragement.

He stood with his hands on his hips, sleeves rolled up, and ready for action.

Muriel ran through the timings of the day, beginning with a 'dawn raid' by volunteers in the wards, who would push leaflets through letter boxes reminding people to vote. At each of the polling stations across the constituency, other volunteers would be 'telling' throughout the day, noting voters' polling card numbers. This was a way of tracking whether those who had pledged support on the doorstep, had actually voted. The data from this process would be fed to campaign HQ. Later in the day yet more volunteers would go door to door, to chase people who had yet to vote.

"It's a well-tested process," Muriel said, wrapping up the briefing.

"Those of you who have registered to be at the count, should report here after the close of polling at 10 p.m." she added.

"Now go home, and get some sleep!" said Tom, as the group broke up.

There was a lot of good-humoured backslapping and handshaking, and the occasional embrace as the group dispersed. It was late in the evening, and people did indeed want to get home.

Suddenly the room was empty. Tom sat down on one of the chairs.

"Well Tom," Muriel began. "Who'd have thought…?"

He looked up and saw her beaming face. He stretched his arms above his head, to release the tension he was feeling.

"I just knew that you had that extra something," she continued.

"Let's not tempt fate Mu," he cautioned.

Muriel waved him away, saying that one of the volunteers was coming to help her set up for the morning. He would then see her home, across the square.

"Now sits expectation in the air," Tom said to himself, as he drove home, recalling a line from Henry V.

CHAPTER FORTY

At the same time, Lord Markham was having a different kind of meeting.

"For the record, I am Detective Inspector Isobel Bannister of Thames Valley Constabulary, the gentlemen next to me is Detective Inspector Brian Fergusson of the Serious Organised Crime Agency".

Izzy's voice in the sterile atmosphere of the interview room sounded flat, but the news that SOCA was involved made Markham's solicitor sit up a little straighter. Izzy repeated the charges that were laid against Markham, and asked if he had anything to say.

"No comment," came the not unexpected reply.

Markham didn't need a solicitor to tell him that the police would have to prove the charges against him in front of a jury; there was no point in saying anything which would help them do so. This was not his first encounter with the judicial process.

"Except that this time it's a criminal charge," his solicitor had cautioned him when they met, before the interview.

"This is not a question of interpreting a contract, it's the evidence against you that the jury will be looking at."

Markham's smirk did not reassure the solicitor, who was familiar with Markham's sharp, but legal, practices.

"A bunch of layabouts from a council estate, who weren't sharp enough to dodge jury service? We'll run rings around them!"

"If new evidence comes to light, they could bring more serious charges," the solicitor tried to inject a note of caution into the conversation.

"The charges are very general and vague," replied Markham.

So it was that when they gathered in the lifeless interview room that Markham's demeanour was one of indifference. The presence of the SOCA representative gave the solicitor a queasy feeling that this time things were not going to go well.

"Lord Markham, we will be making an application under the Proceeds of Crime Act 2000, to seize your assets."

Fergusson's words were directed towards Markham, but he was looking at the solicitor as he spoke, to ensure that he understood. The solicitor nodded meekly, while Markham's face remained impassive.

"No comment," replied Markham.

The solicitor stole a sideways glance at Markham, whose gaze was fixed on the painted brick wall behind the two police officers. He then looked at the file which was open in front of Fergusson. There was a list of the shell companies which he had set up for Markham over the years. This did not look good, he thought.

"Lord Markham, we will produce evidence of criminal conspiracy to commit murder, in relation to the death of Jack Sawyer, a journalist who you spoke to......." began Izzy.

"No comment!" Markham's response was laden with exasperation.

Izzy recited a series of allegations against him, concerning the death of Jack Sawyer which Markham stonewalled. Fergusson fared no better. Izzy's calculation was that by letting Markham's solicitor understand the nature of charges they intended to bring, he'd recommend co-operation, for a lenient sentence.

"Interview terminated," announced Izzy, reciting the time as she stopped the recording.

Round one to us, thought the solicitor. They're obviously getting nowhere with this.

Izzy and Fergusson retreated upstairs to the open plan office, while Markham was taken back to his cell. The solicitor had again asked for bail, and was reminded that Markham had been remanded in custody in the magistrate's court.

"Thoughts?" ventured Izzy, as they entered the room.

"He fancies himself as a poker player," responded Fergusson. "Cool hand Luke."

"Well then, let's see who is the better player," replied Izzy, with a mischievous smile.

"I wanted to see what cards he thinks he's holding, without showing too many of ours."

"He may think he's got a good hand, but I'll bet he's probably only got a high card, which is that we have to prove our case," Izzy continued.

"At the very least we've got a full house, which might persuade a jury, and if we can wheedle any other evidence from anywhere, we could nail him with a straight flush."

Fergusson looked bemused. Obviously not a poker player, thought Izzy.

"A *real* poker player looks at the hands of their opponent. If there's a lot of shuffling, it means they're not sure which cards to play. No shuffling and they've got a good hand, or they're going to bluff. My bet is he's bluffing."

"He could get lucky with the jury," said Fergusson, sounding dubious. "We have to prove our case beyond a reasonable doubt," he added, to remind Izzy that a jury needed to be comfortable with their verdict.

"We have to lead on the conspiracy to murder angle," she replied. "If this becomes a trial about fraud, we'll lose them."

"Murder is your department, Izzy, I content myself with fraud and embezzlement!"

"His luck could run out," said Izzy, to herself.

****

"You scrub up well, Tom!" Matt's voice filled the kitchen in Shepherds Cottage.

He was fingering one of the election leaflets they'd be giving out in the morning. A picture of the candidate stared out from the paper. Tom had decided against an image of him shaking hands with the Party Leader, as he wanted to make his campaign personal and local.

Tom was on his feet bringing another bottle of wine to the table. The late supper was welcome, after a long day. It felt good to see Shepherds Cottage full of people again, despite the lingering smell of smoke and water. Matt had arrived just before Tom, they were all unwinding.

There was a knock on the kitchen door, which made Anna jump and made Matt sit up. It was late for people to come calling. Tom put the bottle on the table. He walked over to the door and listened. He knocked on the inside of the door.

"Open up Pathfinder!"

"It's a friend," Tom said as he unlocked the door and opened it.

Although Anna and Matt had heard tales about Sid, and the exploits he and Tom got up to in the Balkans, they had never met. A slight figure dressed in a black

253

windcheater and black jeans walked into the kitchen. A gust of cool air came with him.

"This is Sid," said Tom, as he introduced Anna and Matt.

"How do," said Sid, laconically. Tom noticed that Sid's nose twitched, he wasn't used to the new aroma in the house, despite the smell of the cooking.

Tom gestured to the table and Sid sat down and pulled off a woollen cap, revealing closely cropped dark hair. Sid declined Anna's offer of food or drink. But her warm highland voice elicited an approving smile from him.

"I hope you're keeping him honest!?" he said to Anna.

"Doing my best!" she replied with a flash of her eyes and a wide smile.

Tom had opened the wine and topped up glasses. Anna stuck to fizzy water. He renewed the offer to Sid, who shook his head.

"Got work to do," he explained.

"You're the chap…" began Matt, recalling Tom's stories from the Balkans.

"My guardian angel" interrupted Tom, not wanting to get distracted by war stories.

"I thought that was my job!" Matt replied in a hurt voice.

"You're my spiritual protector, Sid gets things done," Tom said, trying to keep things business like.

"We look out for each other," Sid added, putting a cap on things.

"Busy day tomorrow," Sid continued. "I need to know where you're going to be. I will orbit around the neighbourhood, and see what I can spot."

Matt obligingly reached behind him, to a pile of papers on the dresser. He passed Tom the large scale map of the constituency, which was covered with a plastic film.

"We'll take the smaller roads and where possible go across country," Tom began.

There was no point having a Land Rover if you weren't going to use it, he had told Mike. It began as a time saving measure, but could now give them the edge over any pursuers. Sid nodded his approval.

"But, you'll have to go around the towns on foot," he observed.

"We'll have plenty of helpers," added Tom.

"Human shields!?" asked Matt.

"Witnesses!" responded Tom.

"Needs must," said Sid, seeing the disapproval in Matt's face.

Matt simply raised his eyebrows and pursed his lips. Maybe this was a conversation they would have afterwards, thought Tom.

"Mobile coverage is not great on the Downs," Tom said, moving on. "But I reckon we save time, so it's worth the risk."

Now it was Sid's turn to purse his lips, but he said nothing.

"Oh great, I'm going to get my bones rattled up there!" Anna had pulled a face of disapproval. "I hope mini-Scobie doesn't object! I'm supposed to appear elegant, and I'll arrive looking like a scarecrow!!"

"You'll be fine!" said Sid, smiling at the image of a wind-blown, dust covered Anna giving out leaflets to startled locals.

Tom handed Sid a sheet of paper with the outline of their whistle-stop programme. For a few minutes they pored over the map, just to make sure that they all understood.

"Who is going to be at the count later?" he asked.

Tom found a copy of the list of the people the Party had asked to be admitted to the count as scrutineers. It included Party officials, such as Henry and Muriel, Tom as candidate, plus an adequate number to monitor the counting of ballot papers.

"Have the plod got copies of this?"

Sid pronounced himself content, and made his farewells.

"What'll he be up to?" asked Matt, after he'd left.

"Best we don't know," replied Tom. "Sid has his own ways of doing things. He'll appear when and where he thinks best."

Matt gave his cousin a sceptical look.

"I'd bet my life on it," he added.

CHAPTER FORTY-ONE

So far, so good thought Muriel. It was mid-morning on Election Day, and things were humming along nicely. The dawn raid had been carried out, volunteers and activists were out and about across the constituency. The ward committee rooms were running, and reporting the morning's voting figures. Henry had been despatched to take over the operations of a ward run by one of the bandits, whom Tom suspected would not make any efforts to chase up the voters. He would manage the scrutineers at the count later. Polling numbers were being inputted by a team of eager young techies, who seemed to speak their own language. She was standing by the kettle contemplating a cup of coffee, when it stopped without warning.

"Power's gone," said one of the techies from the PC at the other end of the office.

"Can you save the data?" called Muriel, thinking fast. She flicked a light switch on the wall – nothing.

"We've got the last input, but nothing new," came the laconic response.

One of the local activists who knew his way around the building went to find the circuit board.

"All normal here," he called.

Muriel looked out of the window, she could see that the electrical store across the square still had its lights on, so this must be a local power cut.

"OK folks, we'll need to use our mobiles to keep in touch, if the power has affected the phone lines."

"I'll call the electrical folks," said the same activist.

This can't be a coincidence thought Muriel. The opposition parties wouldn't pull a stunt like this, as it would lead to a complaint to the Electoral Commission. She remembered an old army saying that Tom often quoted – no plan survives first contact with the enemy.

"Got to be sabotage," she said to herself.

She spotted a young activist, grabbing an early lunch munching a sandwich.

"Ed, put your Boy Scout hat on! Go outside and have a look around for anything like a cut cable, or a manhole cover disturbed and get back here as soon as you can!"

The youth looked momentarily startled at such an odd request, the penny dropped as he saw the techies looking at blank screens. He stuffed the sandwich into his mouth and made for the door. Muriel picked up her mobile and called Tom's number. She caught him leafletting, at least he wasn't in between places, where the signal might drop.

"We've spoken about this possibility," said Tom, after Muriel's report.

They had gone through various scenarios some time ago. Tom had suggested an alternative HQ site, as a contingency. In previous elections, she and Henry had run the campaign from their house. They agreed that if needs be, they could use the house as a back-up.

"OK everybody!" said Muriel after she ended the call, "we'll relocate to my house."

Leaving some caretaker volunteers to redirect people, Muriel led a crocodile across the square. The techies had unplugged the PC, screens and printer, and cradled them as they walked. As she marched her charges in file, passers-by called out to wish her good luck.

The moment she got through the front door, she heard the phone ringing in Henry's study. One of the volunteers ran ahead of her and picked the phone up. They were back in business.

"I found a junction box with wires pulled out," said a breathless Ed, who had been sent across the square to report.

"OK, please go and tell the police, Ed. Tell them to inform that nice detective lady, they'll know who I mean."

He turned on his heel and went. Muriel set the volunteers to work, rearranging furniture and plugging things in. It felt good to have the house full of the noise and bustle of an Election Day.

"Just like old times!" came a familiar voice.

Muriel turned around to see Louisa Miller carrying two baskets of supplies for lunch. Despite herself, she gave her a beaming smile.

"Welcome to the refuge!" she said wearily.

"Supplies for the troops, I was told what happened and sent over here."

Another volunteer came and relieved Louisa of her provisions. Muriel felt rather dowdy next to Louisa, who was dressed as if she were going to a garden party.

"Shall I take some flyers around the square?" somehow it didn't sound like a question.

A bundle of leaflets appeared and Louisa swept out of the door like a galleon under full sail. Muriel watched her leave. She turned to go back inside, to be greeted by gawping techies, who had never seen Louisa before.

"Back to work, you dogs!" she said with mock severity.

Amidst much chuckling the youths returned to their task. Muriel allowed herself a smile – just like the old days.

"What else have you got up your sleeve?" she asked no one in particular. "I hope Tom is OK".

****

Maud had decided that she should speak to the journalist about Markham's network before the police, so that her information could be in the public domain, before any reporting restrictions were imposed during a trial. She wasn't sure about the sub-judice rules, but she'd have to let the journalist worry about that.

Sitting alone in her cousin's house, she dialled the number that Louisa had given her. She got through to Georgina's voicemail. It was Election Day, so she might be away for who knew how long. She simply said who she was and that that she would call back later, rather than leaving any message.

She needed to collect her thoughts. How should she tell the journalist enough to ensure Markham's conviction? She understood that knowledge was power. She had spoon fed Jack and then Tom with just enough information to keep them interested. She had to protect her own position while she was still in Markham's office. She couldn't afford the risk that any evidence would point to her as the source. She hoped that she could slip away into obscurity, and re-start her life, maybe somewhere warm and sunny. Her savings should be adequate.

At the second attempt, Georgina picked up the phone "Hi, is this Maud?" her voice was cool, but an underlying anxiety permeated her voice.

"Yes, is this a good time to speak?" asked Maud. She could hear a rustling of paper, probably a note book being opened. "Maybe you want to record this, Georgina, to ensure you get everything?"

Georgina agreed, there was probably a recorder running anyway, thought Maud.

****

Georgina listened as Maud set out the facts about Markham's business empire and his network of influence. So far so good she thought. She had let Maud tell her story, as she accumulated a list of questions.

"I think it's time that Charles Markham got what's coming to him," Maud said tentatively.

"Perhaps if you ask me the questions you want, I'll see if I can help…."

"Who killed my colleague Jack Sawyer?" Georgina asked, trying to keep her voice even.

"Charles dealt with someone he called the pest controller," Maud began. "Sometimes directly, sometimes via Donald Johnson."

"How can we prove it?" Georgina's journalistic instincts reasserted themselves.

"Those whom the Gods wish to destroy, they first make very clever," she replied, mis-quoting Euripides.

"Charles Markham came to believe that he was too clever to get caught by what he called flatfooted coppers, but he went out and bought some, just in case….."

"Why now?" Georgina asked.

"All my life I was looking for a great cause" Maud continued. "My mother worked for SOE during the war. I always wanted to be worthy of her. Charles gets inside your head and discovers how you think. He persuaded me that he was a on a mission to re-energise the country, but we'd have to cut a few corners. I bought it."

There was a pause, "but slowly, slowly he just became greedy. I didn't complain, because life was good.

261

"There was a time, once, when he'd look at me the way he looks, looked, at Gill. Good days, happy days" her voice drifted away."

Another pause, "when I came across Jack in the market square, he came straight out with the facts about Markham's dealings with traffickers and gunrunners. That got my attention. Then along came miss twinkle toes – Gill Wynne, and he seemed bewitched by her."

Georgina wasn't sure whether Maud's motivation was revenge for being side lined by Gill, or a genuine sense of remorse at how her dreams had faded. "Sometimes you just know," Maud said, as if reading Georgina's mind.

Maud sounded relieved, as if she had unburdened herself. "I'm sorry about Jack," she said. "I liked him, he was onto Markham, but got too close too early."

Georgina went cold at the mention of Jack's name, as if his spirit was hovering close by. She was still processing the information she'd been given.

"Donald has gone to Northern Cyprus," continued Georgina. Maud's reaction showed that this was news to her. "There had been some talk between Markham and Donald, but nothing specific, I suppose that makes sense," she said.

"My understanding is that Markham has put out a contract on Scobie," added Georgina. Tom had told her this, but in confidence, just in case. This was not public knowledge. "How could he do that if he's in custody and Donald is out of the country?"

"There are phones in Cyprus," Maud replied, trying not to sound too exasperated at this question.

"What I mean is, Markham might have sensed that the police were closing in on him, did he have a doomsday plan?"

Maud recalled a phone call Markham had made, which she couldn't quite hear, despite being only feet away. Markham had said something about dead men don't tell tales. She thought it might have been a reference to the demise of Gill Wynne. Georgina listened as the tale unfolded, hardly daring to breathe.

"There is one person you should ask about all of this," Maud suggested. "Someone who as far as I know hasn't been wrapped up in the police or your own investigation."

Georgina dropped her pencil, another conspirator?

CHAPTER FORTY-TWO

The Yeoman was your typical country pub. Sitting alongside the Ridgeway, it attracted walkers and day-trippers. Tom had sent text messages to his core team, suggesting a rendezvous at one o'clock. The weather was mild enough for them to sit outside, the better to see who was approaching, thought Tom.

"We've got things working Okay, now," reported Muriel, tucking into her ploughman's lunch. "The resilience plan worked well, it's just like old times!" she smiled.

"The polling this morning was steady, workers and parents dropping off their kiddies," she continued.

The busy time on a polling day would be in the late afternoon and evening. People would need reminding to go and vote by a process called, quaintly, knocking up.

"So, we'll be knocking up from about four o'clock?" asked Tom, also chewing his way through a ploughman's.

He saw Anna's face, which was red, trying to suppress a giggle.

"Ooh err, missus!" she said, mimicking a music hall comedian. "Never heard it called that before!"

"What a sheltered life you do lead!" teased Tom.

They continued discussing where Tom should be in the afternoon, identifying schools and shopping centres. Mike noted the distances and the time it would take to move from point to point. As Tom took a sip from his glass of cider, his phone rang. He saw it was Izzy.

"Uniform are at your house, someone was spotted poking around," she explained.

Tom caught Anna's eye, who read his expression. She looked serious.

"No sign of a break in, but someone was seen acting suspiciously," she continued.

It was an obvious time to go and look at Shepherds Cottage, the whole vale knew that Tom would be out campaigning. It could be a burglar, or paparazzi, sniffing around.

"We'll leave someone there until later," Izzy said.

They ended the call. Tom quickly shared the news and moved on. Anna looked pensive, but Tom gave her an 'it's Okay' smile, which she returned. He saw Mike glance across the car park, to where Molly was parked. Reassured that all was well, Mike got to work on his ploughman's.

"Hope that Matt's hotline to the Big Man upstairs is in good working order," Mike said, to no one in particular.

"Hmmm," Anna replied, with a mouth full of food.

They were enjoying the enforced break. There was little they could do until the evening period. The others at the pub took no notice of the party, despite the posters festooning Molly parked outside. Groups of walkers came and went, in search of lunch, or to go off walking.

"Back into the wagon folks!" said Tom eventually. "I think we ought to get over to Long Barrow, to see how they're getting on."

Tom was concerned that the Chairman of Long Barrow Ward was quietly on the side of the bandits, so an unexpected visit might sharpen him up a bit. After the inevitable visits to the loo and searching for phones, files and keys, the group dispersed. Mike drove Molly out into the country lanes, heading uphill across the Downs.

Once they had left, one of the walkers sitting at a nearby table, took out his phone and made a call.

****

"Afternoon troops!" Tom breezed into the Long Barrow Committee room, which was a mirror of campaign HQ. A group of volunteers sat around a table covered in sandwiches and half-drunk bottles of wine. Tom had asked Mike to pull up about 30 yards short, so that he could approach without being heard.

"Er, hello Tom," said one of the volunteers, who recognised him.

The volunteers were a merry bunch, but Tom wondered how much effort they'd put in during the day. He asked where their Chairman was.

"Gone to get some more supplies!" responded another volunteer, raising a glass.

Anna walked into the room, still trying to flatten her hair after their breezy trip across the Downs. Several of the men dragged themselves to their feet, out of politesse. Two women remained seated and gave Anna blank looks.

"Paying a house call, doc?" asked the self-appointed leader of the group.

Anna took in the sandwiches, and the collection of bottles. She and Tom exchanged glances.

"A little bit of leafletting, I think!" Tom announced to the room in general.

He picked up the bundle of leaflets due for the afternoon delivery, and thrust them towards the leader of the gang.

"I'm sure Doctor Macdonald would love the chance to get to know this area a little better."

"It'll blow away the cobwebs," echoed Anna, picking up on the idea.

Tom suggested that he'd wait for their chairman to return, and they'd catch them all up later. Like a bunch of reluctant school children, the group collected a bundle each and trooped out. Anna followed behind, blowing Tom a kiss and a cheery wave.

"How was the polling this morning?" he asked one of the volunteers who remained behind.

"Er, dunno, I only came at mid-day," came the desultory reply.

Came for lunch, thought Tom. He'd have to give the Ward Chairman a talking to, he decided. No harm if one of his fellows heard it.

Having spotted Tom's Land Rover outside, the Ward Chairman was at once apologetic and eager to please as he came in.

"Going well, Tom!" he said.

"Looks like it!" was Tom's icy reply. "We haven't had any polling data from you all day".

"Had trouble with the internet," was the sheepish reply.

"Can I see the polling figures?"

"Erm, let me see…."

Tom remained still and let the Chairman flounder amongst a pile of papers on a trestle table. The other volunteer was also shuffling papers, trying to be helpful. The only sound in the room was the rustling of papers, punctuated by the mumbling of the Ward Chairman and his stooge. Tom decided that this farce had gone on long enough.

"Oh dear, looks like we'll have to put you into special measures."

The Ward Chairman looked up from the table, puzzled as to what this could mean.

"I'll get someone from campaign HQ to come out here and brace things up a bit!"

Mike's breezy entrance broke the tension. He had pulled Molly into the driveway of the house, once the surprise factor had been achieved.

"A bit of local leafletting is in order," said Tom.

"Good oh!" said the Chairman, attempting to recover from his loss of face.

As the group gathered up leaflets, the silence was awkward. Good, thought Tom, let them feel awkward.

"I'll be in the wagon, outside," said Mike sensing the atmosphere.

CHAPTER FORTY-THREE

Realising that this was a chance to win the Ward Chairman over to his side, Tom gave him what he hoped was his brightest smile.

"The weather has been kind," he began.

What else would two Englishmen talk about? They walked on awkwardly. Soon they caught up with the rest of the group. Time to show who's boss, thought Tom.

"OK folks," he gave them the same smile, "loose blob down the street."

He was met with blank stares.

"Is that some sort of code?" asked Anna, still trying to straighten out her hair.

Realising that he had used army speak, he explained that they should split into two groups on each side of the road, and leaflet as they went along.

That seemed to break the spell, and the group set off, chattering merrily as they went.

"Many hands make light work!" said the Ward Chairman, recognising the change in the mood.

As they made their way along, stuffing letter boxes high and low, Tom was aware of the sound of Molly approaching.

He turned around to see Matt flashing his headlights. Something must be up. He looked to see where Anna was, she was chatting happily to one of the women in the group. Mike drew up to where Tom had stopped. Anna's sixth sense made her stop and turn to look.

"Message from Izzy" said Mike, "call her ASAP."

Tom realised that the mobile signal was patchy where they were, maybe Izzy had been unable to get through.

Mike was the second contact number for the day. He looked at his phone, hardly any signal.

"Can you drive me up to White Horse Hill?"

Stuffing his bundle into the arms of the Ward Chairman, he waved Anna to join them. She too gave her bundle to her companion, who gave her a smile and a wave as she left; good PR Tom noted. They all squeezed into the front of Molly and Mike set off.

"Rubbish signal here," said Mike, "just got her voicemail from about fifteen minutes ago."

Tom's mind was racing, trying to figure out what this might mean. With the windows open, the rush of warm Spring air was welcomed by all, except Anna, whose hair began to blow into her face.

Mike found the picnic spot at the top of White Horse Hill. An elderly couple was having a late lunch at the picnic table there. This time it was Izzy's phone that went to voicemail. Tom left a short message telling her the time of his call and hung up.

"I'll try Sid," said Tom, as he punched in the numbers.

Sid's phone went to voicemail. Tom winced; both out of contact at the same time.

"Let's sit tight here," he said.

Mike switched the engine off, as Tom and Anna got out into the warm afternoon.

"What's the plan?" asked Anna, as she regained control of her hair.

"Something's up," he said, anxious not to worry her.

"We've got a good signal here, so we can wait until we hear what the story is."

As he was speaking the couple at the picnic table looked over towards them.

"Tom Scobie?" said the lady.

"Good afternoon," replied Tom, with his best campaign smile on.

"Doctor Macdonald?" the man added.

Anna made a little curtsey in acknowledgement. "Have you voted yet?" asked Anna sweetly.

"Nah, not worth it," he said, chomping his sandwich.

Anna was more annoyed than Tom at the offhand response. But she was cut off by Tom's phone ringing. It was Sid.

"He's running and I've lost him," he said. "Picked him up after you stopped for lunch. He's got some local low life on his side, acting as a spotter."

"OK, we're at White Horse Hill" said Tom, "should we go firm here?"

"Best thing, 'til we've nailed him down. He's on a scrambling bike. Izzy's got her folks looking for him."

Tom looked at his watch. Polling closes at 10 o'clock; they couldn't stay there until then.

"I've got a call into Izzy, I'll get an update from her and decided what to do."

"Roger that," replied Sid and ended the call.

Both Anna and Mike were close enough to hear the exchange. Mike nodded as the conversation unfolded. So far their tactic of keeping moving had given them all a sense of safety, but Sid's call changed that. Anna was still and quiet. Tom worried about her reaction to yet another threat. He put his arm around her.

"Okay?"

"Not worth it indeed," she muttered, in a voice just loud enough for them to hear. "I'll remember that, matey, when you come in for a prostate examination."

The couple at the picnic table continued eating and chatting to themselves.

The next call was from Izzy.

"Where are you Tom?"

He explained. Izzy suggested they stayed put while a car was sent to escort them back to safety, in campaign HQ. Tom was happy with that idea, and she ended the call.

While the couple carried on with their picnic, Tom pulled out a map from inside Molly and spread it out on the bonnet. "I reckon we've covered plenty of ground today, I'll let Mu manage the knocking up. I just hope nothing happens before the count."

As he spoke, the sound of a siren could be heard approaching. Tom looked up. "Mount up!" he said.

The picnicking couple looked up in amazement, as a big blue and yellow police car, lights flashing and siren going drove into the car park. Tom waved at them, and Mike gunned the engine into life. The two vehicles departed, covering the picnic table in dust.

CHAPTER FORTY-FOUR

Henry Makepeace ran his eye over the list of people who were authorized to attend the count as scrutineers. A copy had been given to the police, to monitor admission.

"I can't vouch for everybody, as the other parties have their own lists too," he said. "Plus, there'll be media there as well, after what's been happening."

He was standing with Tom in the small room in the Constituency Association office. Muriel was running the evening sweep up of late voters, to ensure that everybody voted before the close of the polls at 10 o'clock.

"But, as far as I can see there are none of the bandits here," he added. "One or two new faces, but I doubt if Markham has been able to get his claws into any of them."

Since the sighting of the suspicious character earlier, Tom had been safely installed in campaign HQ. Anna had gone to the Makepeaces' house, where Matt was deputed to look after her. A police lady stood by the front door. An approximate description had been circulated, and police patrol cars were driving around the area. Foot patrols close to the market square had been increased, the Chief Constable had authorized extra numbers of Special Constables, to augment the effort. It was hoped that such an obvious police presence would deter the killer. Tom wasn't so sure.

"It's me he's after," said Tom, to himself as much as to Henry. "I've got to be at the count, he'll know that."

Henry saw where Tom's train of thought was going. "I'll make sure that there is only one entrance to the Town Hall," he said, making a note on the list.

Tom nodded his approval. "Sid is on the list?" he asked.

Henry nodded. Tom felt easier.

"I'll give my briefing to the scrutineers after polls close," Henry continued. "The ballot boxes won't all arrive at the count before eleven o'clock. Do you want to be there all night? The result is usually called between two and three in the morning, so we can call you once it looks like we're getting close."

Tom needed to think about this. Normally he would want to be with his troops, but he needed to be sure that Anna was safe.

"You don't have to decide now," said Henry, folding up the list.

Tom nodded his thanks. He would need to speak to Sid, Mike and Matt, to agree a course of action. If he could avoid a heavy-handed police presence at the count, he'd be happy, but the killer was still at large.

"This is meant to be a celebration of democracy," mused Tom, "not a sham election like a police state".

His phone peeped; he saw it was a message from Sid.

NOTHING SEEN – INBOUND. WITH YOU IN 10.

"Sid'll be here shortly. I'll have a natter with him, and I'll let you know what I'll be doing, Henry."

Henry gave him a thumbs up, and went off to see how the final round of knocking up was going.

Tom texted a response to Sid, suggesting he go to the Makepeaces' house. They could grab something to eat there, while they planned out the rest of the evening.

Suddenly he felt bone weary. He recognised the symptoms, too much adrenaline and not enough sleep. That's when people make mistakes he thought to himself.

CHAPTER FORTY-FIVE

"Well, *mon cousin*, you've got there!"

Tom smiled, despite himself. He'd rarely seen Matt in such an ebullient mood. It was a weary but merry bunch of party workers who sat around the Makepeaces' dining room table. Pasta never tasted so good, thought Tom as he shovelled another forkful into his mouth.

"Who'd have thought a year ago, that my little cuz would be standing for parliament?"

Tom tried to stay calm, a glance at the clock showed a few minutes after ten. Mike saw the direction of his glance.

"Polls have closed, well done boy!"

All things being equal, in a safe seat such as Ridgeway, it should be a formality to attend the count and pronounce his thanks to all of those who had helped him achieve this wonderful result. Then the work would really begin. A coronation, except things were not quite equal.

And there was Anna at the other end of the table, in her favourite Aran pully, slightly too large for her. It made her look even more vulnerable. Her eyes and her smile were wide with happiness, as she chattered away to one of the volunteer helpers. That's the smile I married, thought Tom. After all of the recent dramas, she could still summon up that winning smile.

He began to speak, but his voice croaked.

"Don't speak Tom," she said in her gentle doctor knows best voice. "Just enjoy the moment."

For a moment they all ate in silence.

"In Moscow, a policeman has just been born," said Tom, puncturing the mood.

Amidst the laughter, he explained the saying he'd heard once on a trip to Moscow.

His mind was drawn to Izzy and her colleagues who had Markham in custody, and who were even now looking for someone who was trying to kill him. That brought him back to the matter in hand. He caught Sid's eye, also forking pasta off his plate, but Tom saw from his expression that he was not joining in the celebratory mood. Sid nodded an acknowledgement to Tom; enjoy this moment – we've got a long night ahead.

There was a rap on the door. Sid was there in an instant. Muriel's voice could be heard in the hallway chatting to Sid. This was her house, after all.

"Good evening all!" she said, entering the room and taking in the scene in her dining room.

Mike stood up and made towards the sideboard, which had several bottles on it. Tom began to stand, but Muriel waved him to stay seated.

"Thanks Mike, I'd love one!" she said, as he gestured towards a bottle.

Anna headed towards the kitchen, "I'll refresh the pasta," she said over her shoulder.

Muriel found an empty chair and sat down at the table, Mike appeared and offered her a glass of wine. She took a moment to look around the table. She met Tom's eye and they both smiled like schoolchildren.

"Here's to you Tom!" She raised her glass to Tom, and then around the table.

Tom raised his glass in return.

"The team that connives together….!" She began.

Once Anna had supplied the food, Muriel explained that once the ballot boxes from the Polling Stations arrived they would be opened, and the process of batching and counting would begin. The process would be closely watched by scrutineers representing all of the parties, including the candidate from the Front for the Liberation of Occupied Berkshire, who had campaigned to have the county boundary restored to its pre 1974 lines.

"The boxes have begun to arrive," Muriel said, as a conclusion to her remarks.

The group ate in a companionable silence, as the pundits on the TV gave their predictions about the outcome. Tom's eyes drooped. He was shaken awake by Anna jabbing him in the ribs.

Eventually Sid caught Tom's eye and tapped his watch. They'd agreed that he should put in an appearance at the count, once it had begun.

"Better get on parade, boss!" Sid said, to which Tom nodded his agreement.

Tom stood up, to get changed out of his dusty clothes, into something befitting a newly elected Member of Parliament. Anna walked up the stairs with him, into the guest room where Tom's clothes were hanging.

"I'd give you my lucky rabbit's foot, if I thought you believe in that stuff," she said, as he pulled on his suit jacket.

"No more than you!" he said, as he did up his shoes.

"As long as you believe in me and I believe in you, we'll be fine," she said smiling up at him.

"Always!" he said, as Sid rapped on the door. He gave her a hug, and held her, wanting to draw strength from her. He would need it if things got dicey.

"I'll be over later," said Anna giving him one of her special looks, she had announced that she was not going to stay cooped up in Henry's house, and Tom had reluctantly agreed as long as Mike was with her.

And quickly they were out into the cool of the evening.

"Evening gents," said the WPC by the front door.

As they walked across the square to the Town Hall, they noticed a few yellow jacketed members of the Thames Valley Constabulary wandering around the market square, a visible deterrent to any trouble makers.

But life went on, as the sound of voices from the nearby pub echoed across the square. As they walked, Tom remembered another occasion when they'd walked together.

"Remember Mostar?" he said.

"Ha!" Sid retorted. "You nearly got us both killed."

"Hardly my fault, it was payday for the local militia men, and we just happened to be passing!"

"A good job they were too drunk to shoot straight, or punch straight come to that," Sid chuckled at the memory.

"Happy days!" answered Tom.

"Oi, oi," Sid's tone had changed.

He veered off towards a row of motorbikes parked by the edge of the square. He walked up to a scrambling bike. The street lights in the square showed that it had a good coating of dust.

"Could be that our boy's already here," he said, glancing around the square.

****

Georgina's head was spinning, after her talk with Maud she had called all of the elves together.

"There's a piece of this jigsaw we still haven't even found," she heard her voice sounding shrill, she took a drink of her cold coffee to allow her time to settle her nerves.

"A *very* reliable source has just given me information that another conspirator, or bandit, or whatever we call them, is unaccounted for." She was going to have to spell out her fears to the elves, so they knew what to look for.

"There is a contract out on the life of Tom Scobie." There was a collective groan from the elves. Georgina didn't know whether this was out of concern for Tom, or that there was more work still to do.

"Either Markham or Donald Johnson has made contact with a killer," she went on to set out the time line of Donald disappearing and Markham being arrested.

"This means that there may be someone around Tom Scobie who can ensure that the job gets done. They can lead the killer to where he is." She saw that they were still processing this new information.

"The source was unable to identify this person, but there will be some link to Markham. Please have a good look back through your own notes and records, and see if we've cut any corners, or made assumptions that we can't prove."

They didn't need telling, they got straight down to it. For the first time in a long time, Georgina regretted giving up smoking.

She would need to tell Tom, even if the story was incomplete. A phone call would be too garbled, so she would have to go to the count and tell him what she had discovered.

"I'll take Dermot with me Shazza, I might need a bit of help," she called to her colleague, as a lanky figure stood up from his desk and picked up a camera bag.

They walked out of the anonymous looking building into the car park. As she opened the doors, she wondered aloud "who would want to kill a newly elected Member of Parliament?"

"No honest man," came Dermot's reply in his languid Belfast twang.

****

Inside the Town Hall, the counting was well under way. Piles of ballot papers had been allocated to each of the polling districts in the constituency. As boxes were opened, the first task for the counters was to turn them all the same way up, and batch them into bundles. This was to verify that the number of ballot papers tallied with those given out at the polling station. Once this was complete, the count proper could get under way.

On their way in, Sid had taken aside one of the policemen and told him about the scrambling bike. Tom headed over to where Henry was presiding over a laptop.

"So far, so good!" said Henry ebulliently.

He had commandeered an alcove in the corner of the hall, and bagged a trestle table for his laptop as well as supplies of coffee and biscuits for the scrutineers.

"The telling and knocking up seems to have worked."

As the counters turned the ballot papers over to be batched, the watching scrutineers were able to note whose box had been ticked. It was a rough estimate, but helped to see how actual votes matched up against pledges.

Tom gave Henry an appreciative slap on the back, he'd want to concentrate on this phase of the exercise, so Tom made his way around the large hall. He saw other candidates and their supporters wearing their variously coloured rosettes.

"Improperly dressed sir!" one of the party volunteers handed Tom a rosette, which he pinned on to his lapel. He'd left his in Molly.

The scene was one of quiet bustle, as counters counted and scrutineers scrutineered. Tom glanced at the clock, wondering when the result would be announced.

"Clock watching already!?" a local journalist had sidled up beside him. "I'm here to see democracy in action," he added with a smile. "How are you feeling Mr Scobie?"

"Watching the result here, as well as nationally," he said cautiously.

"Catch you after the result?" the journalist said, and wandered off to get some more quotes from the other candidates.

All over bar the shouting, thought Tom, as he walked up to one of the other candidates, from the Green Party, who he recognised from a gathering of all the candidates at a local library.

"I hope that you're going to do a better job than the last bloke," she said.

"*If* I'm elected, I'm here to serve everybody, irrespective of how they voted," he said, trying not to sound too contrived. "I was lucky enough to have a grandfather who encouraged me to be curious about bugs and beetles, as a little boy, and I still am!"

That got a weary smile from her. "I'll be calling," she said. Tom carried on wandering.

"Helloooo!" came a familiar voice. "I've never been to an election count before, so we all decided to come and see!"

Anna had found a puffer jacket to replace her beloved parka, of blessed memory. She looked cosy inside her down cocoon. She gave him a hug, which he found he was reluctant to end. Mike and Matt had found the coffee and were wandering around the room, with their passes hanging from lanyards. They went to join them, Tom tried to explain the process, but had to admit it was his first time too.

Tom caught sight of one of the techie folks who were helping collate the results; he was wandering around looking lost. He spotted Tom and walked towards him.

"I'm looking for Henry," he said. "He went to the loo a few minutes ago…."

Well, thought Tom, he's a man of a certain age. He sent the young fellow back to continue his work, and continued walking around, catching the eyes of other scrutineers as he did so. The returning officer told him that all the ballot boxes had arrived and been opened, she pointed towards a stack of boxes in the far corner of the hall.

He caught sight of Georgina as she entered the room; she looked pale. Next to her was a photographer, with a camera slung over his shoulder. She introduced her colleague distractedly.

"Tom! – we think there is another bandit still unaccounted for," she began.

As she spoke, the lights went out and they were all plunged into darkness. There was a collective groan, as people reached for lighters or pocket torches. Tom found the torch he used for evening deliveries in his pocket and flicked it on.

"Everybody please stay where you are!" came a loud voice, probably the Returning Officer.

Tom grabbed Anna's hand, and held onto it.

"Interesting," he said, "this happened at campaign HQ this morning."

A torch beam shone in his direction, and Sid arrived beside them.

"A distraction," he began, "somebody has probably found the main circuit board, and flicked a switch".

"What gives?" Georgina sounded unsure of Sid's meaning.

"We may find out soon enough," Sid continued. "Can we get you somewhere less exposed".

The lighting flickered back into life, to a collective sigh of relief. They walked over to where the campaign team was based, a group were huddled over the laptop. As they walked, Tom introduced Anna to Georgina, explaining that she had taken on Jack's work.

"Still no sign of Henry," said the youth who Tom had met earlier. Georgina grabbed Tom's arm, he saw her eyes were wide with alarm.

Anna saw Georgina's anxious expression, and she saw that Tom was trying to grasp some sort of puzzle.

"Could it be?" Sid ducked out of the group and went off, probably in search of Henry thought Tom.

Tom's head was spinning, too much wine and coffee and not enough sleep. Had Henry played him for a fool, all this time? And what about Mu? He recalled that Mu had encouraged him to stand, while Henry had been lukewarm. Was he one of Markham's gang all along?

"Er, what makes you think Henry is one of the bandits?" he was still trying to absorb the possibility.

"I spoke to Maud earlier this evening, to get her side of the story, and at the end she mentioned another character close to Markham, but she couldn't be sure."

"Did she name Henry?" Tom was trying to eliminate every uncertainty.

"No, but...." She began. Tom found his phone and called Muriel.

"Has Henry come back to the house?" he said without ceremony when she answered.

"No Tom," she sounded nonplussed. "Everything alright?" she asked.

He told her about the lights going off, which came as a surprise, as the lights in the house were unaffected.

"Something's cooking," she said, thinking out loud "maybe Henry went to investigate."

"Maybe," Tom replied "let me know if he surfaces". They ended the call. In response to Georgina's anxious look, he shook his head.

"Not there," he said, repeating Muriel's possible explanation. "I don't want us to panic," he said in a low voice to the group who had gathered around him in a protective huddle.

"Nothing doing," said Sid, as he re-joined the group.

"There are police everywhere," began Georgina "how can someone slip away like that?

"Obviously one exit wasn't covered," came Sid's reply. "That trail bike was parked in the square bold as brass, somebody knew the set up here."

Tom's heart sank, Henry was the one person who would be expected to know the arrangements for the count, and could identify any unguarded routes.

Izzy came into view, with a uniformed colleague. "Looks like somebody found the main circuit board and flicked the light switch," she added in a low voice, trying to appear nonchalant. She saw Anna and gave her a quick smile.

"We're just doing a walk around to see if we can spot anything," she added.

"Shall we walk then?" suggested Tom, "got nowhere else to go".

As they began to walk, the radio on the shoulder of the PC squawked into life. Izzy's phone rang at the same moment.

"Code black, guv," said the PC as he acknowledged the message.

Izzy nodded, as she listened intently to her phone.

"Keep me posted," she said, putting her phone away.

"One of the fire escape doors is open, looks as if someone left whilst the lights were out," she said.

"Or managed to get in," said Sid.

CHAPTER FORTY-SIX

"So we're locked in?" asked Georgina, whose instinct as a journalist rebelled at the thought of any restrictions on her liberty.

"You've got your media pass on miss," said the uniformed PC as they continued walking, "so you can leave if you like."

"And miss all the fun?" said Dermot, who unslung his camera in anticipation of some news worthy snaps.

He was met with an unsmiling stare from the PC.

"Something just doesn't smell right," Tom said, in an impatient tone. "If Henry opened the door, he either wanted to get away, or he's let someone in, and then made himself scarce."

He pulled out his phone and found Henry's number. Anna was still holding his hand, and she gave it a squeeze, while he waited for the call to connect.

"It's just ringing," he said, "no voicemail." He ended the call. "He'll see that I've called, if he's looking."

"I suppose he hasn't gone upstairs for some reason?" he said, pointing towards the gallery that ran around the hall. Izzy waved at two uniformed PCs, and indicated that they should go upstairs.

At that moment, Tom's phone rang, it was Muriel. "Hello Mu, have you found Henry?" he tried to sound cheerful, giving Anna a smile. She managed a tight smile back.

"Tom!" he could hear the fear and anxiety in her voice. Anna saw his reaction. "One of the pistols from Henry's gun cabinet is missing." Tom shot a glance at Izzy, who was speaking to her colleague. She caught his eye and came closer.

"I was just having a look around here, and I saw that the door was unlocked. I don't know what to do, Tom." He could hear the hysteria rising in her voice. Her husband was acting out of character. Something bad could happen, and Henry had gone off the radar.

"Was it the Webley?" he asked. He needed to know which of his pistols Henry had taken. "The one with the dark brown handle," he added for clarity.

"Er, I think so," she replied, trying to be helpful.

"Sit tight Mu, hang on a second."

He looked at Izzy. "Can you get your WPC to go inside the Makepeaces' house and ensure that Muriel is safe, it looks like Henry has taken one of his pistols out, and has gone wandering."

Izzy nodded to her colleague, who spoke into his radio.

"What on earth…?" Mu began.

"OK Mu, let the WPC in, and she'll stay with you." He ended the call.

All the while Dermot had been snapping away, having drawn away from the group to catch the drama. Georgina seemed to be in a daze. Too much was going on, her brain couldn't process it all.

"Henry's not the killer," Izzy said. "We mustn't drop our guard. I want to keep you here Tom, plus Anna, where you're safe." The uniformed PC informed her that the WPC was with Muriel, and that there was no sign of Henry in the house.

"Perhaps Henry has run out of road…." Anna began. "After all this….."

"Suicide?" asked Tom, reading her thoughts. She nodded.

"Perhaps it's not too late," he began. "Where would he go?" He called Sid over. "What d'you think Sid?" he outlined the quandary about Henry.

"We can track his phone if you like." Izzy overheard, "I'll get *my* folks on to it!"

Sid looked sheepish, "only trying to help!"

"It'll depend on whether he's gone away into the Downs where there's no signal," added Izzy, as if answering Tom's next question about how quickly they could run Henry to earth.

Tom was getting impatient with the to-ing and fro-ing. On the one hand, Izzy was trying to protect him from an attempt on his life, and on the other Henry was wandering like a lost soul. If he really was one of the Bandits all along, there was a chance to turn him against his former patron, and redeem himself. He felt he owed it to Mu to at least make the effort.

A thought came to him. He noticed that Sid had wandered off to get some coffee and a bun. Looking around the room, he saw that Izzy was speaking on her phone. He squeezed Anna's hand "let's go and have a chat with Sid," he said as he led her over towards where he was standing.

"Can you spot Matt"? he said, as they walked.

"I'll seek him out," she replied and walked away to look for him.

"I've seen that look before," said Sid, taking a bite out of his bun. "What's cooking"?

"How quickly can you track Henry's phone?" asked Tom. "He can't be far away, he was here ten minutes ago."

"Let me grab my laptop. Have you got his number"?

As he spoke Anna reappeared with Matt, who was chewing a sandwich. "Great food here, I might do this again!"

"Alright team," said Tom without ceremony, "I have a cunning plan."

****

Tom thought he knew his way around Wandage, but quickly saw how the town centre had changed over the years he had been away. Together with Sid and Matt, he had managed to get out through a side door while Anna and Georgina had diverted Izzy with small talk.

"The Returning Officer reckoned it'd be a couple of hours before the count was complete," said Matt, who had been part of Tom's diversionary plan. "So you won't be missed just yet."

"You were right about the change of shift, Pathfinder," said Sid, who was pleased to have got one over the flat footed coppers, after Izzy sent him away with a flea in his ear. They'd slipped out while the uniformed police were coming and going.

"Hopefully we can run Henry to earth before Izzy and co clock that we're not there," echoed Matt.

"Give me a minute" said Sid, putting his laptop onto the roof of a parked car. They were in a dimly lit side street around the corner from the Town Hall where the count was taking place. As Sid fiddled with the settings of the software to locate Henry's mobile signal, Tom allowed his eyes and ears to adjust to their surroundings.

Matt wandered a short distance further along the road. Tom had suggested he 'orbit' him and Sid, who had his head down over his screen. Another pair of eyes and ears would be useful. As his eyes adjusted to the dim light, he noticed cats prancing among the dustbins and caught the sound of discarded crisp packets blown down the street by the breeze.

Beyond the activity around the Town Hall, there were one or two late night revellers staggering home from the pub, or from the local chippy. After a couple of minutes Tom walked up to join him, as Sid picked up his laptop and began to follow.

"Not far away," Sid said in a low voice. As he drew alongside, Sid pointed with his left hand, as he balanced the laptop with his right. He was pointing down an alley way.

Tom crossed over to the opposite side of the road, so that he might peer around the corner, and look down the alley way. He dropped to the ground and shuffled forward on his elbows until he drew level with the corner.

Sid waved to Matt that he should get onto the same side of the road, and close up behind where Tom was lying. He closed his laptop and shoved it into his back pack, which was slung over his shoulder.

Tom edged himself forward so that he could see and hear what was down the alley way. His senses were as sharp as they had ever been. A breeze brought him the smell of either brandy or whisky, as well as the small sound of what sounded like someone sobbing.

He felt his phone buzzing in his jacket pocket, probably Izzy wanting to know where he was. Oh well, he thought, it was only a matter of time before she saw he was not there. No time to lose. He made out what he thought was the form of someone sitting on the ground with their back against the wall. It looked like Henry was trying to summon up the courage to end it all. He had to be quick.

Shuffling back, he stood up slowly and drew the other two in close. He quickly explained what he had seen and what he thought was in Henry's mind. They had to move fast and hope that his senses were dulled by the booze.

"Time to save the lost sheep, Matt," muttered Tom. "Sid, stay here and watch out. Matt and I will rush Henry and grab his gun before he has a chance to react. He can't shoot us both."

Sid nodded, he couldn't see Matt's expression, but he could only imagine what it was like being told you had a fifty fifty chance of getting shot. Welcome to our world, he thought to himself.

As they got ready, Tom could hear Matt puffing, as if he were about to run a sprint, which they both were. There was no real plan, they'd just have to manage as best they could.

"Now!" As they ran, the figure became aware of their approach.

"Wha…?"

In the dim light Tom made out the shape of the pistol, which Henry had picked up.

"Henry, its Tom!" he said, identifying them.

"Tom…?" was as much as he could manage before the pistol was pulled out of his hand by Matt, who had got around him.

"Come on, mate," said Tom, as he and Matt recovered their breath. "Let's get you back home eh?"

Matt grabbed him as they both hoisted him up to his feet. He held Henry steady, as Tom recovered the bottle and gratefully took the pistol which Matt passed to him. They led him gently back up the alley way, where Sid had been keeping a look out.

"I'd better check in," said Tom, "I think we've been rumbled by Izzy!" Tom quickly explained that they were taking Henry home, rather like a benevolent school teacher with an errant pupil who'd had too much cider.

"I'll get a colleague to join you, Tom." Her no-nonsense tone told him that Henry was going to be assisting the police with their enquiries. But at least he would be safe.

CHAPTER FORTY-SEVEN

As they traipsed across the familiar square, heading towards Henry's house, a wave of weariness washed over Tom. They carried on silently, all of them exhausted by the tension of the preceding moments. Like an electric shock, all of Tom's senses screamed danger.

"We're sitting ducks!" he said.

Sid reacted straight away, like Tom he had forced himself to snap out of the collective torpor.

"Lend a hand, Matt," Sid said, as he grabbed Henry under the armpits. Together they lifted Henry off his feet and began hustling him towards the door of the house. Tom ran ahead of them, with the bottle in one hand and the pistol in the other.

As he ran, Tom caught sight of a figure out of the corner of his eye to his left. He saw that the figure was moving tactically, and was carrying something that looked like a pistol. He went cold. He needed to alert Izzy and her colleagues of the danger.

Instinctively he raised the pistol into the air, and pulled the trigger. He remembered how heavy the Webley was to fire, and it felt like an age for the gun to go off. The noise of the shot in the square reverberated and echoed into the night.

He saw a group headed by Izzy entering the square, the gunman saw them too. Tom guessed that the shooter was weighing his chances. Izzy and one of her colleagues had pistols drawn.

"Armed police!" her voice cut through the night.

The shooter took an aim at Tom, so he started dodging around which would make him a harder target in the dim light. In frustration, he threw the bottle towards the shooter, and did a rolling dive to his left. He was vaguely aware of a door opening and light coming into the square as Henry was safely shepherded home.

As he got up, Tom felt the pistol in his hand and for a moment was tempted to have a shot at the gunman, who was also moving around to get a good aim at him. The light was too dim for either of them to fire an aimed shot, but the gunman might just let loose and hope to hit him. He had to keep moving.

"Drop it!" Izzy's voice again, as she and her colleague continued running straight towards the shooter.

The shooter turned towards Izzy, as if to fire. A jolt of rage went through Tom. Another woman was going to be killed because of him. Ivana's face flashed before him.

Behind them, Dermot had moved into the square, to get a better view, and hopefully some award winning photos. His street sense took in the scene in an instant. He moved closer to the action. A blizzard of strobe light exploded as Dermot fired off his camera. The gunman was dazzled.

It was enough for Tom who was able to lunge towards the gunman. At the same time Izzy collided with them both. They all went sprawling on the floor. There was a thud as Tom's fist found the head of the gunman. The other policeman pulled the pistol away, and the gunman was overpowered.

Emerging from the melee, with his tie askew, and minus his rosette, Georgina, who had run after Dermot, saw Tom dusting himself down. She just about remembered to breathe and gave him a broad smile.

"Well Georgie, looks like you've got yourself another scoop!" he said.

****

294

The bright lights of the Town Hall washed everything and everybody in a pale light. Tom stood on the raised stage, along with the other candidates, as the returning officer intoned the result. The words seemed to lose their meaning as he thought of how this all began. He saw the expectant faces, still eager, even at two o'clock in the morning.

Tom's acceptance speech was short; deliberately so. For the first time he felt the full emotion of the moment. He dutifully thanked the Returning Officer and her staff, as well as congratulating his fellow candidates on their well-run campaigns. He thanked his campaign team, and looked forward to serving the people who had put their trust in him.

As he stepped down from the stage, he was surrounded by a crowd of supporters, still able to raise a cheer despite the hour. Despite the heavy police presence, the excitement in the square was momentarily forgotten.

As agent, Mu had put on a brave face and gone through the motions as the count was announced to the candidates, before the public announcement. Tom thought she looked awful, still unable to process what had happened, and what the future might look like for her and Henry.

And there was Anna, who had managed to find a posh frock from somewhere, beaming at him with pride. He drew her to him, and hugged her tight. This time, it was he who was sobbing.

"Well, we got there....." he mumbled. She reached up, and brushed his cheeks.

"Congratulations Tom, I'm so proud of you!" She gave him that winning smile of hers. "Now the work really begins!"

****

In the interview room at Wandage police station, Izzy sat opposite the gunman, now wearing an overall. His face bore the marks where Tom had, as he explained in his witness statement, used reasonable force to restrain him. He was accompanied by the duty solicitor. A colleague sat beside her as she began to speak. Her voice was brittle. She had got to know Tom and Anna, and felt responsible for protecting them.

"You've failed in your mission," she said coldly. "Tom Scobie has just been elected Member of Parliament, and the man who offered to pay you has already been arrested. His assets have been frozen, so you're not going to get paid for this day's work."

Her colleague watched the reaction of the shooter, as the revelations sank in. Izzy was laying it on with a trowel, he thought. He could see the weasely eyes of the man looking back and forth at them both.

"He's no use to you now," she went on. "He might just throw you to the wolves, in a plea bargain."

Careful Izzy, thought her colleague, don't lead him on. It could bite you in court.

"If you co-operate, we'll have a word with the Crown Prosecution Service," he interjected. He was relieved to see Izzy nodding her agreement.

"Can I have a word with my brief?" said the gunman.

CHAPTER FORTY-EIGHT

If a week is a long time in politics, the days after the 2010 General Election seemed like an eternity, as negotiations were opened to form the first peacetime coalition government since the Second World War. The events of election night in the sleepy and very safe constituency of Ridgeway were of passing importance in the national consciousness, and the news story moved on to who was getting appointed to what job.

Georgina had made sure that the full story of the events on election night were laid out for the population of Ridgeway, but was constrained by the *sub- judice* rule about naming suspects. But those who knew, knew. Life went back to normal after the excitement, people had jobs to do and bills to pay.

Izzy was all business, as she entered the Constituency office, a few weeks later. She had phoned Tom to arrange a meeting as soon as possible. This didn't sound like a routine update. She had asked if Muriel would also be present.

Poor Mu, thought Tom, Henry had been released on bail and was co-operating with the police. Louisa had taken Mu under her wing, and made sure that when she spoke to the police there was a lawyer present, but the police didn't suspect her of any involvement. Similarly Maud had been interviewed under caution, but she was bailed by Lady Mary, who stood surety for her good behaviour. She agreed to appear as a witness for the prosecution.

Anna thought Mu was in a state of both shock and grief, when Tom described their first meeting after the election. Tom's instinct was to trust Mu to continue in her role, as a further Association Chairman was sought. To his relief most of the Association Executive Committee agreed with his judgement, they'd had enough turbulence over the preceding few days, and at least Mu represented continuity.

Izzy was precise with her language; Tom wasn't quite sure what she made of the decision to retain Mu in post, as the wife of a potential suspect, but she didn't raise the matter. "Charles Markham has now been charged with the murder of Jack Sawyer and Gillian Wynne, as well as the other conspiracy charges already alleged."

Tom noticed the cautious language, but he could see a twinkle in those smart brown eyes of hers.

"Gill sent us a message from beyond the grave" began Izzy. "She obviously didn't trust Markham one bit, despite their 'alliance'. A poisoned pill, if you like, in the form of a diary."

"To be opened in the event of my death?" suggested Mu. Izzy nodded.

"We've got him!" she said, unable to hide her smile. "He's completely boxed in. The gunman that we picked up, has also confessed to the murder of Jack Sawyer."

Tom shuddered at the memory of the night visit to see Lena to retrieve the trove of papers Jack had accumulated.

"Markham's part in the criminal enterprise has now been unpacked for us, in all its glory," she continued. "We're passing on what evidence we can to our Interpol colleagues, to put out Red notices for Donald Johnson, and others involved in that racket."

Tom nodded approvingly, and he saw Muriel dabbing a tear away. "I'm sorry to put it in such a callous manner…." Izzy said, as she saw Mu's reaction.

"The suspect has explained that Henry had been coerced into opening a side door into the building where the count was being held. His plan was forestalled by you, Tom, deciding to go out."

"I just knew something was wrong, and didn't like the idea of standing around...." Tom began.

"We'll have to disagree on that, but as things turned out...." Izzy said.

"Henry was put in an impossible position," she said gently to Mu "and he saw there was only one honourable way out," she added. "Fortunately Tom thought otherwise."

There was an awkward silence in the room.

Mu nodded and gave them both a tight smile. "I do hear on the grapevine that Lady Mary is planning to divorce Markham," she said. "He'd put most of his portfolio in her name, to avoid the tax authorities," she added.

"Lady Mary is also helping us with our inquiries," said Izzy. "She might avoid jail, but she'll have an uncomfortable conversation with the tax folks."

"How is Markham faring?" asked Tom. "Seeing his empire crumbling before his eyes."

"He's on suicide watch," Izzy replied matter-of-factly. "Someone like that, often can't face the reality of what they've done."

Tom nodded. "Still, I'm taking no chances, until he's behind bars. Brother Mike will be keeping an eye on Anna and driving me around, whilst I'm down here," he added.

Izzy nodded; once bitten twice shy, Mike would be on the lookout. "After all, you'll have to look after the little one....." she added.

"I want Anna to feel safe," Tom continued. "I'm going to be away in Westminster."

Anna was contemplating the opportunity to redecorate the house, after the fire, and was talking about a move to a bigger house.

"What was that saying of yours Tom?" said Muriel, looking up from the papers on her desk.

"The team that connives together, survives together," Tom provided the answer. "Between us and Sid, I reckon we make a great bunch of connivers!"

Tom looked at Muriel, he could see a shadow had come over her face. Too many bad memories, too many ghosts in the room. Izzy sensed the heaviness in the room, and stood up to leave. "Well, I've got villains to catch! I'll leave you to get on with...."

She waved a hand across the papers on Muriel's desk; gave them both a smile and headed towards the door.

"If you succeed in sending Markham down, I'll put you in for the Queens Police Medal." Muriel said to Izzy's back, as she was leaving.

She turned, and looked over her shoulder. "Er.... I've already got it!" She gave Muriel a cheeky wave and a smile, and went on her way.

"Full of surprises, that girl!" said Muriel, smiling after her. "And you too, Tom. I'd no idea you could be so – resourceful!"

"We've come a long way in a short time, Mu," he replied, as he looked around the room. "If Malcolm Miller had played along with Markham, he'd be sitting here now, and Donald Johnson would be sitting where you are. The good people of Ridgeway would be none the wiser......."

"Well, they're getting wiser now!" Muriel said with added passion. "The local paper and the nationals are full of Markham being charged with murder. And those photos of you and the gunman in the square – that's award-winning stuff. You did all that Tom."

"Jack Sawyer started it, and Georgina and her team picked up the baton, not to mention the formidable Maud!" he said. "If only Jack had managed to get sufficient evidence on Markham......."

"That bent copper would have sat on it," Muriel interrupted. "Gill Wynne would have won the nomination, Markham would've seen to that."

"Another ghost," said Tom.

"What if......" she said, looking out of the window.

"Would you do it all again Tom?" Muriel asked. "Henry told me about something you said at the selection interview. The banality of evil...." Muriel reminded Tom.

"When this began, I was stirred up by the idea that Malcolm Miller used me to discover something that he could use to discredit Markham. He didn't think about the wider picture, the people whose lives were involved. They were little people far away. I'd seen what happened to those little people."

Muriel sat still as Tom unfolded what sounded like a personal credo.

"When I saw how Markham was manipulating the system to get his puppet installed in Miller's place, I thought there's something thoroughly rotten going on."

"He made a mistake underestimating you Tom", Muriel said.

Tom made a face, this isn't about me he thought, but then he sat forward.

"When he came after me I couldn't quite believe it. The business of forcing us off the road, it was so crude in its simplicity."

"I'm just sorry that Henry couldn't find the moral courage to confront Markham sooner, the story could have had a very different ending," said Muriel almost to herself.

Tom wasn't sure what to say. "Markham ensnared people," he began, but stopped himself from making Mu feel worse. "Markham was brought down by those closest to him, once they realised that he had feet of clay, or perhaps they sensed that the good times were over."

"I'm surprised that the Party took no interest in this," he added.

"Perhaps that'll be your next campaign?" Muriel said, brightening at the thought. "After all you've won the heart of a very capable campaigning journalist!"

Tom sat back in his chair and glanced around the small office. His gaze fell upon the black and white framed photo of Winston Churchill.

"What was it the old man said?"

Muriel glanced up, seeing him looking at the picture.

"This is not the beginning of the end; but it is, perhaps, the end of the beginning."

****

Back in the cottage, Tom was pottering about the house when his phone rang. It was an anonymous number, so he answered warily.

"Mr. Scobie?" an officious sounding voice asked. Tom replied cautiously that it was indeed him.

"One moment please, I have the Prime Minister for you."

Tom thought it was nice of the PM to call, probably a quick congratulatory call to all the newly elected MPs.

"Er, hello Tom" came the very recognisable voice of the new PM "Congratulations on your result".... So far, much as expected, thought Tom.

"I'm sorry to hear that you've had some, er, problems locally, I'll get the Party Chairman to call you about what happened."

Ah! Somebody has been reporting back, probably the Area Campaign Director.

"The reason I'm calling, Tom, is that there may be something you can do to help the government."

A ministerial appointment? thought Tom.

"We'd like to make good use of your, er, particular skills that you used in your former employment. It concerns a matter requiring delicate handling, and one for which we think you might be well suited."

How am I going to explain this to Anna, he thought.

THE END

About the author

Nick Watts has worked in Westminster, in a variety of guises, since 1991. During this time he has seen the travails of the Major Government, the arrival of New Labour, Brexit and the subsequent political convulsions. He has worked with MPs and Peers from all of the main political parties, and has led delegations on overseas visits. He has a good understanding of the kind of people who become politicians, and the pressures they have to deal with. Ridgeway is his first book.

Printed in Great Britain
by Amazon

18579527R00181